"A beguiling romance lovingly told, The Inheritance meets readers at the intersection of tested love and slow restoration. Costea weaves her debut with an artistic sensibility and an open heart that is sure to find a "keeper shelf" place alongside Cynthia Ruchti, Jolina Petersheim and Francine Rivers. The Inheritance isn't merely a story rather a rallying cry to fight for love, encouragement and hope."

—Rachel McMillan, author of *The London Restoration* and *The Mozart Code*

"Raw, real, and uplifting, The Inheritance is a story of family, faith, and finding one's place among it all. With strong themes of redemption and forgiveness, this story will resonate with anyone who has been part of a less-than-perfect family, friendship, or marriage. Laura Costea is one to watch!"

—Jennifer Deibel, author of *A Dance in Donegal*

"The Inheritance is a sweet, clean read that provides a much-needed reminder that God's redeeming work is never done—and that His second chances are always worth taking."

—Rachel Dodge, bestselling author of *The Anne of Green Gables Devotional: A Chapter-by-Chapter Companion for Kindred Spirits* and *Praying with Jane: 31 Days Through the Prayers of Jane Austen*

"Small-town life, big dreams and redemption. Laura blends these beautifully into a story that captures the heart. This story tells of the hope we can have in Christ, who makes all things new. I know you will enjoy this book that paints the story of city life in California to the country life of the Midwest."

—Laura McCollough, author and blogger at artandfaithcreative.com

"I was drawn to The Inheritance because of its unique confluence and exploration of culture, religion, and relationships. In the midst of a Jewish girl's journey to becoming a Messianic Jew is a delectable mish mash of rugelach and caprese, conversations on the Bible and Torah, prophecy, art, and more. This is a relatable, fun story about Jewish and Italian culture, marriage, faith, and reconciliation."

—Michelle Ami Reyes, Vice President, Asian American Christian Collaborative, and author of *Becoming All Things: How Small Changes Lead to Lasting Connections Across Cultures*

"I was rooting hard for Hope and Peter's relationship and the story moved me to tears more than once. A sweet yet realistic love story."

—Sharla Stenerson, creator of the *Stuff I Wish I Could Say* podcast

The Inheritance

A NOVEL

LAURA COSTEA

prologue

Today

Work-gnarled hands gripped the steering wheel and guided the old Ford up the hill. She was proud of those hands. They'd done a lot of good in her life. She glanced in the rearview mirror to catch a glimpse of the sunset, and looked instead at two wrinkle-lined eyes; her hands weren't the only thing that had gotten older lately.

She strode up to the front door like she knew the place. What would they think when they saw her? What would they say? But this visit had been delayed long enough. And now, her being here could change their lives… their futures.

Now or never. She raised a bold hand. And knocked.

part one

HOPE'S BEGINNING

*"It is said that the darkest hour of the
night comes just before the dawn."*

Thomas Fuller

chapter one

Western Nebraska, Some Years Ago

Peter stretched and yawned. What a dull day. But every day was the same here.

He was itching so bad to get outta this town, he almost wanted to crawl right out of his skin. But he couldn't get out. At least not today.

"Pete!" The command came from behind the barn. He hated being called Pete. "Pete, I need you over here!"

Peter sighed, stuffed his hands in his jeans pockets, and sauntered towards the voice. He was in no hurry to get to the other side of the barn, to the voice that belonged to Jim Bailey. His dad.

He paused just long enough to pull a cigarette from his pocket, light it, and take a long drag, before he rounded the corner to see what all the fuss was about. Jim Bailey heard his son's footsteps approach, but didn't look up from the trailer hitch he was working with. "I need you to help me back up into the barn," he grunted, turning red from the effort of adjusting the hitch. Jim always lost patience more quickly on a hot day. "We gotta unload all this hay before the sun goes down. Can't find your brother – " His voice was barely audible now, he was bent so low over the hitch. Then something snapped. "Aww…" Dad mumbled a few curse words under his breath. Peter was still nursing his cigarette when Jim stood, put a hand on his aching back, and finally looked at him.

"Get that thing away from my barn!" He exploded, finally looking Peter in the eye.

"I'm not gonna drop it, Dad. I'm not a kid." Peter took another long breath and stared Jim straight in the face. He was taller than Dad, had been since he was 17 years old, and it felt good.

But all of Peter's six feet didn't intimidate Jim. The shorter man wasn't afraid to push his parental weight around. He took a few steps closer till he could jab a finger in his son's chest. "No flames… no smoke… not even a spark… anywhere near my barn." His voice dropped lower. "You hear me?"

Peter didn't nod, didn't speak. Simply rolled his eyes and stepped a few paces backwards – then made a big show of dropping the cigarette on the ground and putting it out with the heel of his work boot. "There. Satisfied?" He spread his arms out wide in a mock show of innocence.

Jim scuffed some dirt over the discarded cigarette to make sure it was really out. Then he went back to his work, but not before giving Peter a dirty look.

"Here. I can replace that wire later. It's just the brake light. Just help me back her in." Jim Bailey was neither a young man nor a trim one, but he jumped into the driver's seat of the truck as if he were a spring chicken.

It comes with practice, I guess, Peter thought morosely – practice at the only thing Dad had ever cared about. The one thing Peter would never care about. As he walked behind the truck and waved Dad in, his mind drifted away on his dreams. He was off, and soon – by this winter, at the latest. He was taking his guitar to California and wiping the dust of this godforsaken Nebraska town off his boots for good.

Jim shifted the truck into park and hopped down from the driver's seat as nimbly as he'd stepped up into it. He unhitched the trailer, then climbed back into the truck. "Start unloading," he hollered over the low rumble of the engine. "I'm heading to the house to find your brother." The family's old farmhouse was half a mile east, and down a low hill, from the barn – Jim never walked it. Every moment counted for a busy cattle rancher.

"Well, can Todd come help in the meantime?" Peter hollered back.

"I send my ranch hands home every day at 4:00. You know that. This is a job for my sons." Jim had one hand on the driver's side door, and he was leaning over impatiently. He was ready to get this over with.

Peter checked his watch. It was already 6:30. "What about dinner?" He hollered at Dad's retreating back.

"You eat after they eat," Jim hollered back over his shoulder and slammed the door.

Peter's shoulders hung low as he looked up at the mountain of work before him. 50 bales of hay. Each weighing 50 pounds. And all of it needing to be done within the next two hours. Dad would want the barn organized– and swept – before they brought the cattle in for the night. He took a moment to gaze out on the open fields. Hundreds of acres of them. The prairie grass blew softly in the wind – almost like the dance of the ocean – but Peter didn't notice the dance. He only noticed that it was too hot and dry for work like this. Heat waves rose above the horizon and shimmered strangely. It'd been a record week for heat, this last week in July.

He turned to stare down his task one more time. So many things had to be done just so – all because of Jim's preferences. Deep clean the barn on the first Saturday of every month, Pete. Feed the cows before you feed yourself, Pete. If it was his barn, he'd do things differently. But it never would be his barn. California would make sure of that.

Peter donned his leather gloves and grabbed a pair of hay hooks. If he had to do all this work – and he had to achieve at least some appearance of work before Dad got back with Rob – at least he wasn't going to let it ruin his guitar-playing hands.

But wait. Rob had gone into town to pick up Gina. If Dad was going to wait for his favorite son – and Peter felt sure that he would – they wouldn't be back down for another hour at least.

He had time for a little enjoyment. He deserved it, being left alone with all this work. He slowly, deliberately, removed one glove and with his free hand, pulled another cigarette from his pocket.

He worked quickly – not noticing when the sun went down behind the hill and Dad still hadn't returned. Not noticing the beads of sweat that fell from his forehead as he hooked, lifted, flung the hay. Forget body mechanics. All his anger towards his Dad fueled the fire and made his work go faster than it ever had. He didn't even notice when a small something fell into the hay. Not until he'd stacked the last bale high, straightened, and put a hand to his mouth, did he realize.

He'd dropped his cigarette.

∽

San Diego, California

"Race you to the top!" Without looking back, 19 year-old Hope thrust her hands into her horse's wiry black mane and lifted her seat out of the saddle. The moment Pirate settled into a regular stride – a long, easy lope – she felt the rhythm of her breathing slow to match his.

They did make it to the top first. Anna's horse was slower, and Hope knew it. She could hear Anna's laughter as the older, stouter Arabian horse moseyed his way up the hill.

Hope seized the extra moment to breathe deep, and take in the beauty all around her. Yes, this was her favorite place. Up here, she couldn't hear any shouting. Mom and Dad had never been best friends, but lately, between Dad's long hours at the hospital and Mom's mood swings, Hope had tried to avoid being home whenever she could.

And here, at the top of the hill, with her two best friends in the world, she had no worries. Up here... she was safe. She could close her eyes, and breathe, and listen. If only paints and an easel weren't impossible to carry on horseback, it would be perfect.

"I see that dreamy look in your eyes. Come back, Miss Prophetess." Anna had reached the top. Hope felt sure that if her cousin could reach her, that playful comment would've been accompanied by a jab in the ribs.

"Oh, you remember my old nickname?" Hope rested, forearms on Pirate's mane, enjoying the sun on her back.

"How could I forget? We used to play that we were descended from Queen Esther herself. Or better yet, King David."

"Hmm. Well, if we were really the stock of kings and queens, I think we'd make it to the top a little faster, don't you?"

"I meant to lose," Anna said in her confident, sing-song voice. "Just trying to be a good older cousin. Uncle Rosie made me promise to look after you, you know."

"Yeah, ten years ago!"

"What can I say, I never break a promise. Anyway." Anna softened her voice. "What's got you distracted today, Hope?" Hope's favorite cousin was as gifted at seeing directly into her heart as she was at cheerful teasing.

"I was just thinking. I can see my future from up here." The wide valley spread below. The horses dotting the pasture. The lower Olympic-sized arena where jumpers ran through their courses. The covered, smaller arena carved out in the middle of the hill, where disadvantaged and differently-abled kids received their riding lessons. For some of them, it was the closest they would ever get to walking.

"You and me both. You'll be the owner, and I'll help you manage."

"Fun joke, cuz."

"Not a joke. If you can get Uncle Rosie to buy the place when Miss Heidi retires – and I've no doubt you can – I'll help you run it. I already talked to Jake about it."

"You mean it?!" She'd hug her cousin if she could reach her across the divide their two mounts created. A sparkling smile – Hope's best feature, she'd been told – would have to do for now.

"Yup. Now speaking of Jake, I better get home if I don't want to find the baby playing video games when I get back." Anna rolled her eyes and turned her horse. She loved to tease everyone, especially her husband.

Hope needed to steal one more moment of beauty before she headed back down the hill. The only daughter of a successful doctor, she knew she was privileged. She knew she was lucky; not most nineteen year-old girls had their own horse, their college classes paid for, a huge extended family to love them, and a gorgeous beach close by that was so quiet it felt like her own. But at the end of every day, when she came home from the horses or from school or from playing with her nieces at the beach, the loneliness would set in, and that lucky feeling would fade away. She'd taken, lately, to extending her outings as long as she could, to bottling up all the loveliness she found and attempting to carry it inside her. But it would evaporate the moment she walked in her family's front door.

This time, when she let her cocoa-brown eyes fall on the valley below, she didn't find the easy light green that normally covered these pastures in late July. The fields were straw-colored, and the straw was blowing in the breeze. No, not straw – corn. Hope knew she was seeing with her mind's eye, but it felt so real. She blinked her eyes, quick, to clear away the image. But she felt that tug again, the tug that pulled her towards quiet, towards listening. So she tightened her hold on the reins and held her horse still.

The golden afternoon light trickled down through the leaves all around Hope, reminding her of the way honey looked when it dripped from a spoon. The golden voice she missed from her childhood spoke straight to her heart: *There is more.* She closed her eyes and tried to capture it, tried to tuck God's words and the sound of His voice into a place in her heart where they'd never be forgotten.

Ten minutes later, she and Pirate walked into the wide, sunlit barn aisle. Horses munched hay contentedly in their stalls, stamping the occasional hoof to ward off a fly. Heidi's students were just finishing up, and Anna was brushing her horse outside. Grooming Pirate in the pre-dusk quiet of the barn was Hope's favorite daily ritual.

She hung up her saddle in the tack room and grabbed her lunch pack with one swift motion. Then she led Pirate up to the hot walker; not because he really needed it – his breathing had already slowed to a regular rate – but because he needed the practice. If she was training him to be a steady ride for students, then he needed to be accustomed to every appliance on the ranch.

After attaching Pirate to the walker and clucking him on, Hope pulled down the tailgate of her forest-green pickup truck and hopped up on it. "What you got for dinner?" Anna called out in her singsong way and hopped up next to her.

Hope opened up the cooler sack. "Oops. I grabbed Dad's stuff by mistake."

"His bagels and lox? Oooh, a few patients out there are gonna meet a grumpy doctor today!" Anna made a grumpy monster face, just like she had when they were kids.

Dr. Rosenberg was a hard worker, like most of the Jewish men that Hope knew. He was also a modest man. He didn't require much. But he did like his bagel and lox to sustain him in the last four hours of a twenty-hour shift. "I know," Hope sighed. "Can you imagine Dad eating my peanut butter and jelly?" Hope looked down at her accidental dinner. "Still, though. No sense letting it go to waste. You want some?"

"You know I do." Anna broke the sandwich in half and gulped down her portion. How she kept her trim figure, Hope never knew. Hope was fit, too, but she had to work hard at it. "Ok. I really gotta go now. Thanks for the ride!" Anna hugged her slightly taller cousin and jogged off to her car.

Hope stretched her arms into the air, then reached behind her head to untangle her curls and re-do the bun that had come loose. She hopped off the back of the truck and lifted the tailgate back into place, then went around to the front door to put her lunch sack away.

She checked her phone quickly before closing the door. She had three missed calls, all from Dad, and one text message, reading just one short line: *Come home now.*

Peter was doubled over, his face just inches from the pungent hay. Breathing it in, thankful, for once, that he'd been raised among it, that he wouldn't have an allergic reaction from looking at hay like some of the city folk who came every year to gawk at a real cattle ranch.

No, he needed every ounce of concentration to find that cigarette. But where had he dropped it? His heart threatened to pound out of his chest – but he picked his way through slowly, deliberately. If he tore bales apart and searched frantically like he wanted to, then not only would his hours of neatly-stacked labor be for naught, but Dad would know something was wrong the moment he stepped into the barn.

Peter put both hands on his knees in a tripod stance to catch his breath. It was pointless. He'd searched twenty minutes already – but he could search for twenty hours and never find it. How stupid he'd been. The stress, the fear clutching at his chest – all for a few moments of pleasure. Of rebellion, if he was being honest.

Looking for a cigarette in a haystack had to be worse than looking for a needle. A needle couldn't start a fire. But then a thought struck Peter – what if the pounds and pounds of hay he'd stacked snuffed out the flame? Didn't fire need oxygen to burn?

And water. Water could stop a fire. The moment the thought entered his brain, Peter grabbed the hose from the side of the barn and pulled it around, grunting from the effort. He had to do something before Jim got back. He couldn't water the hay itself – it would rot, and be ruined. But he could drag the hose in a big circle around the hay, making puddles on the ground.

He was almost ready to roll the hose back up when Dad's voice broke in. Peter hadn't even heard the truck pull up. "What the – What do you think you're doing?!" Jim Bailey stopped in his tracks. "How did all this water get here? Peter!" Dad only uttered the second syllable of his son's name when he was beyond mad and into livid. "Don't you know it's mosquito season? And – why?" Dad grumbled and cursed under his breath as he walked around, surveying the mess.

Before Dad could force the truth out of him, Peter took off. He took long strides down the hill – half a mile was nothing to his long, athletic legs. He needed some air.

Cicadas chirped in the few trees that dotted the walkway; an eagle cried overhead; hidden grasshoppers warmed up for their evening concert. But Peter heard none of it. He only heard the thumping of his own heart, and another voice that pounded along to the beat of it: *You're a failure. You're a failure. You're a failure.*

chapter two

The sun was setting behind the low San Diego hills by the time Hope pulled her green pickup into the driveway. It was basically its own street, their mile-long driveway, and she made her way carefully, so as not to disturb Mom's oleanders or the rosebushes. As Hope rounded the last bend, she shifted into park, and sat back in her seat for a minute. All her energy was gone. Then she noticed Dad's car next to her. *Strange,* she thought. He wasn't expected home till 10pm at the earliest.

Hope tried, but couldn't remember a time when Dad had come home early. If anything, he usually arrived later than planned. *A doctor's work is never done,* he would say. *Least of all an oncologist's.*

"Hello?" Hope called as she opened the door, half hoping no one would respond. Maybe they'd gone somewhere with Mom's car. She dropped her bag on the porch. She'd come get it later, along with the boots that she removed and piled next to it. Nothing that carried a trace of barn dirt was allowed into the house. She crossed to the laundry room where she always left a change of clothes waiting. She quickly replaced her riding breeches and oversized top for a clean pair of jeans and a comfy light-blue long sleeve. Then she washed her hands – all the way up to her elbows, in fact – in the deep laundry room sink. If Mom was home, she was more likely to see Hope if she didn't smell like a horse.

She padded in her socks across the vast marble entry and over to the staircase. Still no sign of Mom or Dad. She was about to head to the kitchen, but stopped in her tracks when she heard the soft click of their bedroom door. Then Papa stood at the head of the stairs, where he watched her a moment. As she plodded up-stairs towards him, she noticed the lines around his eyes and the slight slump of his shoulders. If someone who didn't know him well were to look at him, they might only notice the thick mus-tache, the professional clothes that he wore even at home, the aura of authority that hung around him. But she knew him better. She could see that he was tired.

"How's Mom?" Hope asked softly. She was surprised to hear that her own voice sounded as tired as Dad looked.

"I've got her settled down now. You can go in." He passed Hope without looking in her eyes. Probably to go to the kitchen.

Hope sighed a sigh that went down to her toes. She took the steps one at a time, willing her feet to go faster but unable to make them do so.

After a soft knock at Mom's door and the sound of a whis-pered, "Come in," Hope kneeled beside Mom's bed. No trace of the sunset could be seen through the thick, drawn blinds. No hint of the delicious-smelling jasmine that grew down below could come through her windows. Mom was in pain again. But this time seemed even worse than last week.

Sweat beaded on Mara's brow. She kept squinting up her eyes in a grimace. "Is it the headaches again?" Hope went for a wash-cloth and dabbed at her mother's forehead.

Mara just shook her head and bit her lip.

Hope sat back in the rose-colored wing-backed chair and won-dered what she could do to help. She was happy to come home early, happy to be there for Mom – but why? There had to be some-thing she could *do*.

Then she noticed Mom's hair. It was a source of pride for Mrs. Rosenberg to have her hair curled by noon every day. But today it lay flat against her head, and it was growing damp from the beads of sweat.

"Hey, how 'bout I wash your hair for you? Would that help?"

Mara grimaced like she might decline, but then gave a slow nod.

Hope helped her mom over to the bathroom, found a chair for her to relax in, and waited for the water to get hot. When Mom finally leaned her head back in the sink, Hope started massaging her scalp with strong fingers, and asked, "There. Doesn't that feel better?"

"Yes." Mara took a deep breath for the first time since Hope had walked in the room. "That, and the pain pill your father gave me. It's helping."

Hope was used to playing mother while Mara played the child. But there was something different about tonight. Now that they were in the light of the bathroom, Hope could see the stains made by tear tracks that lined her mother's cheeks. And why had she needed a pain pill? If it was strong enough to relax her, it must've been stronger than Tylenol. But if it wasn't the headaches, then what was hurting her?

"Mom, is something troubling you? You don't look... normal." Hope didn't know how else to say it. She went to move a piece of hair from her mother's face and touched her cheek in the process.

"Stop! Stop it, I told you!" When Mara looked up, her eyes were round with fear. Like those of a hunted animal.

Mara writhed away from her chair, away from where Hope was standing, and fell hard onto the floor. She curled up into a fetal position and sobbed for a moment. Hope froze. Trying to recover, she placed a gentle hand on her mother's shoulder. "Mom, are you ok? I just want to..."

Mara snapped her head back, and her hand too. Her arm pulled back as if ready to strike Hope in the face when she screamed, "Out! Out, I said! Don't come back!" Then her voice rose beyond a scream and she was shrieking wildly. "Get out!!"

Hope left the sink running and ran from the room.

Orange flames licked the night sky, but Peter didn't see them.

He only heard the ringing of the phone. Hollered shouts from his parents' downstairs bedroom. Some shuffling – then the sound of the front door slamming.

For a moment, he thought he'd roll over and try to go back to sleep. 5:00, his normal wake up time, would come early. But then he heard muffled tears – Mom.

"What is it?" He was asking her a moment later, after he'd donned sweats and taken the stairs two at a time.

"A fire! A prairie fire!" She collapsed in his arms. "Oh, Peter. *Mio Dio, mio Dio!*" Peter's Italian mother switched to her first language when she was stressed. She covered her face in her hands and sobbed, shoulders shaking in her thin summer nightgown.

"Mom, where's Dad? Where's Rob?" He threw a coat over her, then herded her out on to the porch to try to get a better look. The windchime Mom had bought this summer rattled and swayed in the wind like a warning. He squinted his eyes and trained them on the spot a half-mile away where he would be able to see the barn, if it hadn't been the black of night.

Where the barn should be was a faint orange hum.

"At the barn… they took the tractor to the barn!"

Peter squeezed Teresa's shoulders with his strong hands, then jumped into his big white pickup truck that was always parked in front of the house. He fumbled with the keys that were always left in the ignition, hands shaking so violently that it took three tries to start the engine.

He sped up the hill as fast as he could, almost flipping the truck at the one bend in the drive. He cursed under his breath and steadied his hands on the wheel. White knuckles. Hands shaking.

"Dad!" Peter yelled when he burst from the truck and saw the flames erupting from the roof of the barn. His hands flew to the top of his head as he tried to take it all in. He didn't know what else to say. How had this happened? Had it been his fault, really?

Todd, the ranchhand, and Rob were both manning hoses attached to spray trucks. Dad was behind the wheel of one, and a neighbor had driven over with another. When Dad saw Peter, he jumped out of his truck, the family's two border collies at his heels.

The flames reached up into the sky, as if they were trying to touch the stars. Peter heard a snap… a crackle… how long before the whole barn came tumbling down?

Jim was shouting. "We gotta get 'em out!" Peter couldn't make out the words over the din of the wind and the crackling flames. But he understood Dad's body language, when Mr. Bailey Sr. tossed a bandana to him and wrapped another one around his own face. "Cover us!" Jim shouted back to the two men wielding spray hoses.

Peter wasn't sure how much coverage two men with hoses could offer him when he was walking into a literal furnace. A gas mask would help. Or fire-retardant clothes. The thought struck him that Mom would be praying; and he was surprised by how much comfort that idea brought.

A blast of hot air pushed Peter back, but he willed his fight-or-flight response to turn off, and followed his dad anyway. On they fought through the heat and the sound of beams cracking, the two dogs on their heels, all the way to the back of the barn. Jim grabbed the two long leather stockwhips that he kept hanging on the back wall for mustering cattle. "Hi-yah! Hi-yah!" He shouted while cracking the whip. Peter choked on the smell of smoke entering his lungs and tied his bandana a little tighter. It was no use; the cattle were scared senseless.

It was taking too long. Could they make it, if it took much longer? Their most trusted dog started nipping at the heels of the cows in the back. That dog was smart. He set off a chain reaction; the cows in back butted into the cows ahead of them, until every last head of the 500 cattle had been chased from the barn.

Peter burst from the burning structure and collapsed onto the ground. Maybe he should get farther from the fire; but all he could think about now was filling his lungs with air. That had been too close.

Jim thought of one last thing; he swung the twenty-foot long metal gate shut to prevent any brainless cattle from heading back into the death trap. Rob and Todd continued spraying, but their drops had made no difference. Peter watched from his spot on the ground as Dad stood, hands on hips, taking deep breaths and surveying the damage.

The barn would be a total loss. There was no denying it. Thank God they'd gotten the cattle out.

"Should we try to round 'em up, Dad? Lead them down to the pond?" Rob was asking. Jim didn't seem to hear him.

Jim was looking down. Down to the dry cottonwoods where the cicadas lived, the elms that lined the driveway down to the house.

One cottonwood was all ablaze. The flames jumped to the cottonwood next to it. It wouldn't be long before they were all on fire.

Was the wind picking up? Was it Peter's imagination, or were embers from the fire actually blowing sideways?

"The house! It's gonna head to the house! Peter, get up! Go, go, go!"

The men wrestled the hoses as the spray trucks followed behind them. More neighbors arrived; news travelled fast in this little community of ranchers. The sun was rising at the edge of the horizon when an east wind picked up and the men cheered.

The fire was turning away from the house. They'd really beat it. Peter collapsed in a heap on the ground next to Rob, then uncharacteristically threw an arm around his brother. Maybe fighting fires brought them closer. He laughed at the idea and wiped the mingled sweat and soot from his brow with his forearm. Mom had come up, ignoring Dad's protests that she stay near the house, and brought water for everyone. He chugged a bottle in under a minute.

The rising sun shone through the now-empty frame of the barn, giving the black boards an eerie look. Dust they'd all kicked up during their fight slowly settled along with the floating ash from the fire. Peter looked down the hill. They'd lost five trees, but managed to save the rest. And the house. Thank God they'd saved the house.

The men were so elated by their success – a prairie fire in July was no joke. But it had been no match for them. The mood was almost celebratory, until Roger, Miss Hazel's dear husband from the next farm over, looked up the hill with wizened eyes. New flames licked the waving prairie grasses; the tongues of orange moved faster now than they had before with the wind pushing them uphill and with a feast of grass before them. The men hadn't put out the fire; they'd redirected it. He shushed everyone with a single motion.

"Wait," he cautioned, and raised a hand to silence their back-slapping and water-chugging. "It's headed for the town."

Hope sat on her flowered bedspread, trying to muffle the sound of her tears with a pillow. She took a few deep breaths, then stood to retrieve her brushes and paints. She couldn't wash away Mom's pain. But she knew how to paint away her own.

She settled herself at the easel and slid her brush across the paper. It would only be a few moments, she knew, till the brush took on a life of its own. Till a story played out on the paper in front of her before she'd even decided what to paint.

A rose with a thorn. A beautifully deep, red rose. With another, smaller, rose attached to it at the stem. The smaller rose was shaped like a heart, and it bent away from the tall, straight one. And a petal fell down…

As the petal fell, it began to look more like a drop of blood, and fell upon the thorn. As the straighter rose took on a darker, deeper color, so did the small one. Tears fell down Hope's face as she realized what she was painting: Mom's pain had become her own.

Her door swung open without a knock. She sat up straight in her chair, startled, and turned the easel to the side. Why did she feel the need to hide her artwork from Dad? Would he even know what it meant? Would he care?

Dr. Rosenberg seated himself in the soft blue reading chair by Hope's nightstand. He was silent for a few moments. Then with a shuddering breath he said, "I can't believe this. I'm going to lose my marriage. And all because of you." His shoulders slumped and his head fell into his hands. Hope wondered if he might cry, but he didn't.

Hope let him sit in silence for a few moments. Then he exited with a little huff and a shake of his head.

Her eyes went back to her painting.

The second rose was too dark. But her paint wasn't dry yet. She'd try to blot it.

She grabbed a paper towel from her stash, but blotting quickly turned to rubbing. Before she could stop herself, there was a hole in the paper – ruined. She was surprised when a scream rose from somewhere inside and she had to stop it by clapping a hand over her mouth. She gently pulled the now-useless painting off the easel and crumpled it, then kneeled on the floor and sobbed.

But after a few moments, she unfolded the crumpled paper and looked at the two roses again. Maybe Mom's pain wasn't what made Hope's heart bleed. Maybe her worst fears were right. Maybe Hope was the one who had started it all.

After all, it was Hope who brought home boots caked in mud. Hope whose hobby cost the family so much money. Hope who wasted hours painting, instead of measuring up and becoming a doctor or a lawyer.

Maybe the kindest thing she could do would be to leave.

She stood quickly. She'd do it now, before she could change her mind. She ran first to the jack-and-jill bathroom that connected her room to the guest room, and scrubbed her face quickly in the sink. When she glanced up, her reflection was almost frightening: eyes wide, hair disheveled, just like Mom's had been tonight. She turned quickly to scrub her face with a towel, then hurried back to look around her room rapidly. What should she take? What does one take when one is leaving her home forever?

She pulled a duffel from under her bed and began filling it quickly. Her choices didn't make sense: one sweater, all her underwear, a few skirts; but she didn't want to overthink it. She paused when she realized she'd have to wait until Dad was asleep. Or at least occupied.

She stepped out of her room and down the hallway, grateful her feet were padded by warm socks and the soft beige carpet Mom had picked out just last year. The sound of rushing water greeted her ears. Dad was in the shower.

It was now or never. She ran back in her room, shoved her riding clothes into her duffel – she'd wear her boots – and took the stairs two at a time. She stopped to grab her keys but thought better of it; Dad had bought her the car. It was only right that she leave it here.

She had some money in her checking account. Not enough to buy a car... but enough to get by, for a little while. There was no reason why she couldn't keep her job at the ranch. She'd just have to find a place to live, that was all. She'd start by walking to Renee's house. Her friend lived at the bottom of their hill and had always been a safe place for Hope. She could spend the night there without fear of questions, and regroup in the morning. Maybe go to Anna's for a couple weeks.

No one heard the door *click* quietly as she left. She took a long, cleansing breath of the cool San Diego night air. It was good just to be out of that house. Long walking strides turned into a jog. The sooner she made it out of their mile-long private driveway and onto the street, the better. Eventually, the pounding of her feet and the ragged sound of her breaths were louder than the pounding of her heart. This was the best thing. There would be nothing for Mom and Papa to fight about if she wasn't there. A fleeting thought lifted her spirits: maybe Mom's pain would even go away.

She looked up at the moon, up at the stars. Orion's belt and the Big Dipper hadn't changed since she was a little girl. God would take care of her now, just like He had then. She walked on, slow but resolute, until she noticed an older man standing in her driveway.

She scarcely had time to stop in her tracks before he was standing in her path. Short brown hair, rumpled corduroy pants... where had he come from? Nobody should be in their driveway at this time of night. But for some reason, she felt no fear, only peace. Like he was supposed to be here.

"Nice night," he said. "Beautiful stars." His voice was quiet but strong, his smile winsome. He was near enough to put an arm around her shoulders, which wouldn't have seemed odd at all. The two strangers stood in silence a moment. She took a deep breath and felt her heart rate start to slow down. She looked at him and smiled. He spoke again. "You're a good girl, Hope."

She wasn't surprised that he knew her name; it seemed right that he should know everything. She just looked down at her feet, and unbidden tears sprang to her eyes. A good girl. How long had it been since she'd heard that phrase? He did put a hand on her shoulder now, and that small kind touch was enough to turn her quiet tears into sobs. When they abated, she looked up, but he was gone. She knew now what she had to do.

She turned around and walked back into the house, while the stranger stood, out of sight, until she was safe inside.

The door clicked behind Hope and she sighed a heavy sigh. It was good not to run – she would leave one day, and soon, she hoped. But not like this. Today, she needed to turn around and face her problems.

But knowing it was right didn't make it easier. Her feet felt like fifty pounds of lead as she trudged up the stairs. But as she reached the top, the Golden Voice she had heard at the barn just this afternoon wrapped around her tighter than any embrace, and His words filled her heart like honey: *More. There is more in store for you than this.*

chapter three

Rob guided Peter's truck down the county road. Peter had been too stunned to drive; Dad and Rob both thought it was the smoke inhalation from the barn that had done it to him.

"Where are we going?" Peter asked faintly, wrapping his arms around his shaking chest.

"Dad said to follow him, so that's what I'm doing." Rob gestured to the pickup in front of them. His voice was strained from anger and exhaustion. And smoke.

Peter's eyelids were heavy. He remembered the last few minutes: hurrying to pick up Mom at the house. Teresa sobbing and wailing; it was her home, she didn't want to leave. Todd and Rob picking her up and plopping her beside Dad in the cab of the big truck. Dad hollering at their ranch hand, Todd, to take the tractor; it might be able to get to places that they wouldn't. Rob shoving him into the truck and shouting that they had to leave.

He almost fell asleep in the midst of this nightmare when a sound overhead awoke him. A loud crack – a branch falling. It had been burned off an ash tree above, and fell down just ten feet in front of them.

"Hold on!" Rob hollered.

Peter's eyes shot open and he saw the predicament. The flames were licking the left side of the road, taunting them; on the right side was a hill too steep even for his rugged four-wheel-drive. He glanced in the rearview mirror: everything behind him was an inferno. The only way out of this fire was through.

Rob gripped the steering wheel and pressed the pedal to the

ground. It worked; the truck plummeted over and off the flaming branch; but Peter thought he could smell burnt rubber. The tires. He thought again that Mom would be praying. *We'll make it.*

"That was too close," Rob shook his head.

A sudden thought occurred to Peter. "Has anybody called 9-1-1?"

"Huh?"

They had fought prairie fires on their own before. But Peter couldn't think of a time when one had raced its way toward the town. He couldn't remember anyone calling for help. He asked it again. "Has anyone called 9-1-1?"

"No, I don't think so. Here." Rob grabbed a cell phone from the center console and handed it to Peter.

The woman's voice on the other end of the line was so cool, it was surreal. "9-1-1, what's your emergency?" She asked. Like fires happened every day.

Peter's throat was too dry to speak. She asked again. "A fire. There's been a fire." She asked a few more questions and instructed him to stay on the line, but within moments, the call was dropped.

"Well, they'll be on their way," Rob said as he watched Peter put the phone away.

"Yeah, but who knows how long they'll take. Stupid volunteer fire department. Everyone who's qualified to hold that hose is fast asleep right now." Peter folded his arms over his chest and glared out the window.

Rob said nothing. They were pulling up to the hospital now. It was the easternmost building of the town, and the place where Rob's pregnant wife was working.

Jim's two sons' feet hit the pavement even before his did. "Wait here," he barked at Teresa, but he needn't have bothered. She was too grief-stricken to move.

The fire was just behind them. They'd outdriven it in the last mile, but Peter could see it steadily climbing if he looked back down the hill.

When the four men walked into the hospital, they didn't know that embers from falling ashes littered their hair, their shirts, their arms. They didn't know they looked like they'd just left a war zone. Jim, Peter, Rob and Roger stood stock-still, stunned momentarily by the cool air and the quietness of the ER. One nurse strolled across the waiting room, glancing at a chart. Her only patient, an older man, was waiting in a chair for her to call his name. It was obvious they had no idea of the danger.

"We have to get out now!" In a room where you could've heard a pin drop, Jim's voice boomed like a bomb.

The stocky nurse shook herself a little, lifted eyes that said *don't mess with me,* but raised her eyebrows when she took in their appearance. "Excuse me?" She asked.

"Gina!" Rob ran to his wife, calling her name.

"What is it? What's wrong?" She hurried from behind the desk and over to him in her blue scrubs, stethoscope clanging against her chest. Her legs were still quick for a woman six months along.

He pulled her close and spoke directly in her ear. "There's a prairie fire. You have to evacuate the hospital, now."

Gina looked at him a moment, thinking. Cool as a cucumber. She was the favorite nurse of more than one doctor for that reason. Then she ran to the nearest patient room and punched the Code Blue button. Within seconds, four more staff members were in the room.

"We have to get everyone out, now! There's been a fire!" She started barking orders.

"What about supplies? Should we bring an IV kit or medications?"

"Leave it. Anyone from ICU will go in the ambulance; there's an ACLS kit. Any patients who are stable: just disconnect their IVs and get them to the parking lot. These gurneys roll for a reason. Let's go!"

Gina knew her nursing duties didn't change just because her location did. She grabbed a notepad, made sure she had a couple pens in her pocket, and instructed her coworkers to do the same. She'd take notes on her patients' conditions and document whatever she could on the drive. She could input her notes into the computer when they got back to the hospital.

A matter of minutes later, 25 patients and the eight staff members on duty that night were grouped in the parking lot, united by the flames not a quarter mile away that had them mesmerized. Peter held out a hand. It looked like rain; but when he looked at his palm, it was ash, chunks of gray ash, falling from the sky. The fire hadn't weakened; it had gotten stronger, as if it was hungry for more. Peter looked over at the farthest wing: the maternity wing, he knew; it was already ablaze.

Roger and Todd were waiting for them. They loaded three patients and a nurse into the bed of Roger's grey work truck, and three more patients who could sit into the cab of the tractor. The two technicians who were on duty would drive the ambulances; but the five nurses and one doctor were needed to ride with the patients. How they fit everyone into three pickup trucks, two ambulances and a John Deere tractor, Peter would never remember. All he knew was that ten minutes later, he was behind the wheel of his now-unrecognizable truck, and next to his mom, trying not to hear her tears. The vehicles got in a line – the tractor last – and the drivers waited for Jim to do one final head count and give the signal to leave. Gina was on her phone in the bed of Peter's truck, her notes on her lap, giving report to the hospital in Red Bluffs. When they put her on hold, she ordered Rob to call the mayor, who they'd all gone to high school with, and urge him to order a mandatory evacuation. Nobody asked if she was following the right chain of command. This town had protocol for tornadoes; it had a plan for blizzards and hail storms. But they'd never dealt with a fire like this. The only plan they had for a prairie fire was the one they'd always stuck to when times got tough: neighbors helping neighbors.

Rob had given up the fight to get her into the cab to protect their unborn baby; she insisted on staying with her two patients, who lay on a pile of blankets in the bed of the pickup. So Rob stayed with her, arms wrapped protectively around, legs anchoring her on each side, holding the phone to his ear while he waited for the mayor to pick up.

"Wait." Roger's voice was hoarser even than usual from the smoke and the stress. He'd gotten out of his own truck, stepped over to the group and motioned for all to listen. "Let's pray."

The respected man didn't need to say anything more to get each head to bow. "Lord," began Roger, "thank You for getting us away from the fire safely. And thank You for helping us get every patient out of that hospital. Please protect us on our drive out of town. Amen." Fire or no fire, a farmer's prayers were short and simple; he knew God didn't need fancy words. Roger cleared his throat and hopped back to his own car. "Aright. Let's go!" He'd be leading the way to town.

It was fifty miles to the nearest city and the closest hospital. Peter added a silent prayer that his truck would make it that far. On the way, they passed fire trucks and sirens blaring. Finally, help was coming.

The next morning, Hope woke up puffy-eyed, and late. Saturdays she was normally up by seven to cook breakfast for Mom and Dad, then be ready to head to the 10am *Shabbat*, or Sabbath, service. But it was almost nine when she pulled her weary body out of bed and slid her tear-stained pillowcase off her pillow to wash it.

How come everything ached? Was that what guilt did to people? And what had she done, anyway?

Last night wasn't the first time Mom had gone to bed early with a headache. It wasn't even the first time Mom had tried to strike her. But it was the first time Hope had thought of leaving. When she'd returned to the house and knocked on Mom's door again to check on her at 11pm, Mara had let her in, but pretended like the scene in the bathroom had never happened. Maybe she'd forgotten. Normally, Mom would apologize, and have some explanation for her outbursts. But this time, after the anger passed, her mouth stayed a thin, quiet line.

Hope hugged her naked pillow to herself and felt a few stray tears race down her cheeks. She wiped them away hastily; but even more shameful was the fact that she'd cried herself to sleep last night. *Come on, Hope.* She busied herself with making her bed and opening the window. *You're not twelve anymore.*

Saving money – and helping Dad take care of Mom – had seemed like a good idea a year ago. She'd traded in her dreams of early entrance to vet school for the dream of being a good daughter. But that was one dream she'd never fulfill. Mom wasn't better. If last night was any indication, then she was actually worse.

Hope stood at the open window of her second-story bedroom

and looked out upon the valley. She had the best view in the house. *Father, what do I do?* She prayed silently. No answer.

She changed into dress pants and her favorite red blouse, pulled her curly mane back into a ponytail, then headed downstairs. She'd never been able to master the messy bun, like many of her friends. There was just too much hair, too much *messy*.

She took the stairs slowly this morning, and smoothed her blouse as she did. Mom said red clashed with her skin tones. Made her look pale. But today she didn't care. She also didn't care if Dad skipped *Shabbat* to stay home with Mom, as he often did when Mara wasn't feeling well. She was going, even if she was going by herself. She'd sit with Anna and enjoy her little nieces.

By the time Hope reached the kitchen, she only had thirty minutes to make and eat breakfast before it would be time to leave. She cracked some eggs into a pan and turned on the coffee pot. Still no sign of Mom or Dad, so she turned on the radio for company.

Her favorite country deejay announced the next song, but then a more sober tone came into his voice. "A small town in Western Nebraska – a town that actually boasts more cows than people – suffered a devastating fire last night. The fire chief is calling it a prairie fire, but no one knows how it started. Get this, Allison, the town doesn't even have a full-time fire department – only a small volunteer-run station, can you believe that?" He made a *tsk*-ing sound as if to say *poor small-town folks*.

"Wow, no, I can't believe it. So what did they do when they noticed the fire? How did they put it out?"

"Well, in true small-town fashion, neighbors all rushed in to help each other. They were even able to evacuate the local hospital using pickup trucks, ambulances, and get this – a *tractor*. But by the time fire trucks from the neighboring city arrived, the hospital and about ten other buildings were engulfed in flames. Officials say the fire is contained now, thanks to the hard work of the firefighters and a surprise thunderstorm that showed up on their heels…"

"Where is Nebraska, anyway? Isn't it in the South somewhere?" The female broadcaster's voice dropped mockingly when she said the word *South*.

"I believe it's somewhere in the middle, Allison… you need to catch up on your geography," Sarcasm dripped from the male deejay's voice, putting him in danger of losing his position as Hope's favorite. "Anyway, as I was saying. The fire is contained... no casualties have been reported... but several injuries. The fire chief on duty is saying the hospital, at least, is a total loss, but it's too early to tell how much damage has been done to the other structures..."

His words died off with the *click* of the radio. Hope was done listening to this. She didn't even have the energy to change the channel.

She had enough worries of her own.

A whole month had passed since the prairie fire had blackened their land and taken out not only the Bailey family's farm, but four of the neighboring farms as well, and a good chunk of the town. After the fire flattened the hospital, it had taken a turn north and also demolished the town's one and only hardware store, along with 12 family homes. 17 more family homes had been deemed damaged, but fixable. Some folks had insurance to take care of the smoke damage. Others had paid off their mortgages so long ago that insurance had gone by the wayside, and they had to rely on the help of family and friends or hired workers to get their homes livable again. Peter's guitar had also been burnt to a crisp, having been left in the barn where he'd practiced that fateful day; but nobody seemed to care about that.

In true Midwest fashion, neighbors stuck together. Though 29 families in all were displaced, not one became homeless. Roger and Hazel had gone to her brother's in Southwestern Colorado while their house was renovated. Two families were bunking here, with the Baileys. Gina and Rob had moved out of the guest home and into the main house to make room for an older couple with grandchildren. One of Gina's coworkers, Ali, was also bunking in the main house with her two little girls. The house seemed overstretched to the men involved, but Teresa was in her element, with so many people to cook for and talk with.

One of the things she didn't tire of talking about was the way the fire had stopped. Right on the heels of the firefighters had come a not-uncommon, but not expected on that day, July thunderstorm. First hail and lightning had come: the kind of hail that normally forced folks inside. A steady rain followed it, assisting the hardworking but few firefighters in their work. And somehow, even with all the burnt buildings and injuries, there had been no fatalities. Mom gave credit to the angels; Dad, to their own speedy work; Peter was just grateful.

He'd confessed to Teresa just a few days after the fire about the cigarette. His mom was his best friend, and the secret was eating him alive. He couldn't carry it alone any longer. Mom had wept and begged him, "Don't tell your brother. And especially not your Dad. They will…" She had uttered the word in Italian first, then he'd helped her find the right English one … "They will *alienate* you."

Everybody knew the fire had started in their barn, yet nobody had asked why. This town couldn't afford their own fire marshal, so there would be no investigation. They weren't a curious people; the fire was just accepted as fact. Yet somehow, Peter's secret being safe didn't ease his mind about it.

Gina was at the table now, barely able to reach her plate over a ready-to-pop belly. "Morning, Peter," she said in her cheerful way around a mouthful of toast as he came down into the kitchen and poured his coffee. She turned when she heard a knock at the door. "Who can that be?"

Peter held his coffee in one hand and opened the door to find three of his neighbors, all with tools in their hands, their trucks running in the Bailey's driveway. "What's all this?" Jim asked as he came up behind them, mail in hand. He handed a stack of envelopes over to Peter, put his hands on his hips, blocking the gentlemen from entering until he had his answer.

"This is an old-fashioned barn-raisin'." The tallest of the men, Tom, turned and looked Jim square in the face.

"Excuse me?" Jim asked as if they had offered to come and take down his barn, not build one.

"Look, we know you don't like askin' for help," Tom continued.

"I'm not asking."

"I know that, I know." Tom softened his voice a little and held up a hand to quiet Jim. "But I also know that your insurance refused to build you a new barn because you never put in sprinklers like they asked you to. Now don't give me that look. You know news travels fast in this town." Jim hadn't just given him a look; he'd turned on his heels and looked as if he was ready to walk away. Or punch something. But he turned back and looked at his old friend; not relenting, but listening.

"Now. You saved my mother," Tom jabbed a thumb towards his own chest, "And his daughter," now the thumb was aimed at the dark-haired man standing beside him, "In that hospital fire. We know you were just doin' what neighbors do. We know we don't owe you anything. We're just here to help you like you helped us."

Peter watched his father's face, wondering if he'd mention that they didn't need a barn – the cows were gone without a trace. But knowing this town, the men already knew. Dad didn't actually seem able to say anything. Peter had never seen Jim cry, but he'd never seen him closer to it than on this day. He watched his dad open his mouth, then close it; then simply motion the men down the driveway. "Well, come on then. I don't have all day."

Before he left, Tom offered Peter a hearty slap on the back. "Thank you, for all your help, Son. You're a hero, you know that?"

Peter's eyes fell at the word. Hero. If they only knew.

As the men headed down the drive, he thumbed through the mail. A letter for him. He tore it open quickly. It wasn't just any letter – it was an acceptance letter. Their response time was quick. He'd make his own way, and he'd do it before he ever had to see one more nasty Nebraska blizzard.

Guitar or no guitar, he had to get out of this town.

It only took Peter two weeks to pack up, nail down a new place to live, and find a roommate. He'd even been able to secure an interview for a part-time job as a janitor at the hospital near the school he'd be attending. Life was easy when you were young and determined and you didn't care about anyone else's opinions. But if he'd had two years, he wouldn't have been able to convince his dad that it was the right thing to do.

"You're making a mistake, Son."

Peter rolled his eyes. Why did Dad have to follow him out of the house? The decision had been made. Though Mom had railed at him with tears and reasons to stay when they'd first talked, at least she knew when to let him be. At least she had the sense to stay inside today.

"Yeah? You know all about that." Peter hollered back, one hand on Ali's car door. His family didn't even care about him enough to give him a ride to the airport. He'd had to bother a friend instead.

Jim flinched but kept walking towards him, kept pressing. "California's expensive, Pete. You're not prepared." Dad's mouth was set in a hard line, his hands shoved deep in his pockets.

"Oh, and you were prepared when you violated a building code? And lost everything?" Peter didn't really care about the barn. Or the cows. But it was ammo against Dad – ammo that hit the one area where he was weak.

"If you go now – like this – don't bother coming back." Jim spoke quietly; he probably didn't want Mom to hear. But he was in Peter's face now, a finger in his chest.

"Fine!" Peter didn't mind being loud. Let Mom hear. Let Ali hear. Let the neighbors five miles away hear.

He climbed into the passenger seat and slammed the door, watching Dad and his stooped shoulders walk back up to the house. It took him a moment to turn towards Ali. "You okay?" She asked softly, putting a hand on his.

"Yeah," he lied. He slipped his hand out from under hers and pulled the acceptance letter from his back pocket, where it had been burning a hole. He stared at it just to feel that momentary surge of pride. If Dad knew what he was really doing, he wouldn't be so quick to judge this move.

But Peter wanted to keep it a secret. He wanted to do this privately, and finish something all the way through for once in his life. He wouldn't tell his family until it was done, until he could come back and make everything right.

chapter four

Hope sat in the hard plastic chair, and held Mara's hand, and waited for someone – anyone to explain it all to her.

Two months had passed since the night when Mara had kicked Hope out of her room, but she still hadn't bounced back. Typically, when Mara had her dark moods, she'd stay there for two or three days. Sometimes as long as a week. But two months? This time, it was as if some dark invisible force held her mother down. Would she ever come back up?

"Mom, are you okay?" Hope whispered the same words that had crossed her lips at least four times since she'd arrived an hour ago.

Mara opened her eyes but seemed too tired to keep her eyelids open, and let them drop. "Yeah, I'm okay," she whispered, her voice empty.

Hope let her shoulders hang down, looked up at the IV pole, and sighed. Morphine. Why did Mom need Morphine?

She sat up a little straighter. "Mom, are you going to tell me what's wrong?" Her voice sounded loud in the white sterility of the room. Mom just rolled over. She wasn't going to answer. The same way Dad hadn't answered this morning when he'd called her in the middle of a class and summoned her to the hospital with no explanation.

But Mom turned back and opened her eyes wide. "I will tell you when your Dad gets here." Hope caught a glimpse of a tear running down her face. Hope lifted a strand of sweaty hair that was stuck to her mom's cheek. "We want to tell you together." Mom looked away; her voice was all trembly.

Panic clutched Hope's chest. Was Mom dying? Hope stood up quickly. She needed to get some real air. Not this stuffy hospital air. Before they told her anything that could change everything, she needed to get outside. To feel normal.

"Ok. Well, I'm gonna go get a cup of coffee." Hope waved her hand lamely in the direction of the door. "You want anything?"

Mom didn't answer, just closed her eyes again. Hope donned her lavender cardigan and pulled the long strap of her purse over her shoulder. She'd call Anna with an update while she was out. Not that there was any news worth updating her on.

The Med-Surg hallway was a busy hum of nurses in their squeaky shoes and green scrubs. But one man cut through the crowd effortlessly. There was nothing about him that would catch the eye, ordinarily. But Hope didn't have an ordinary eye. She had an uncanny ability for seeing every detail in a person's face, and she knew somehow that she'd seen this one before. She noticed the man's soft blue eyes that were gentled by smile lines; she noticed his rumpled corduroy pants; she noticed his brown hair, and how it was thin on top. She noticed how his face was an open book. One she'd like to read.

He nodded and smiled as they passed each other, and she placed him. He was the man who had stopped her from running away on the night Mom first got sick. When she turned on her heels to try to talk to him, he was more than ten paces away from her, walking quickly in the direction from which she'd come. She sighed and continued on. He looked busy, whoever he was.

A few moments later, Hope broke down in the cafeteria. Something about the warm cup of coffee in her hands and Anna's voice on the other end of the line made her carefully crafted walls come crumbling down.

"No one will tell me what's wrong with her." Hope sounded like a little girl as the words came tumbling out. She felt like one, too – it was all she could do to keep from curling up, wrapping her arms around her knees and rocking back and forth. "All I know is that she's been getting weaker every day for the past two months. Why are they keeping it a secret?"

Anna sighed and sympathized through the phone. Hope clung to the device with both hands; but she was alone here. Anna couldn't help her. Anna couldn't help Mom. "I'll call you later," she whispered before hanging up.

"God," she sighed. "Father, how can I help her?" She wiped her eyes, then stood to force her feet back up to the second floor.

She passed more nurses, more patients dragging IV poles, more distraught family members, without really seeing anyone. Her mind took her back, instead, to last spring, and Mom's empty side of the bed. It was the morning after she and Papa had had one of their arguments. Hope and Papa had woken to find her gone, and her car gone too. No note, no phone calls. Just gone. That morning, Hope had opened all the windows in Mom's room, the first time they'd been opened in weeks – the forgotten daughter was desperate for some fresh air, desperate to hear the sound of the robins heralding the morning, desperate for some kind of assurance that everything would be normal – that this day would roll over into the next, and sometime, Mom would come back.

It had been a long three days; but she had come back. And she would come back this time, too. Hope hugged herself as she walked down the cold hallway and tried to believe it.

She took a deep breath. Yes. Papa and the doctors would get on top of Mom's pain. Mom would come home from the hospital, and Hope would finally urge the thing she'd been wanting to say all along: that Mom get help. That in addition to the doctors, she talk to someone. Hope would even go with her.

Filled with a new resolve: things would get better, and Hope would help; she stepped over the passage of room 221, the weight off her shoulders. Her eyes scanned the room quickly. The bed was empty; the sheets rumpled down at the foot. The IV bag swayed lightly on its pole, and its tubing hung down to the ground.

Mom was gone.

"We lost a patient?" The young man in the janitor's uniform asked in a booming voice. He was the closest human to the nurse's desk, so he was the one her words had fallen upon; but she had no words left. She just nodded and leaned on the counter that surrounded the nurse's desk with one hand.

A nurse Hope recognized, but couldn't place, came up and put a hand on her arm. "Maybe she just went out for a breath of fresh air. Let's go and see." Her hold on Hope's arm was surprisingly strong; maybe she'd noticed how weak Hope was feeling and wanted to make sure she didn't fall over. The nurse waved a hand in the young janitor's direction, beckoning him to follow them. He put down the trash can he'd been about to empty, ripped off his gloves, and instead of following, jogged ahead to the nearest door marked "Exit" and held it open for them.

The two women walked quickly but quietly out the door. Hope was glad for someone to hold her up. The bright sunshine felt disorienting and out of place when they came out into the parking lot.

"Any idea where she would've gone?" The young man asked, his arms crossed over his chest and his feet spread far apart. He looked like he was ready to run.

The nurse who was still holding Hope up with one arm looked sharply at the janitor. "Peter, go," she said urgently. He took off running in the direction of the highway that roared above them, faster even than Hope could've imagined he would.

The nurse noticed Hope's confused expression. "We had a psych patient run out to the highway yesterday," she explained, her voice clipped.

Hope grew more confused. "Why?"

The nurse just looked at her, a somber expression on her face.

"O-oh." If Hope had felt weak before, she was near-nauseous now. She doubled over as if feeling the pain of every patient who'd ever walked through that hospital. The nurse led her over to a bench that was strategically placed at the entrance to the parking lot.

"Let's just sit here." The older woman put her arm around Hope and they sat in silence, waiting for Peter to return. "I'm Esther," the nurse said after a moment.

Suddenly Hope could place her. "I remember you. I'm sorry."

The nurse who'd worked with her papa for as long as Hope could remember, who'd been at every holiday party and even attended her Bat Mitzvah, waved off Hope's momentary forgetful-ness. "It's different when you see somebody out of context."

Peter was walking back to them with long strides now, hardly looking winded. The bright San Diego sun seemed to almost reflect off his features, and Hope wondered what kind of daughter she was – noticing how well-made this young man was, when her mom had just run away and was maybe even in danger. She didn't have time to rebuke herself, though, because then he was in front of them – "No sign of her," he announced, and sat down in the bench across from the two women.

"Good. I didn't think so. But better safe than sorry." Esther tightened the arm around Hope's shoulders and with her other hand, lifted the small hospital phone that hung around her neck. She pushed a few buttons, and when someone at the desk picked up, she said, "Lacy, it's Esther. Get Dr. Rosenberg. Tell him to meet me in the parking lot."

Hope looked up at the calendar. It was October 21st. One month to the day since Mom had left.

"I want to do something, Dad," Hope's thoughts burst out upon Dr. Rosenberg that morning while they shared some eggs and rugelach together. He eyed her wearily over his newspaper. "I mean I'm tired of sitting around here, just waiting for her to come back." Hope made the mistake of letting her voice rise and her hands with it. Papa noticed her emotion and hid his face behind the news-paper again.

She sighed. It's not that Dad had done nothing. It was more that he'd given up. He'd come straight back to Room 221 that day when Esther had called him, and questioned all the nurses. The staff knew the Rosenbergs well, since Dad was a hospitalist on that unit, and they'd tried to help as much as they could.

After that, Dad had checked Mom's credit cards, but she hadn't used them. She must've gone to family. They'd both called her phone multiple times, but it was off. Hope had even tried calling her grandmother in Canada, but the woman had hung up before

Hope had gotten around to her question. Hope wasn't surprised. Missing person or not, Grandma had never had time to talk to her.

The only place where Dad had stopped short was filing a police report. "If she wants to come back, she'll come back," he'd explained gruffly to Hope when she'd asked him about it. He didn't believe that it was any sort of illness that had driven Mom away; but that she was just angry and didn't want to be with him anymore. Hope had sighed and accepted his decision.

Dad could sit here if he wanted to. But Hope had to do *something*. She quietly put her bright blue coffee mug in the sink and hurried upstairs to call Anna. Anna would have an idea.

"Why don't you bring some flowers to the nurses?" Anna asked her over the phone a moment later. "There's too much worry in that house of yours. Do something that brings a smile to someone else." By the way Anna's voice came in and out, Hope could tell she was cradling the phone against her shoulder. She heard little Cora's voice in the background and hurried off the phone.

Flowers. Yes, that was perfect. Instead of sitting here wondering when Mom would come back, she'd do something to brighten someone else's day. She would be like Miriam of the Old Testament. She'd use whatever instruments she had to honor the Lord, no matter what ocean she'd just walked through.

She hurried to get ready, to curl her thick mane – an exercise that could make any woman sweat – and make her bed. An hour later, she was entering a different world, her only pair of boots that weren't barn boots squeaking with every step, and a bouquet of fall flowers held like an offering in both hands. All was quiet, except for that squeaking. It must be a slow day on the Med-Surg unit. She walked under an air-conditioning vent and shivered, then pulled her teal knit sweater tighter around herself. Why was it so cold in here? Maybe that was why Mom had left, she thought drily. Hope tried to push down the sorrow and held her head a little higher.

She was pleased to see a familiar face ready to greet her at the nurse's station. "Well, hello, Hope." Nurse Esther put down the chart she'd been reading and came around the counter to give Hope a hug.

"Hi, Esther. These are for you." Hope handed her the bouquet awkwardly. Now that she was here, she didn't know how to behave. How to talk.

"Me? Why, thank you." Esther laughed good-natured-ly and placed the vase on the on the tall counter where everyone could see it.

"Well I mean, they're for all of you…" Hope offered lamely. She almost said *and thanks for taking care of my runaway mother,* but stopped the words before they made it to her lips.

"Well, let me introduce you to everyone. Everybody, this is Hope, Dr. Rosenberg's daughter. Hope, this is Esme, Mark, and Maria." Esther gestured to the three nurses who had also been working at the desk.

"Hi." Realizing that each of them probably saw dozens of patients every day, and might not remember, she explained herself. "My mom was a patient here a while ago… I just wanted to say thank you."

"Any news?" Esther asked quietly. The gentle nurse cocked her head.

"Not yet." Hope answered quietly as she looked down at her folded hands.

Esther *tsk*ed and nodded. "And how are you?"

"Oh, you know. Runaway mother. Depressed father. Only daughter here trying to hold it all together." She had meant to be funny but her words came out in a pathetic, choking sob. But the words were out in the open air before Hope could stop them. The nurses didn't seem surprised, but each gave a nod or a knowing smile her way. The one called Mark ran off to answer a call light, and Maria picked up the ringing phone. They hadn't been shocked or offended by her emotion; they just listened, then went back to life as usual. She should've known she'd be safe around these people. They'd probably seen everything and couldn't be surprised by her honesty. She loosened her hold on her sweater, realizing she wasn't so cold anymore.

"Well. You've come all this way just to brighten our day. The least we can do is get you a cup of coffee." Esther spoke in a no-nonsense way and placed a quiet hand on Hope's arm, steering her down the hall. The motherly touch made tears spring to Hope's eyes. She couldn't have protested, even if Esther had given her a moment to do so.

Halfway down the wide hall that was so white it was almost blinding, Hope scrubbed at the moisture in her eyes with the sleeve of her sweater. As she did so, she snuck a glance back in the direction from which they'd come.

"Looking for someone?" Esther had caught her.

"Oh… no," Hope answered quickly, but by the teasing smile on Esther's face, she knew that this woman she admired had guessed correctly that she'd harbored a small hope of seeing Peter today. A month had passed, but yes, she still remembered his name – the way he had run all the way to the highway, no questions asked, just to help her. She would've liked to thank him.

"It's not the best coffee, I'm afraid, if you're a true connoisseur." Hope was, but she didn't want to say so. "But it's warm, and it's free," Esther went on as she ushered Hope through the door to a room marked Family Room. "This room is available for any of our families to use. So anytime you come to visit your Papa, or bring us flowers, you come on in."

Hope chuckled. If she was going to be greeted by friendship and coffee, maybe she would make the flower-bearing thing more regular.

"Let's sit down here." Esther guided her to a round table with four of the hard plastic chairs positioned around it. Hope wondered how many conversations had happened here. She knew from what her Papa had told her that hospital Family Rooms were the places where doctors told family members that their loved ones had died or were dying. She looked around; maybe that was why this room had lower lighting, and a few boxes of tissues scattered around. How many families had heard news here that would change their lives forever? She wasn't the only one who'd ever had a hard day inside these walls.

She wrapped her hands around her warm mug of coffee and let her shoulders soften. Warm noontime light filtered in through the window and fell across the table. Voices called to each other outside the door, and beeping persisted, but in here she felt safe.

"I've known your parents for a long time, you know." Hope

had been so lost in thought she'd almost forgotten Esther was there. She had a bad habit of doing that.

"I know." She tried to pretend like she'd been tuned in the whole time they'd been sitting there. Looked at Esther's face, smiled, and took a sip of coffee. "Dad says you're his favorite charge nurse." She lowered her voice as if to confide a secret. "Don't tell the others."

"Actually, I've known them outside of the hospital. Both of them."

Hope stopped mid-sip. "You mean... Mom and Dad?"

Esther nodded. "I used to be your mother's teacher. In Hebrew school."

Hope was confused. Esther seemed the right age to have been a teacher to one of her parents... but Hope's family still attended the same synagogue that her parents had frequented growing up. How come she'd never seen Esther there? She was about to ask when she realized that the reason might be personal. So she waited instead for Esther to go on.

"I like to think I got to know Mara pretty well. Every Saturday for twelve years gives you that chance, you know. And she was a sensitive girl. Sensitive and sweet." Esther took a sip of her coffee, too, to give Hope a chance to wipe away the hot tears that had suddenly sprung to her eyes. "She was a lot like you," Esther added.

Now she might really lose it. Hope would never be like her mom. Never, not ever. Only her respect for the older woman kept her from saying so. She put her coffee cup down so quickly that hot liquid sloshed out of it. "Sorry," she muttered, keeping her eyes averted from Esther's. But she felt the nurse's eyes on her as she stood, grabbed paper towels to clean up the mess, and refilled her coffee cup – not that she needed more. But she needed something to hold.

She was just sitting back down when she heard the door open behind them.

"Well, hey. I thought I saw you." The deep voice was aimed in her direction, and suddenly Peter was standing right in front of her chair, as if they'd known each other all their lives. She hadn't noticed before how blue his eyes were.

"Oh... hi. Just visiting with Esther here." Hope prayed her

words came out smoothly and didn't betray the way her heart was churning inside her. She leaned forward in her chair and wrapped her hands around her mug, hoping she looked casual. He was the kind of man who took over any room he entered, she could see that easily.

He was tall… she wondered briefly, if she were standing next to him – would the top of her head reach the bottom of his chin? Then she tried to push the thought away as she looked nervously at Esther, who was watching them both with a sort of guarded smile.

Peter went to the counter for his coffee, and got a teasing reprimand from Esther. "That coffee's for staff and family members, you know." Peter winked at her and made a big show of only pouring a tiny drop into a cup. When he leaned against the counter, Hope noticed that he was dressed differently today. Today his scrubs were green, not the nondescript hospital blue, and when he turned around and leaned against the counter, she noticed that the nametag clipped to the front pocket read: *Peter Bailey, EMT student.*

"You're a student, too?" Hope asked him.

"Janitor by night, firefighter student by day. At least, that's the plan." When Peter sat down in the empty chair next to them and stretched out his lanky legs under the table, she noticed that every feature was chiseled, as if he'd been carved out of stone. His hair was dark and thick, like hers. "What a nice surprise," he commented. "To come for a cup of coffee and find two beautiful ladies."

Esther rolled her eyes at his flirting and stood. "I better get back to the desk. Don't want to get called into Dr. Rosie's office." So she knew Hope's Papa's family nickname. Maybe it was true. Maybe she did know Hope's parents more than Papa had ever let on. When Esther was halfway through the door, she turned to reprimand Peter one more time. "You better get back to your instructor, Son. You know he had to go to bat with yours truly to even get you all in here." Peter winked at Esther and lifted his coffee in a mock salute, but did not stand up.

Hope took a deep breath when Esther closed the door. She had hoped to run into Peter again today; but she hadn't been prepared to be alone with him. She stood to go. "Well, I… I better get home."

"Wait." Peter's voice softened and the teasing tone went away. "How's your mom?"

Now it was Hope's turn to lean against the counter. "No news yet." She remembered why she'd wanted to run into him in the first place. "Oh… I wanted to say thank you… for chasing her down. I mean, for trying to find her that day. For running all the way out to the highway. Thank you."

"No problem." He shrugged his shoulders as if he were trying to play it off like sprinting after patients was no big deal; but she noticed something that looked like a smug smile on his face.

"So… have you worked here for a while?" She asked, knowing she should go but wanting to stall at the same time.

"No. Just moved here in September, in fact."

"Oh. Well, I could show you around, if you like…" she offered lamely, then wished she could backtrack. Had she just asked a boy on a date? And she hardly even knew him. What would Papa say?

But he seemed pleased, not annoyed with her. "That would be great." He stood slowly so he could pull his phone out of his scrubs pocket. "What's your number?" And he leaned against the counter next to her.

Her feet were lighter when she left than they had been that morning… than they'd been for many days. Months, maybe. She'd done two brave things today. She'd given a boy her phone number. And she'd gone back to the place where she'd lost everything.

"You ready, Hope?"

"Ready, Papa."

Hope slung the strap of her duffel over her shoulder and fairly bounced out of the room. Ran back to get her favorite cherry-red hat. Today was the first day she'd tried to straighten her hair since Mom had left. She'd rushed, burned her finger and a few strands of hair, and given up. The results were subpar. She sighed at her reflection in the mirror, and placed the hat neatly atop the mass of half-straightened dark frizz. Better.

She checked her phone one more time before dropping it into

her purse. The text message from Peter made her forget her frizzy hair. *Since you're going downtown anyway today,* it read, *you should come meet us at the coffee shop.*

He'd asked about her weekend plans yesterday – she'd been delighted that he'd asked, and devastated that she had to tell him she was busy. He wasn't giving up though, she realized as she read his message one more time. She liked that.

Who's Us? She replied, wondering.

Yours truly, Esther, and a couple other people from work.

What could Esther be doing with a handful of young people, downtown on a Saturday night? Now Hope's curiosity got the better of her. That, combined with her desire to see Peter, made the idea irresistible. *Which coffee shop?* She asked.

The one on 10th and L, he replied. *I'll be waiting for you.*

She giggled. *I'll try.*

When she met her father in the hallway, she tried to suppress her smiles. This would be their first family event since Mom had left. Not that Mara had ever been too eager to come along. But at least she'd been there. Dad was a somber presence on the way to the car, so Hope put a lid on her bubbly mood. She didn't want him to think she'd forgotten about Mom.

As she buckled her seatbelt, she thought of a distraction. She could ask him about the plan she and Heidi had dreamed up just yesterday. A plan he surely couldn't say no to.

"Papa, I just remembered," she started, rolling down her window to let in the sunny fall air. She paused as she watched flaming red and orange leaves fall from the oak trees that lined their driveway. "Heidi said she could help me set up my own therapeutic riding stable. Right here." Hope beckoned to the expanse of land around them, then turned towards her father as Dr. Rosenberg eased the car down their long, winding driveway. Why did they have to live so far from the family? Hope was eager both to see her cousins and to share her latest news.

Papa stared straight ahead, giving no indication of having heard her. She remembered not to bounce in her seat or to talk with her hands... Papa might listen if she talked slowly and told him only the facts. So instead of continuing with her story or trying to drag him along with her to dream-land, she quietly folded her hands in her lap and went on. "We have the space for it. All these nice, flat acres. There's room for a barn and an arena. I could ask Anna and Jake to help with building plans. We could use the money that was supposed to go towards my college expenses. Heidi can help me advertise and get certified by the state so I can take foster children." She took a deep breath to deliver her last pitch. "I know Mom never wanted horses here because they'd tear up the grass. But I'd keep them on the upper hill, away from the house, so you can't even see them." She stole a glance at Papa. His mouth was in a thin line; he said nothing. She heard her own voice coming out weaker than before: "I drew up a business plan so we can talk about it." She leaned over to pull the four-page typewritten plan out of her bag.

When Papa finally spoke, he was a few steps behind. "Miss Heidi?" He asked.

"Yes, Miss Heidi." Hope wrapped her arms around herself, like one of Miss Heidi's warm hugs. Heidi was a stable owner and a riding coach; but Hope saw through her mentor's business side, and knew that she did it out of a love for kids as much as a love for horses.

Hope had started showing horses when she was 12, and back then, three-day eventing had been her favorite. The smooth, calculated moves of dressage brought her peace; the thrill of the jumping ring made her feel alive; but the beauty and the race of cross-country was where she could breathe, really breathe, no matter what was going on inside.

So she'd dreamt of going to the Olympics. Until Miss Heidi had opened a therapeutic riding center for disabled and disadvantaged children. And all Hope's dreams had changed. When she saw what happened to children who couldn't walk the moment they were set upon a horse; when she saw the change in children who wouldn't smile, the moment a horse nuzzled them; she knew that she was meant for no other life. She was meant to help heal children through horses. And if she could do it here, then she wouldn't have to leave Papa. He wouldn't be alone.

She sighed and settled back in her seat, waiting for his answer.

He looked out the front window a moment longer. Then finally, he said, "I thought we agreed that you were going to go to college first, before we would talk about starting your own business."

"I know… but I thought I could do both." Hope's voice grew smaller. She tried one last time to be brave. "I could take online classes. They're cheaper than attending on campus, anyway. This is important to me, Papa…" At the look in his eyes, she let her voice trail off.

"College first. Then we'll talk." His face was as resolute as his firm grip on the wheel.

"But Papa, if you would just listen…"

"I have listened. This conversation is over." And he gave her a look that needed no words.

She sighed and leaned over to slide her four-page business plan back into her bag.

It was twenty minutes before either of them spoke again.

Hope broke the silence first by clearing her throat. "Did I tell you Anna's gonna be there?"

"Yeah. I wasn't sure if she'd make it out with the little ones." He took a deep breath and kept looking straight ahead. Maybe the rest of the drive wouldn't be so bad, if they could stick to easier topics.

"Just wait till you see them. They're getting so big. And Grandma Leah…" Hope stopped. Was she looking forward to seeing her grandmother? The woman had stepped in and helped in a big way this year. She'd gotten them through their first Mom-less Yom Kippur, one of the most important Jewish celebrations of the year. She'd even gone with Hope to pick out a dress for prom last Spring when Mom wasn't feeling well. But still… there was something about the woman that made Hope want to hide.

"Do you think Mom will ever come back?" She whispered quietly to the window. So much for easier topics.

"Humph," was Dad's only reply.

Hope sighed without looking at him. The Rosenbergs were the only family in her tight-knit community who'd had a parent just take off like this. It was so unheard of that the relatives just tiptoed around it. She shouldn't be surprised that Dad did too.

There were only two times when she allowed herself to process it. The first, when she was painting; and the second, when she was with Anna.

"Auntie Hopey!!" Anna's children squealed and Anna herself threw her arms around her younger cousin. Hope looked so grown-up today... she was getting prettier every time Anna saw her... but there was a sadness that hung about her too. Anna would never say this to Hope, but when Aunt Mara had left, it had made her grateful for her own mother, who picked up the phone every time Anna called for advice or just needed a friend.

I'll be that friend for her today, Anna thought, as she embraced the girl-turning-to-woman in the parking lot. The cousins linked arms like schoolgirls and headed into the synagogue.

The girls squished together in the long red benches, each with a tot on her lap, Hope having waved off Anna's husband Jake so he could mingle with relatives and she could assume her Auntie duties. Baby Cora wasn't such a baby anymore – at four years old, she was learning her way, and definitely learning how to *get* her way, as evidenced by little hands digging through Auntie Hope's purse for the crayons and chapstick she knew would be there. Little Josephine was snuggled up to her mama's chest, seemingly overwhelmed by the crowd. Hope smiled. She loved how Anna taught her kids to call Hope "Auntie," even though she was really their second cousin – or was it a first cousin once removed? Oh well, whatever her true position, she was grateful that Anna hadn't reduced her to it. She needed all the family she could get.

Now everyone was settled, and the program was passed out and announced. Today was Lily Stein's Bat Mitzvah. A few cousins would take turns singing, and the rabbi would read the sacred texts in their ancient Hebrew.

Hope sat back and relaxed into her seat. There was something so haunting about the melodies that came. They swelled and filled the room and made her heart ache. Though it had been years since she'd finished Hebrew school, she still understood the words. They spoke of waiting and lament, of hope and deliverance. But she had a feeling, that even if she were only a passerby who happened upon this service and stumbled into the synagogue... she would know. She would know that the songs were stories, and the texts were too.

God, though my father and mother forsake me... You never have. And you never will. It wasn't the first time one of David's prayers from the Psalms had risen up unbidden in her heart. Hope dug in her purse for some paper for Cora, but when that was rejected, she let the child doodle in pen on her own wrist and forearm. Love tattoos, she told herself as she admired Cora's scribbles. It was nice to have some evidence of having been loved. She relaxed with the child in her arms, and let the music heal her heart, as she listened.

Later, at the reception upstairs, many arms were flung around Lily, who looked extra-radiant tonight, surrounded by the attention of her relatives. Hope pressed a small gift into her cousin's hand and told her how special she was. Then she stepped to the outskirts of the party, and walked along the crowd, giving herself a moment to simply take it all in.

Not one conversation could be picked out, but rather many mingled together as the group who knew each other so well talked, and laughed, and sometimes shouted comments or greetings across the room. There was a cadence and a rhythm to their talking, as if they belonged together – because they did. Their dress was formal but simple, women in sensible dresses and men in suits and ties. There wasn't a blond head in the whole of the large room; Hope laughed as she thought of the surfer-and-swimmer culture that surrounded them in Southern California. Something like 99% of the girls at her high school had been blond. Maybe she and her family were an odd group, to outsiders. But not to each other. To each other, they were just right.

The traditional spread of bagels and lox, vegetables and other goodies tempted her from a corner table. They laughed, they ate, they gossiped. No one asked about Mom; Hope didn't know if she was grateful or if she wished they'd ask. Family members started leaving, and Anna came up to her, baby girls all bundled in coats. "We're gonna walk around a little. Get some ice cream. See you later?"

Hope's eyes widened. "Take me with you?" She pleaded.

Anna clucked her tongue as she thought. "Hmm... better ask your Papa."

A moment later, Hope was begging Papa to let her go like a little kid. She left out one tiny detail – how she intended to use the ice-cream expedition to look for the coffee shop Peter had told her about. Papa got nervous enough any time his only daughter went out into the unknown without him. But she'd stay safe, and she'd keep her phone with her.

Hope knew that the family and the food must have put him in a good mood when he only hesitated a moment before agreeing. "But stick together," he emphasized, wagging a finger at her. She would. She'd stick by Anna. Then, if she found Peter and Esther, she'd stick by them.

She sidled up to Anna and took Baby JoJo on one hip. "Ok. I'm ready."

A moment later, they were trotting down the sidewalk. Jake reached down and took Josephine from Hope, lifting her atop his shoulders. Anna and Hope walked with Cora between them, each holding a hand and lifting her up in the air every time they counted to three. The cool November air and the promise of ice cream had energized them.

Hope looked around while they walked. Downtown San Diego was home to a different group of people than the one she'd always known. The people here were like the buildings; all different, all beautiful.

When they stopped at the ice cream parlor, Hope looked up at the street signs. 12th and L. So they were only two blocks from Peter and Esther's meeting place. She opened the door for Anna and the girls, then stood in the doorway as her family loyalty wrestled briefly with the thought of an adventure. She looked up at Jake, who held the door for her. "I think I'm more in the mood for coffee than ice cream." Her voice sounded to her like someone else's. "There's a coffee shop two blocks down this hill. Do you mind? I'll be quick."

Jake looked at her, but there was no suspicion in his eyes, as there would've been in Anna's had Hope delivered this little speech to her best friend. "Let me walk you," he said, pulling away from the door. "Be right back!" He told Anna, who stood at the counter with their little girls. Anna nodded back to them, releasing her hair from JoJo's little fist while pointing out ice cream flavors to Cora.

Hope kept up easily with Jake's long strides. "So, how're the horses doing?" He asked her. He knew all about Hope's obsession; she and Anna were cut from the same cloth.

"Good," she answered. She told him about how she was already picking out which shows she'd compete in with Pirate next summer. About how Heidi had made her an assistant teacher in the kids' classes. She left out the business plan she'd tried to discuss with Papa on the way over. It was pointless to talk about it now.

They passed 11th; almost there. "You know, Ben was asking me about you the other day." Oh. Maybe this was why Jake had agreed so easily to walk with her. He wanted to talk about his brother.

Hope sighed. She and Anna had grown up with Ben and Jake. Ben was sweet, and thoughtful, and she'd thoroughly enjoyed going to his prom with him last year; but she didn't feel any sparks when she looked at him. Not like she already did with Peter. "He's a good friend," she said shyly to Jake, trying to be kind. It was awkward talking to him about this.

Jake smiled and let the matter rest. Then he opened the door to the coffee shop. "Well, here you are, m'lady," he said in a singsong way, taking a bow. Hope giggled and stepped through. She went straight to Esther, still in the day's dark blue scrubs, but with a bright smile on her face that could've fooled anyone as to her hard day's work. Esther stood from the little round table she'd staked out and wrapped Hope in a warm hug.

"I'm so glad you came, Hope." The woman held her at arm's-length. "I had a feeling you could use a friend."

Hope was surprised when tears sprang to her eyes at Esther's remark. Hadn't she just left a roomful of friends? But Esther was right... she needed a friend she could talk to. As close as her family was, they didn't really *talk* about their personal lives together – save Anna and Jake.

Her eyes fell on the small stack at Esther's table – a few books and notebooks. "Let me just grab a cup of coffee. I'll be right back."

A moment later, Hope was back and sitting with Esther, hands wrapped around her warm paper cup, and she could finally ask the question she'd been wondering – "What do you have here?" She raised her coffee to her lips and indicated the small stack.

"My Bible. And some notes."

Hope choked on her coffee, sputtering some of it over the table in the process. "A Bible? I thought you were Jewish." Her voice shook almost as much as her hands, which were trying to mop up her mess with napkins. She only succeeded in knocking over her entire cup.

"Shoot," she muttered as she went down on her knees to inspect the damage.

"You all right, dear? It didn't burn you?" Esther asked as she stood to go for more napkins.

"Yeah, I only spilled my whole cup all over the floor, not myself, at least." Now she didn't have any coffee. And she'd have to leave without seeing Peter. She couldn't be seen sitting at the same table as a Christian Bible. Her heart thudded within her. If Papa were to see…

"Everything ok here?" The deep male voice she'd already committed to memory interrupted her mopping and made her heart pound even faster.

She tried to stand but hit her head on the underside of the table instead. "Ow…" she muttered, going back on her knees and clutching her head. Some night this was turning out to be.

"Here, let me help." Peter took her hand and lifted her to her feet. "Can we get a mop over here?" He hollered to the nearest barista. "You want an ice pack too?" He asked, winking at Hope.

"Oh, no, I'm…" then she realized he was teasing her, and she eased back on to her chair. No more getting up tonight.

Esther returned to the table with more napkins. When she saw Peter, she checked her watch. "*Tsk, tsk*. Peter Bailey. Always late, but worth the wait."

"That's me." He seemed proud of the fact. Hope watched as he gave Esther a quick hug, then pulled out her chair for her. He was so gentlemanly.

"Wait. Let me go replace your coffee. Be right back." He winked at Hope as if he'd read her mind. She turned to protest, but he didn't hear her.

"Oh, let him." Said Esther. "It'll give us a chance to catch up."

Hope smiled and allowed herself to relax into her chair a moment, willing herself not to tip it over. "There was something I wanted to ask you," she brightened. Maybe Esther would know how to answer this question. "The day my mom left," Hope cleared her throat. "The day my mom left," she started again. "There was a man at the hospital. A middle-aged man. Dressed in corduroy.

Kind of rumpled." She searched her memory; there was nothing else to say about him. Esther might not understand if she said something about his otherworldly presence. Or the way he seemed so easy to talk to. So she cleared her throat again and asked as naturally as she could, "Sound familiar?"

"No…" Esther was looking at her funny. "We get a lot of people coming in and out of the hospital." Hope knew this, and Esther knew she knew it. "Is there some reason why he's important to you?"

Hope shrugged. "He was walking towards Mom's room when I was walking out. I just thought… maybe he knew her or something." She didn't add that he was the same man who'd stopped her from running away just a few months ago.

Esther shrugged and covered Hope's hand with hers. "Sorry, sweetie."

At that moment, Peter returned with her coffee. "Hot and fresh, just for you," he said gallantly, placing it down before her with two careful hands.

She couldn't help but laugh, and blush a little bit.

The warm feeling inside – which either came from Peter's attention, or from her new cup of coffee, or a little bit of both – gave her the courage to ask the next question that was burning in her mind. "Now tell me," she asked pointedly of Esther – "What is a Jew doing with a Christian Bible?"

Esther turned over her ornately illustrated blue book, and showed Hope the cover. It read "Complete Jewish Bible." Hope had never seen those two words together before.

"There's only one difference between myself and a traditional Jew." She said, looking hard at Hope. "Mind you, it's a pretty big difference." She put the book down and took a sip of her own coffee. "Traditional Jews are still waiting for the Messiah." She put down the mug and reached out for Hope's hand. "I believe He's already come."

Peter had tuned Esther out long ago. He was staring instead, unashamedly, at the curly-headed girl next to him. He couldn't help but notice how she'd lit up like a firefly when he'd sat down next to her tonight. The way she smiled at him with her whole heart was irresistible.

Now others had come to join Bible study, but Peter's eyes were on Hope's doodles. It was just a simple brown napkin that hadn't been needed to clean up her earlier coffee spill, but she'd taken to it like Michelangelo to a ceiling. Swirls turned this way and that. She kept on doodling while Esther talked, till the head of a bird emerged on her paper. "That's really good," he lowered his head to whisper to her.

"Thanks," she whispered back. They both giggled when they noticed Esther watching them, like a couple of kids in school. The older woman smiled teasingly at them, then went on about how Jesus, who she also referred to as *Yeshua,* had fulfilled all of the Old Testament prophecies. Hope turned her eyes from Peter to watch Esther intently. Peter, too, feigned interest, but he'd heard it all before. Grown up with it, in fact.

A guy who was taller than Peter opened the door to the coffee shop and looked around; then stopped when he spotted Hope. He seemed like he was about to come over. "You know that guy?" He whispered to Hope.

"Yeah. He's my brother in law. Cousin in law." She corrected herself and smiled.

"Good." Peter asserted with meaning. He loved how he could make her blush.

"Thank you, Esther. I'll think about what you said." Hope stood and gathered her things. "'Bye, everyone."

Esther stood to give her a hug. "Take this, Hope," she said, handing her a book. Hope hugged her back and took it.

When the tall guy reached their table, Peter stood to look him in the eye and shake his hand. Hope's curious eyes were on them both, then she turned to leave with him.

Peter sat back down at the table, wishing he could leave with Hope instead. But it would be too awkward now. He glanced down at the table – she'd forgotten her drawing. When no one was looking, he slid the napkin over the table and into his pocket.

chapter five

Peter hustled around the one-bedroom apartment he shared with a guy from his EMT class. Rent was so high in San Diego they couldn't afford anything bigger. Finding a roommate had been easy. Stretching the wad of bills that Mom had forced on him as he left had been harder. But God was blessing him. He'd landed a job at the hospital – yes, just a janitor job, but he was proud of it. Years of shoveling cow manure had taught him not to be afraid of hard work. If he could prove himself, maybe they'd hire him to work in the ER after he finished his Emergency Medical Technician class.

His phone rang, and Rob's name appeared on the screen. He threw the phone off his bed and onto the other side of the room. Rob hadn't spoken to him since Peter had announced his departure to the family. What was the point of talking now?

But curiosity got the better of him with the second call. "Hello?" He said gruffly as he held the device tighter than necessary against his ear.

"Hey, bro." Rob's voice was softer than he'd expected it to be. Peter's ears perked up and his shoulders softened. It was actually good to hear a familiar voice. "How's it going out there?"

"Well. I haven't been surfing yet." Peter wrapped an arm around his chest and didn't try to keep the sarcasm from his voice. Rob had insinuated that Peter was chasing empty dreams and ocean waves while he stayed home to help the family. "But it's good. My class is going well. I'm getting good grades on the quizzes." Peter walked around the room aimlessly and straightened his shoulders as he talked. It felt good to have his own pursuit, something he was proud of.

Rob listened as Peter went on about his job, his apartment and his daily life. After a few moments, Peter forgot to be mad at his brother.

"So… how long do you think you'll stay out there?" Rob asked casually when Peter thought the conversation was wrapping up.

Peter was surprised by the question. Rob knew this class was a semester long. And that Peter had bought a one-way ticket and rented an apartment.

"I don't really know. Awhile." Peter unknowingly puffed his chest out a little more as he spoke. "Why do you ask?"

"Dad's working himself to death out here." Rob didn't add, *I am too,* but Peter knew that's what he meant. He felt a pang in his stomach that might've been guilt, but dismissed it. He was helping his family, the whole town really, in his own way, out here.

They didn't know that EMT school would lead to firefighter training. That he was here to gain the skills necessary to change things at the dingy old Fire Department that couldn't save his town. That he wouldn't come back till he could fix the mess he'd made.

Hope studied herself in the mirror and added a few curls to her unruly hair. She'd need something warm; even in San Diego, November had brought brown crunchy leaves on every path and a chill to the nighttime air. Her grey sweater with the oversized sleeves was so comfy. She pulled it on and looked at her reflection. No — she needed some color. The burgundy top with flowers etched into the neckline was more her style. She checked her reflection again and was almost satisfied, but heard Mom's voice in her head instead – *You really shouldn't go out with your hair like that. It's so frizzy, it looks like you stuck your finger in a socket.* She held it back with one hand – should she do a bun? *You look like a boy, Hope, with your hair pulled back like that.*

She let go of her hair and checked the time on her phone with trembling hands. Why was she so nervous? Probably because no boy had ever really liked her before. Except for Ben, that is.

Wallet, keys, phone, and lip gloss – she shoved them hurriedly into her purse. Papa was at work – she hadn't told him about her date. But she was nineteen, after all. Was confiding in a parent really necessary anymore? If starting her business wasn't part of Papa's plans for her right now, what would he say to a guy? She supposed that's why she hadn't wanted to tell him – he'd disapprove, like he did all of her ideas.

Hope shrugged off the momentary guiltiness and continued packing her purse. A notebook and a pen in case she had extra time to doodle. A book for good measure. She could stall herself no longer, and checked her reflection one more time.

It was as good as it was gonna be. She put a hand on her waist, which was a little thicker than it had been last spring. She knew that working with the horses kept her strong, and strong was better than skinny, but if Mom were here, she would notice that Hope's jeans were just a little bit tight. And she would say something like, *You know, Hope, if you gain weight when you're young, it's only harder to get it off later.*

Again with the memories. Tears stung at her eyes as she realized – even though Mom had left, her words hadn't. Those old comments weren't just part of Hope's memory – they were alive and well inside her mind. They were like a legacy she couldn't leave behind.

She headed out to the quiet of their front yard, where the peace that came at the end of the day was starting to settle. Her mind quieted down like the birds in their nests, and she looked out at the horizon where the sun was tucking itself in for the night. They couldn't see the sunset from their house – too many trees – but she liked to watch the glow behind them change from orange to yellow to pink, then fade. She climbed into her pickup and checked the address again. She'd be meeting Peter at the restaurant, which sounded safer – though she knew in her bones that she'd be safe anywhere with Peter.

After struggling through traffic and circling the one-way streets in downtown San Diego, she mentally added deodorant to her list of things to bring on a date. She blasted the air conditioner on her underarms instead.

~

Peter was watching out the window for her. When he saw the green pickup truck that she'd described pull up, he stood and stretched. She was cute. When he'd called and said in his straightforward way, "I'd like to get to know you," she'd giggled and accepted. He wasn't looking for anything serious – not when he had school and work to focus on. Not to mention the fact that he still didn't know where he stood with Ali. But Hope could be a fun distraction. Someone to talk to.

She was parking now. She could parallel-park her pickup. Impressive. He gallantly took the front steps of the Italian restaurant two at a time to meet her and open her door.

When the curly-headed vision stepped lightly from her truck, he wasn't prepared for the way she took his breath away. She was so different from the girls back home: a little bit shy, but so real you could see all her feelings on her face. Her smile lit up at the sight of him, just like it had at the coffee shop. When she placed a hand lightly on his arm without any prompting, any thought of his life back home vanished from Peter's mind.

"Hi," he put a hand over the one she'd placed on his arm and guided her up the steps. "I thought I'd bring you someplace special," he confided as he pulled out a chair for her at the white cloth-covered table. Low lamps and candles lit the place and more than a few tables boasted old bottles of wine. His job as a janitor couldn't exactly cover a place like this. But his credit card could.

"Wow," she breathed, sitting down and smoothing a napkin over her lap nervously.

"Ever been here before? You've lived in San Diego all your life, right?" He noticed her glancing in every direction, taking it all in.

"No. I mean, yes, I've always lived here... but I haven't seen the inside of a lot of these places. Dad's pretty frugal." She blushed a little. Was she embarrassed that she'd admitted so quickly how she was still tied to her parents' apron strings? But he had been, too, until recently.

"Well, let's see what they've got here." He cleared his throat and lifted his menu. "Hmm. Looks pretty authentic. My mom's Italian, so I should know." He'd always been proud of his heritage, Mom's tomatoes, and the way he'd grown up speaking enough Italian to get by.

Her shoulders relaxed a little. Maybe talking about family made her less nervous. "Oh, is she? Do they live here? Your parents?"

"No, in Nebraska." His eyes dropped back to his menu when he said it. "Dad's a cattle rancher. Or was. He was a cattle rancher." He didn't try to keep the edge of bitterness from his voice.

"Oh. Well, what does he do now?" She asked, looking at him with the face of a girl who had all the time in the world to listen.

And so he talked. All through the waiter's questions of what they would like, and the serving of waters and the bringing of plates. All through each bite and every exclamation on her part. When the waiter came back to ask if they needed anything else, Peter was still talking. He told the story of the fire, how Dad was trying to rebuild the ranch, how he felt so less-than compared to his brother. He told her everything – everything except how the fire had been his fault. That part he left out for another time.

Never in his life had a girl been so easy to talk to. And never in his life had a girl tried to comfort him the way she did when she covered his hand with hers and said softly, "That must've been hard," at the sobbiest part of his story. And so he talked until the lights in the restaurant were turned even lower and the waiter informed them that the place would be closing in ten minutes. He looked at her helplessly, only then realizing he'd taken up the better part of three hours with his talking; but she just smiled, and held his hand, and said, "Come with me somewhere."

"Come on," she laughed and pulled him by the arm. Night had fallen, and though the bright city lights had muted all the stars in the sky, they couldn't touch the ones in her eyes. He followed, content to be led by her.

They entered through the heavy wooden door of a brick building – the sign over top read *Downtown Stomp* in handpainted letters. "Swing dancing?" he asked in surprise when he heard the old ragtime music and saw a few couples dressed up like they were straight out of the 1940's.

She laughed again. Her laugh was like music. "The only kind of dancing Papa ever approved of."

"Are you good?" he asked slyly as she took his hand. He had a feeling she was good at everything.

She just shrugged and started stepping to the music, pulling him effortlessly into a circle where ten or twelve couples were learning a new step. But it was obvious she didn't need the lesson; her feet knew each step by heart.

He stumbled over her once or twice, and would've felt oaf-ish if his head hadn't been in the clouds. As it was, it didn't seem to matter how many times he stepped on her feet or bumped into another dancer. Her laugh only became more hypnotizing with each mistake he made. She led him along so gently he didn't even realize she was taking the part of the male until one of the dance instructors came over and teased him about following.

"How are you so good at this?" he whispered into her ear, grateful that Etta James's "At Last," a slower song, had come on and given him the chance to hold her close.

"Oh, Anna and I used to come here on weekends. Before she got married." She wasn't exactly relaxing in his arms. But she wasn't pulling away, either. He wondered briefly how many boyfriends she'd had.

"To meet guys?" He pulled back to look in her face, careful to keep the smile on his.

"No," she answered simply. "Just to have fun. I like learning new things." With that she did a little twirl and announced she needed a bathroom break.

He watched her walk away. She seemed so content with her life. With her family, with the horses she'd told him about briefly on the walk from the restaurant – with just being alive. Her life seemed so full. Was it too full?

When she came back with that smile again, he realized that it mattered very, very much whether he'd be able to fit into it.

"I'll tell you all about it at the diner this weekend. Nope, you have to wait. Because, I said so! I want to tell you about Peter in person. It's more fun that way." Hope cradled the phone against her ear as she pulled ingredients out of the pantry. Anna relented and both girls hung up.

Hope had been out with the horses all day. Taught two classes, exercised Pirate, and worked a few of the showhorses for Heidi. Now, at home that night, she rolled out pie dough. Her only light came from candles and the dust of the moon that settled on the kitchen counters and her face. She looked out the large kitchen window of their Spanish-style home and watched, for a moment, as stardust settled on the leaves of her favorite tree. Second only to the horses, this was her next favorite way to relax.

And Papa would be surprised when he got home from his shift. Apple pie was one of his favorite treats. When she couldn't find the pie pan, she made it into a gigantic turnover, arranged imperfectly on a cookie sheet. She stood back and enjoyed the look of it – rustic. Rustic, too, was the whole-wheat flour she used... something about the nutty color and the nuttier smell made her think of ages long past. While she worked, she imagined that one of her great-great-great grandmothers might have rolled out dough like this.

Maybe there were women in her family line who baked. Maybe she'd had great-grandmothers who'd stayed.

She put her finished turnover in the oven, blew out the candle, and glanced up at the clock. 9pm. Papa should be home soon. She dusted the flour off her hands, hummed a little song to herself, and headed upstairs.

She flipped on the light in her room and glanced at her reading stack. Esther's Complete Jewish Bible; she picked it up and turned it over in her hands, still amazed that the woman had just given it to her that day in the coffee shop. So far, she'd read some of the Rabbi's comments on the Psalms, then read the first four gospels.

She placed it back down, on top of Josh McDowell's *Evidence that Demands a Verdict*. That one had come recommended by Esther, and she'd picked it up at the library on a day when Papa had been at work. She had turned the last page on McDowell's book last night, so she didn't need to pick it up again. She only did so out of habit, holding it in one hand and the mug of tea she'd brought with her in the other hand, as she settled into her reading chair.

Settling into this reading chair with a cup of tea had become a habit. Just as wondering about *Yeshua* had.

Yeshua was the Hebrew name for Jesus. And there was no doubt in her mind, now, that He was the Messiah. There was just no way that one man could fulfill all of the old prophecies by accident.

A vision trotted through her mind of the little girl she had been – running through the synagogue with the same wild hair she had now. The little girl who'd loved all the old stories so much, she'd sworn up and down that she'd be a rabbi when she grew up. And in those growing-up circles, they did talk about *Yeshua*. He was a great teacher, after all – how could they not talk about Him? She had grown up believing that He was a good man, a good Jew.

But He'd claimed to be so much more than that. And what Esther had said, so gently, made sense. Could a good man claim to be her people's long-awaited Messiah, if it was a lie?

She could picture, now, the look in Esther's eyes the night she had said that. There had been pain in her eyes. Hope wondered if Esther, too, had struggled with this decision – if she had had a father she didn't want to disappoint, a community she didn't want to leave.

But if it was true, then it was worth it.

"Father God, I know you love me. I know you loved us so much that you sent Messiah." She paused. The words felt fresh on her lips. She knelt down and let the soft breeze from her open window fall on her face. Fingered the blue-and-green plaid quilt on her bed, just to have something to touch, before going on. She couldn't deny any longer that Jesus was the Savior God had sent. But could He be Savior... for her?

She went to the window and looked out for a moment, down on the driveway where Mom's car was parked and had been for a while. Would be forever, probably. Hope sighed. She hadn't been able to find the right words to get her own mother to stay. How could she get the One she'd rejected all her life to come?

Slowly, she walked back to her bed and got down on her knees. She tried again. "*Yeshua.* Jesus." It felt strange... but right. The breeze halted outside her window, and her room was absolutely still. She went on. "*Yeshua.* I know now that You are the Messiah. The one and only Son of God. The One we've been waiting for. You must be disappointed that it took me so long..." She stopped. Shook her head. That wasn't His character, wasn't His personality. She knew now that *Yeshua* was a man who sat next to lonely women at wells, who let prostitutes wash His feet, who spent some of His last breaths commissioning a friend to care for His own mother. If there was one thing she'd learned from reading the gospels, it was that Jesus had time to listen. She tried again. "I believe You died for my sins. I need You. I... I can't make it on my own." She took a deep breath. "I know now that You *are* the Savior. Can You be *my* Savior? Lord, I give you my heart... Will You come in? And take over?"

And a gust of hot wind blew into her room. Filled her room. She looked up at the ceiling, half-expecting it to be lifted off the room. Her heart swelled with a sense of being loved like she had never known before — not from Papa, not from Mom, not from Esther or even from Anna. How was it possible to feel so loved by someone who was invisible? "I guess that's one of the mysteries of You," she breathed into the silence. Only the silence didn't feel lonely anymore, because He was there with her.

And as His love came in, the darkness left. She hadn't known that it was there until it was gone. But as she looked around her room, she saw that even the shadows were lighter. A golden light, brighter than moonlight, fell across her bed. It was the same light that had often trickled down through the leaves, and seemed to whisper to her: *There is more.*

She sighed a deep sigh of contentment, not wanting to move. She lingered until her knees ached, not wanting to lose the moment, not wanting to lose Him.

"*Yeshua,*" she breathed, the name now feeling like that of an old friend. "I think You've always been there. I just didn't know Your name."

～

Peter pulled up the drive to Hope's house and whistled. Hope wasn't kidding when she'd told him her Papa made good money. No wonder she'd hinted that he should dress nice, and act nice, too. He'd kissed her and asked, "When do I not?" And she'd just blushed. But as he stepped out of the now-shabby-looking car he'd bought just last weekend with his earnings – and been proud of, too – he was grateful she'd given him a heads-up.

"Dr. Rosenberg," he smiled and shook the man's hand the second Hope's Papa opened the door. He wouldn't give the man time to worry or wonder about him. He'd just talk until Hope came downstairs and they could go out together.

Dr. Rosenberg's eyes narrowed, and his smile narrowed even more, as the two men sat down in the living room together. Peter's plans to keep the conversation going died under that stare. He was grateful when, just two minutes later, Hope bounded down the stairs. "Ready?" she asked, eyeing, in turns, the two most important men in her life.

"Ready." Peter stood gratefully. "Thanks, Dr. Rosenberg. Nice to meet you." The man replied with something that might've been *nice to meet you, too...* but Peter's eyes and ears were only on Hope as they floated through the door. "Well, your limousine awaits, my dear." He opened the door and gestured her into it. "Where to?"

She giggled, and eventually they settled on the beach. It was one place they hadn't been together yet.

They parked, the only ones in the parking lot. For their first beach excursion, she'd take him somewhere quiet, she'd promised. As they stepped out of the car, he noticed how her dark curls hung down her back. "You stopped straightening your hair," he said, touching it lightly with a finger.

She thought a moment before responding. "I've stopped doing a lot of things that Mom wanted me to do."

"Well, I like it." He wanted to do something to take away the sadness that settled whenever Hope spoke of her mom. So he took her hand and said, "Come on, let's run." Her laughter rang out as they pounded through the sand until they both grew tired of running. Then they flopped down on the bare earth, and she leaned against him.

He thought of the warmth that had graced the seaside he'd been to before – only twice – but the beauty of it had settled itself firmly in his mind. There, they hadn't needed sweaters. Here, he and Hope both pulled theirs more firmly around them. Early December brought a chill, even to Southern California. "I gotta be honest. It doesn't compare to Italian beaches. But it'll do."

"Oh, but this is my beach. My Del Mar. I've come here every month since… well, since forever." She leaned back against him and pointed. "See that cape over there? That's where I got stuck when I was a kid. Anna and I swam too far. She stayed with me and helped me keep treading water until my mom swam out to get me." She shaded her eyes and looked up the hill. "And see that house up there? Our old dog Brownie got bitten by the owner's dog. That was scary." He looked at her more closely. She hadn't spoken of a dog before. But her face sweetened even more when she'd said it, if that were possible.

"Brownie?" He teased her lightly.

"I was six, okay?" She leaned into his arm.

"Anna and I even brought the horses here last summer. That was a lifelong dream come true, let me tell you." She closed her eyes as if reliving the adventure. "We promised each other we'd do it every summer, forever and ever. Maybe someday we'll even bring her girls, and they'll ride, too."

He liked this. Dreaming with her. Just sitting on the sand, watching the dark waves build strength and roll up below them. Sitting safe and snug together on the sand. "Hope Rosenberg," he said, pulling her closer, "I think you are just what I needed."

She looked at him with wide eyes. "You need me?" A grin spread across her face that must've been as bright as the one she'd worn on the day she'd brought her horses here. She leaned into his hug. "I think that is the most gloriously romantic thing ever."

"I'm not going to be able to go to Sabbath service with you

today, Papa." She'd been dreading this conversation as soon as she'd realized that it was coming. So her heart thumped within her and her agony only increased as she had to say it again, louder, to get him to hear her, to get him to put down his newspaper.

"Why's that? You love the Shabbat." He was finally looking her direction now.

She sat quietly in the blue couch opposite him, hands folded in her lap, trying to give the appearance of calmness. "Yes. I do. And I always will. But today," she whispered, then tried again, a little louder: "Today I'm going to the Messianic Congregation with Esther."

Dr. Rosenberg was at first shocked, and needed ten minutes of explanations by Hope before he could reconcile himself to what was going on. When he finally did understand, he walked away, paper in hand, muttering words under his breath… his words indiscernible, but his tone unmistakable.

In his absence Hope tried to keep calm, tried to eat breakfast, tried to fold laundry, tried to pray. When he finally came back downstairs thirty minutes later, the conversation was not pretty.

Dr. Rosenberg fought for his way. Hope listened, quieter every moment.

When he was done, she tried explaining, quietly, "I'm still a Jew, Papa. I'm not giving anything up. I'm gaining something." But at this he only shook his head and *tsk*ed.

He sat quietly for a moment, chin resting on fingertips. Hope could tell he was considering his options. "Fine." He finally spoke. "You'll go to the Messianic congregation. But you won't discuss this with any other family members. Is that clear?"

Hope sighed as her shoulders slumped a little. It wasn't the answer she'd wanted. But it was a beginning. She nodded her assent, then went to her room, her heart sinking a little. There was nothing she hated more than disappointing either of her parents.

So she went to her easel. Mom and Dad had only consented to let her paint in her room – on brand-new carpet, nonetheless – if she agreed to keep a canvas tarp under her work at all times. She stepped lightly on it now and began gathering up supplies.

But instead of flipping to a new page, her fingers landed on the pair of roses she'd started earlier. She'd only filled up half the page. The right side was all white. Blank.

Without really thinking, she started to paint *Yeshua* in. His face was gentle, turned towards the flower, and his hand was open, underneath it. Hadn't his family been disappointed in him too? He understood. A drop of the scarlet stain that came from the smaller rose fell onto his hand. He caught it, and the red spread over his hand and up to his wrist. Her pain had become His.

Hope and Anna had plenty to talk about when the two met for their monthly just-girls dinner date the next day at a diner half-way between their two cities. "Jake practically pushed me out of the house!" Anna exclaimed as she sat down in the sticky red seat, huffing from running from the parking lot. Anna knew she didn't have to be on time for Hope; but she did like to make an entrance. "He said, 'I'm not the only one who deserves to have a life outside the home, you know.'" Anna imitated the love of her life with an overly-exaggerated deep voice. "Isn't that sweet? Now, what're we having?"

Hope just smiled and watched her best friend pore over the menu. Moments later, both girls had ordered burgers without cheese, fries and soda. Good thing the place gave free refills. There weren't enough fries in the world to get through all they had to talk about tonight.

"So he said you can keep going there? Wow, Uncle Rosie," Anna's eyes were wide as she slurped down the last of her soda. Hope knew she had promised Papa not to discuss her new faith with any family members, but... Anna was more than family. She was Hope's best friend. She was the one safe place where Hope could talk about anything.

Anna checked her phone. "No news is good news. They love it when Daddy's there to tuck them in at night."

"So how about you guys? How's work going?" Hope flagged down their waiter for more fries.

"Oh, you know. Remodeling old houses is always an adventure." Hope did know. Anna and Jake had been at it for years. Their own remodeled 1900 Victorian was the coziest place Hope knew. That was another reason why Anna and Jake were perfect for each other, Hope thought. Anna had enough creativity and resourcefulness to not only restore old homes, but to keep the original personality intact somehow. Jake had the business head that kept Anna's feet planted firmly on the ground.

What would it be like to be part of a team like that? To work with someone, to live with someone who truly knew you? Hope let out a long breath and wrapped her hands more snugly around the cup of tea she'd ordered. "I wonder if I'll ever have that," she whispered.

Anna didn't have to ask what she meant. She just reached a hand across the table to squeeze Hope's. "Of course you will," she reassured.

Hope sighed. "Well if I do, I'll probably mess everything up." She got up to walk towards the counter for more fries even though her basket was still half full, and used the opportunity to scrub away a few rebel tears that had sprung up in her eyes.

When she sat back down, Anna looked right at her through cocoa-brown eyes whose beauty couldn't be hidden even by the glasses that sat perched before them. "Oh honey. You know that's not true. I've seen how you are with the kids at the ranch. Not to mention your nieces and nephews. You're gonna do fine when it's your turn."

Now Hope looked up from the table. Why was she hiding her tears? Anna knew all of it.

"Really, you will. And if you don't, you can always send the little rascals to me. I will put those kids to work. Auntie Anna will straighten them out so fast!"

For only a moment, Hope pictured it. She imagined her sweet, short-statured cousin putting hordes of children to work at various chores throughout her house. Then Hope laughed so hard she had soda coming out of her nose. This was what she needed. To laugh more.

Soda mopped up and giggling finally suppressed, Hope tried to steer the conversation to the topic she'd been wanting to bring up, and yet avoiding, all evening. "So, you remember Peter?" She asked shyly.

"The guy who stole you from us when we tried to take you for ice cream?" Anna was still bitter.

Hope giggled. "Yeah."

"What about him?"

"Well… we've been on a couple dates." Hope had no idea she looked like the most beautiful version of herself in this moment. She only knew that her voice had gone quiet and her cheeks hot out of shyness.

"Hmm. But he's not a Jew, right?"

"Right."

Anna paused. Reached in her purse for a tissue and some lip gloss. Hope could tell she was thinking. Eventually she spoke, but she kept her tone light, like always: "Well, you said Nurse Esther knows him?"

"Yeah, from work. He's an EMT student. And he has a part-time job there." Hope's words came out in a rush. "He's from Nebraska, but he came out here to make his own way, and take classes to become a firefighter. And he really loves the Lord, and he's passionate about helping people, and…" she had to prove that he was good.

When she finally looked up, Anna was smiling at her from across the table. "It sounds like you know a lot about him already."

Hope fiddled with her soda straw. "We've talked a lot. He even came dancing with me," she added with a smile.

"Is he a *good* dancer?"

"No," Hope wasn't afraid to admit. She giggled. "But he's willing."

Anna checked her phone again. No emergencies from home. "Oh, willing. Sometimes that's better than good. But just take your time, ok? Promise?"

Hope nodded, and the two girls paid for their meal. Emergency or no emergency, it was time to get home.

"I just… I wanna do it right, you know? Being a woman. I wanna grow and mature… how do you do that? What's your secret?"

By now the two girls who looked like sisters were walking out of the restaurant. Anna stopped her cousin, repeating, "The secret to maturity?" At Hope's emphatic nod, Anna put an arm around her shoulders, and said thoughtfully, "You know what my mom used to say. But I don't think you're gonna like it."

"What is it?"

"Time and trials, dear one," she said slowly, watching Hope's face while she said it. "Time and trials."

∾

"Hold him down, now!" Peter's ears heard Charlie's voice and his arms jumped into action at the same moment. It wasn't technically in the job description of an ER Tech to help restrain psych patients. But when it came to cases like this one, it was all hands on deck. The guy must've taken some kind of upper before he got to the ER, and it was kicking in now. He was stronger than your average 250-pound man. He seemed to fly off the gurney swinging, but three more coworkers ran in to help, and in less than a minute they had him back down, restrained to the bed, while the nurse ran to get a sedative. *Danger to self and others,* they'd said about room 23 in report. The guy had already threatened to hurt a staff member, the triage nurse had said. This was the kind of patient they didn't mess around with.

A few minutes later, Room 23 was breathing evenly and resting in bed, and Peter was ready to head back and finish the EKG he'd set up. But as he was walking out of the room, he nearly bumped into a worried-looking woman and a small boy heading into it. "Whoa, can I help you?" he asked, blocking the door. One of his duties, he'd learned, was to help screen visitors. Also not in the job description.

"That's my husband. I need to go in there," the pale-haired woman explained evenly, but Peter could see the worry lines on her face and hear the shaky edge to her voice. She looked like she could use a good meal, or a full night of sleep; or maybe both. Peter looked to the nurse for help.

"Sure, come on in. He's resting now," Nurse Megan replied in her confident, comforting voice. She busily fluffed pillows around her patient; his sheets had needed changing after he'd soiled them in his fight. But Megan hesitated when she turned and saw the little boy. Peter guessed she was thinking what he was thinking: that the boy shouldn't have to see this.

"Hey, could you sit with me right here a minute? I could use a little company." Peter gestured to two seats that were situated right outside room 23. The little brown-haired boy obeyed but didn't smile back. Peter nodded to the mother and saw that a little smile of gratitude had escaped her lips. The boy seemed even smaller as he sat beside Peter. Peter looked at his hunched-over frame. His dirty hands with long fingernails. His very worn shoes and too-small dark blue jacket. *What must life be like for this little guy? Is he the son of this dude?* Peter didn't ask. He knew everything he needed to know… that this little man just needed somebody to care. If anyone knew how that felt, it was Peter.

The little boy looked anxiously behind him into the room that held his family. Peter tried to distract him. "So, what's your name? How old are you?" When those questions were met with a grunt and Peter was refused eye contact, he tried another tactic. "Hey, you see that guy over there? I wonder if he knows his shirt is tucked in on one side, but not on the other." The boy finally looked up and smiled. Peter caught sight of a doctor whose scrubs were clearly one size too small and pointed him out to the boy. When he got an actual laugh this time, he kept going. Maybe it wasn't the kindest thing, making fun of strangers. But he'd gotten the kid distracted. He wanted to be like Jesus to the people who came in here, especially children. He wanted to make them feel safe in what was maybe the scariest place on the planet. The temperature was frigid, the chairs rock-hard, and the beeping incessant. The least a Christian guy like him could do was offer a few smiles and some conversation. So he teased, and he laughed, and he kept that boy smiling, until the mother exited the room, nodded a polite thanks to Peter, gathered her things and her son, and left.

Peter sighed as he watched them leave, then headed into the break room. He needed a cup of coffee. While there, he checked his phone. *Can I stop by?* Hope. Just the sight of her name ignited a warm feeling in his gut.

Sure, if you bring me a burger, he tapped out quickly. Hope and food would be the perfect pick-me-up to this gloomy January day.

Half an hour later, a coworker came to get him. "Your girl's here," he said with a sly smile. Peter raised his eyebrows and finished entering the vital signs he'd just taken into the computer. Then he headed out to the ER waiting room to meet her.

There she was, sitting in one of the hard-backed green chairs, a paper sack from his favorite burger joint in her hand, her long hair dripping from running through the rain outside to get to him. The drops falling from her hair reminded him of their trip the beach together. December breeze forgotten, she'd dragged him knee-high into the surf. They'd played and splashed each other like two lovesick puppies. He'd never forget how she'd spread her arms wide below the sunset that night, thanking God for a beautiful day. It was like she had a direct line to Him or something.

She'd breathed new life into Peter that day, and she'd been doing it every day since. She was doing it here, today, with her bright smile and wet curly hair. He walked slowly over to her – what was he waiting for? When a Nebraska boy found a good woman, he knew better than to let her go.

She stood, delighted to see him. He knelt down in front of her in his pale green scrubs. "Hope, what's the one thing you want more than anything in the world?" He already knew the answer. They'd talked about it just last night.

"A happy family. One that sticks together," she said with her simple smile, her hands in his.

"Well, I'm ready to give that to you." He kissed her hand. "Hope, will you marry me?" He looked up at her with his most charming smile.

"Oh my goodness!" Her hands flew to her face as she shrieked. "Is this real?" When he nodded, grinning, at her, she jumped up and down, then joined him on her knees and wrapped her arms around him, shouting, "Yes!"

He laughed and pulled her to her feet with him so he could kiss her properly. Three or four patients who'd seen the whole thing clapped; one older man with an oxygen tank whistled. Lindsay, the triage nurse who'd been working behind the counter, came out and hugged them both.

"I don't have a ring," he said sheepishly. He should've thought this through.

"Hang on." Lindsay ran back behind the desk. Then, in her businesslike way, she hurried back out and handed him a quick-lock off an unused Foley catheter set.

He ceremoniously slid the lock onto Hope's finger. She teasingly held her hand out, turning it this way and that as if it were the shiniest thing ever. Then she threw her arms around him and kissed him again. "Oh, I almost forgot your lunch!" She pulled back to hand it to him.

He laughed and shook his head. How could he eat, let alone work, on a high like this?

Lindsay patted him on the shoulder before returning to the now-grumpy-looking line of patients at her desk. "Congrats, you guys. I guess good things do still happen to good people."

chapter six

Hope stood and stared at herself in the mirror. She wasn't supposed to be this nervous.

She looked down at her bare arms – the white dress was sleeveless – if Mom were here, she'd notice that Hope's arms weren't as thin as they could be. Or should be. And her curls. Mom would call it "frizz." Her stylist friend Jennifer had hummed and worked and expertly pinned up the dark locks. She turned her head this way and that. Peter liked her curls. She prayed they'd hold up in the humidity.

The back of her dress scooped low – but not too low. It was Mom's. She hadn't altered it, really – only let it out an inch or so in the waist. Mom had always said she could wear this dress when it was her turn. But it felt weird doing so without her.

Out of habit, Hope checked her phone. Nothing. Aunt Roberta had been a good stand-in when it was time to pick out the flowers, the cake, the venue. But there was a gap in every scene where Mom should've been.

She exhaled slowly to try to steady herself – but when Anna handed her the lily bouquet, Hope couldn't hide the fact that her hands were trembling.

"You ok?" Anna asked quietly, noticing Hope's paleness.

"Yeah. Just the jitters, I guess."

"Ok. Well, it's almost time to go. You ready?"

"Yeah." Hope touched up her lipstick and followed her best friend out of the dressing room and under the clear March sky. She took a deep breath; it felt better to be outside. San Diego's Botanical Gardens were a feast for the eyes.

The music swelled, letting her know that the groomsmen were walking her aunts and cousins down the aisle. All her family – except for Mom, of course, and Grandma Leah – were here. When her grandmother had learned that the official conducting the ceremony was to be the Christian pastor from Hope's college campus, she'd declined the invitation and sent a gift instead. Normally, knowing that she'd displeased family members would be enough to send Hope into tears. But not today. She straightened her shoulders. Nothing could shadow her joy today.

But as they passed the water fountain, where a little green hummingbird had just finished getting a drink, something happened to Hope. To her insides, to be exact. She started hiccuping and couldn't stop. She clapped a hand to her mouth and, wide-eyed, stared at Anna. Anna stared back and slowed her walking. "They'll wait for you. You're the bride," she whispered.

Why now? She'd never been prone to excessive hiccups before. A hand still over her mouth, she nodded frantically to Anna.

She could see the crowd now. Their backs, in white chairs spread out in rows. Still she couldn't stop. "I'll go get you some water," Anna whispered, and ran off. Hope hid back a little bit to make sure no one could see – or hear her.

Anna returned, running – but spilled the water all over the sandy path before she could hand it to Hope. When the two girls looked at each other, a fit of giggles erupted. Hope took a deep breath. "Laughing cured me! See? No more hiccups." They stepped forward on the path, and Anna handed her off to Papa by the third palm tree, like they'd discussed. He raised his eyebrows at the two red-faced girls but Hope only put a finger to her lips and said, "Don't ask."

Anna sauntered up the aisle, elegant in her long coral dress, on the arm of one of Peter's friends from work. Hope still felt a little jilted that none of Peter's family had come. She would've liked to meet them. Didn't they want to meet her? But they were too busy at the ranch, Peter had said. Cattle ranching must be demanding. Oh, well. Who cared that they couldn't be here? She was marrying

Peter, not his family. She breathed a silent prayer of thanks to God that Peter had given up the family business.

Anna was at the head of the aisle, and it was Hope's turn. She tightened her arm around Papa's and was proud to look in the calm lines of his face. Of course he'd protested at first – loudly – to their quick engagement and quicker wedding date. But Papa knew when to accept defeat, and he knew when to show up. Her giggles finally died when the first few calming bars from Canon in D played. It was time.

One foot in front of the other. She felt her insides quake again. *Not now*, she told herself. When she looked at Peter's face, everything seemed to calm down, to slow down. Peter, who'd helped her find her smile again. Who'd danced with her every time she'd asked. Peter, who'd tolerated her many tears over her mother not being there, her many questions and all her ups and downs. Peter, strong and tall and steady. Peter.

Papa passed her over to him and sat down quietly, his shoulders slumping a little. She and Peter held hands under the *chuppah*, the small canopy just for them that had been brought over from the Messianic congregation. The flowers that had been strategically placed around it fluttered in the warm March breeze. She closed her eyes and squeezed Peter's hands lightly. Before she knew it, it was time to read their handwritten vows. Anna handed a small piece of notepaper to Hope. She opened it up and read a few words of devotion she'd written especially for Peter, then quoted a passage from 1 Corinthians 13: "Love is patient, love is kind. And I can't wait to practice on you, Peter." Their audience chuckled. Some knew how much patience and kindness were required after the honeymoon.

When Peter kissed her, it was a little longer, a little more needful, than her friends and family might have expected. But Peter wasn't afraid to show how much he loved her, audience or no audience. Pastor Sheldon announced them man and wife, and Peter lifted her hand in a victory salute.

As Peter held her hand to lead her down the aisle, she stole a glance at Papa. It pained her to see his sad eyes, his hunched-over shoulders. But this walk was a victory walk. She practically danced down the aisle with Peter. In this moment, disappointed family members faded into the background of Hope's mind. Peter loved her. That was all that mattered now.

Peter laughed and guffawed along with the friends who came up to the bridal table to slap him on the back. He'd done it; he'd married the girl of his dreams. She was dancing with her dad now. He downed a glass of wine and went to circulate among their friends.

Hope's papa twirled her one more time then passed her off to her prince charming; this felt like a victory dance. Someone handed Peter a wine glass wrapped in a cloth; they whispered in his ear; he grinned and stomped on it. Shouts of "Mazel Tov!" rang from half of the room, while the other half looked on and laughed.

When it was time for toasts, Pastor Sheldon was the first to stand. He took the mike politely, but held it away from his face; his big, booming voice was already amplified by his natural energy and the excitement of the day. There was nothing he loved more than cheering on other young families.

As Sheldon cleared his throat and straightened his tie, Peter thought back to the meetings he'd had with the gentle giant during their whirlwind engagement. Sheldon had asked him, point blank, "What's the rush?" He'd even been so bold as to ask Peter if he was running from something. Or if he was blinded by puppy love.

But Peter had just shrugged and responded, "We know we wanna get married. Why wait?" Peter's new mentor had nodded and dropped the subject. Now, Peter could see, if the man didn't agree with their quickness, he hadn't let that steal his joy. He was just as eager to celebrate as if he'd been the one tying the knot.

Sheldon was quoting his favorite Scripture now, one that he'd memorized: " 'If you have any encouragement from being united with Christ, if any comfort from his love, if any fellowship with the Spirit, if any tenderness and compassion, then make my joy complete by being like-minded, having the same love, being one in spirit and purpose. Do nothing out of selfish ambition or vain conceit, but in humility consider others better than yourselves. Each of you should look not only to your own interests, but also to the interests of others.' That's from Philippians 2. Hang onto the love of Jesus – that's the best marriage advice anyone could give you." He clapped Peter on the back and prayed for him, right there in front of everybody. Hope's Jewish family looked on respectfully; the ones who had accepted the invitation knew about her new faith and knew what to expect. Then with a final, "Whoop!" Sheldon handed off the unused microphone and went back to his own beaming wife.

The toasts continued; Peter felt a surge of heat rising in his chest as he thought about how his own brother, his own father, even his mom, should've been there. There was too much work on the ranch, they'd said. He pushed them out of his mind – back to the past, where they belonged. And gladly took Hope in his arms when Nat King Cole's "Let's Face the Music and Dance" came on.

It was to be a good old-fashioned swing dance party; he wasn't exactly thrilled about it, but one thing he'd learned about Hope was that she was accustomed to getting her way. Being the only child of a wealthy dad could do that to you. "Still happy to lead me around the dance floor?" he whispered into her ear.

She sighed happily and replied, "Dance floor, the moon, Texas – you're stuck with me now, wherever we go."

chapter seven

Hope dismounted off Pirate at the top of the hill, before she reached the barn, looking for Peter; but he was nowhere to be seen.

She'd thought he would enjoy meeting her four-legged friend on this glorious May day. It was the first time she'd been able to get him out here. His work schedule was so busy.

She went on with her work; pulling off her tack and putting it away. Hosing off Pirate at the wash station, cleaning his hooves, and giving him a few extra treats. The sun felt warm on her bare arms. The fresh air, the openness of just being here, lifted her spirits a little.

It hadn't been easy at home. She wondered if that was why Peter had disappeared; was it that hard to be around her?

She chatted with Heidi for a few minutes. Her mentor still expected her to take over the barn; Hope could feel it, even though they didn't come out and talk about it directly. She wondered how practical that was now.

She finally found Peter when she climbed into the passenger side of her little green pickup truck. He was sitting in the driver's seat, looking at his phone. Her mind flashed back to their honeymoon, to that day when she'd spent an entire morning on the sunny Hawaiian beach alone. At first she'd enjoyed the quiet time; but when lunchtime rolled around and there was no Peter, she'd gone up to the room to look for him. He'd stared at her when she entered the room like she was in intruder, the phone against one ear and darkness in his eyes, then waved her off quickly. Later she'd found out he'd been talking to his mom. But she'd thought he wasn't even close to her? She'd asked him at dinner. He'd only stared at his plate and held back any answer. But after all, the woman hadn't even come to the wedding. She couldn't be bothered to meet her new daughter-in-law. Hope couldn't help feeling sorry for herself that day, and lamenting in her heart, *the honeymoon is over before it's even begun.*

But it wasn't March in Maui. It was May at home, a new day. She'd try a new way of getting back to his heart. Maybe teasing would work. "Hey. Didn't you like watching us? Were we that boring for you?" She smiled as brightly as she could and touched his arm lightly.

"It was ok," he replied, shirking off her arm and not looking up.

"Ok?" She couldn't help but be offended, not just by his pulling away but by his words. Horses were her passion, her therapy, her *thing.*

"Let's just get home." He didn't want to talk. Fine.

But by the time he'd maneuvered the car down the steep hill at the exit of Flying C Ranch, it appeared that he *did* want to talk.

"How am I supposed to afford all this, anyway? Horses are expensive, you know." She was shocked by how loud his voice had become, how quickly. He shifted in his seat as if nervous.

She tried responding in the way she'd seen Anna's mom respond when her dad had gotten heated. Softly. Maybe a gentle word could soothe his anger, whatever was causing it. "I'm sorry you feel that way." She made her voice low, quiet, then she paused, thinking of some logical way to answer him. "But you know, I'm working to pay for Pirate. My work here even earns extra income for us."

He hit his hand against the steering wheel and cursed. "It's too much for me! I can't handle it." His voice was explosive now. She put a hand on her seat reflexively, as if trying to hold on for safety.

Unbidden tears sprung up in her eyes. *Not now,* she admonished herself. She willed them away, and remembered something he'd said to her once. "Remember," her voice was even quieter than it had been before. "Remember when we were dating –" goodness, it had been so short – "Remember when we were dating, and I told you about the horses, and you said you didn't really understand, but if it was important to me, then it was important to you?" Maybe if she repeated Peter's own words back to him, words from a time when he'd actually loved her, he'd come back to himself. Come back to her.

"Yeah, well, not anymore! Not this! It's too stressful." He lifted a hand to rub his eyes and swerved onto the shoulder, then cursed again, took a deep breath, and corrected the car, speeding up as he did so. She wished she were driving.

Hope kept silent and prayed all the way home. Prayed for their safety. Prayed for him. She thought maybe he'd cool down on the 20-minute drive home.

When they arrived at the little guest cottage they were renting from Papa, Peter went inside without even waiting for her. Without even looking at her. Slowly she brought her things inside, leaving her riding boots by the door. When she went in, he was on the couch and staring at his phone again.

"Are you working tonight?" She asked softly, trying to start some kind of conversation but too hurt to find something creative to talk about.

"Don't you know my schedule by now? Geez," he stormed off the couch, down the hall into their small bedroom, and slammed the door.

She sat down on the couch, stunned as if someone had hit her in the stomach. A few moments later he was back, having changed into his nicest jeans and a button-down. "I'm going to José's house," he announced, again not looking at her. José was one of his coworkers, and Hope knew that they were friends, but still; didn't married people check in with each other?

"Don't you even want to ask what *I* had planned for today?" She asked, a little shortly.

"You're not my mom." His voice was quieter but he was shaking his head, lips tight and the darkness back in his eyes.

"I didn't mean —" she started, but the door slammed. He was already gone.

Peter came home early the next morning. He fiddled with his keys a moment before unlocking the door to Hope's Papa's guest cottage. Maybe he'd been wrong to take off like that. But she didn't know how the smell of the barn had taken him back. Back to his former life, back to the cattle ranch. Back to his failure. Maybe today would be the day when he'd confess everything to her. Everything. Then she'd understand.

But when he opened the door, there she was, rumpled and sleeping on the couch. He sat down next to her and put a hand on her hip. She rose quickly, startled by his presence.

"You left!" She exploded.

He pulled his hand back as if he'd touched a fire. She'd never yelled at him before.

"You left me here... alone!" Then she hid her face in her hands, a sobbing mess on the couch.

He stood to go. He didn't need this. Between the stress at work, and the nightmare he'd had last night about the fire... he didn't need an emotional wife, too.

But at the door, he turned around to have one last look at her. Tuning out her sobs, his heart whispered a silent prayer that Sheldon had taught him to pray: *Lord, help me see my bride like you see her.*

In that moment, he didn't see Hope the emotional wife.

He saw Hope the abandoned daughter. Hope, the one who'd been left... and who was terrified of being left again.

He crossed the room for the third time that morning and took her in his arms. Her sobs muffled enough against his chest that his voice could finally be heard over them: "I'm here. I'll never leave you."

June 12. Hope's birthday. Peter had had the date circled on the calendar for weeks. They'd both been busy lately; tonight was set aside for celebrating.

He had his favorite Italian opera cranked up loud enough for the neighbors to hear it, if there had been any neighbors. He looked out the window above the kitchen sink at the wide expanse of property. Hope's papa's property. He allowed himself to be grateful for a moment.

When it became clear that Hope and Peter weren't budging from their plans of getting married, or from their timeline, Dr. Rosenberg had given in. Hope had told Peter later that it hadn't been without a fight; he'd tried two or three times to convince her to wait; but eventually reconciled himself, even telling her, "You know, I always knew that when you fell for a guy, you'd fall hard."

But Peter wasn't just any guy, he told himself as he drizzled olive oil in a pan. He was the one who'd swept Hope off her feet. He didn't agree with everything the doctor said. But he had agreed with his plan. *Finish school,* Hope's papa had said, *and you can live here rent-free as long as you need to.* It didn't hurt that the main house was just half a mile away. Anytime Hope needed something, or someone to talk to, she could just walk over and visit with her papa.

He looked around, noticing the little feminine touches she'd placed all around the house. It used to be an airbnb, kept up by Hope's mother, but Hope hadn't liked her mom's style, she'd said with a frown. So she'd redecorated in bright colors... pops of red, bright blue. Pictures of nature and even one of Jesus that she'd painted herself. Aside from the fact that she always left her riding boots lying around, she was a pretty decent housekeeper.

Yes, she'd been working hard. And he was going to make it up to her tonight. He knew he'd been distracted lately. Busy with work. He knew he'd gotten frustrated with her too easily. He'd give her a big celebration tonight, and everything would be back to normal. He sang along to the opera – his buddies in his band back home had always made fun of him for his affinity for the opera, but he couldn't help what he'd grown up with – and pulled the chicken out of the fridge. Mom had sent him her recipe for chicken parm when he'd told her he wanted to surprise Hope for her birthday.

Hope knew he was taking her swing dancing later – but she didn't know he was cooking for her. She didn't know that when she came home from the ranch, she'd walk in the door to find a clean-shaven husband and delicious smells coming from the stove –

His phone rang. Rob. They hadn't talked in a couple months.

He stopped himself mid-goofy dance move to pick it up. He was in a good enough mood to talk to his brother today.

"Hello?" he asked, distractedly, pouring more olive oil down in the pan. You could never have too much olive oil.

Silence on the other end. "Hello?" he asked, annoyed this time. He didn't have all day.

"Peter?" Rob asked quietly.

"Yeah?" He needed this conversation to go a little faster. He'd hang up soon if Rob didn't get to the point.

"Peter. Dad's gone."

"Ok. So, you need help at the ranch? I'll be there in thirty hours." He joked but there was an edge to his voice. So what if Dad was gone on one of his hunting trips? Peter could care less at this point.

"No. He's *gone*. He died just a few hours ago, Peter."

"What?" A wooden spoon clattered onto the floor and the oil-filled skillet lay forgotten as Peter began walking aimlessly around the kitchen. "What did you say?"

He heard Rob take a deep breath. "He woke up with chest pain last night. Mom called the ambulance, and he coded on the way to the hospital. The paramedics resuscitated him, and Gina thought he was gonna be ok when we got there. He was on a breathing tube and all these machines... but then he coded again, and they couldn't get him back the second time. He's gone, Peter." Rob spoke mechanically, as if he'd already told the story a couple of times.

"Chest pain? So he had a heart attack?" Peter tried to catch up. Dad had never had heart problems before. "How did that happen?" he asked loudly.

"Stress, the doctor guessed. Dad's been working really hard on the farm, you know." Rob's voice was quiet now. Peter couldn't help but feel the dagger in his chest.

I shoulda been there, he thought. But what he said was, "What about Mom?"

"She's beside herself. She needs you, Peter."

"Ok. I'm coming." That's what Peter needed. An action plan. He threw the phone down and ran to their back bedroom. He'd pack a few things and get to the airport.

~

Hope unlocked the front door, unable to keep the eager feeling from coming up in her chest. Peter said he had something special planned for her tonight. She'd shower and get dressed up, then they'd go on a date. It would be like old times.

She pulled off her boots and laughed at herself a little. How funny that the "good old times" were only six months ago. How funny that they could have so many ups and downs in that short time. But every marriage had issues, she reasoned, like Esther had told her. You just had to hold tight and remember the good times.

She placed her keys on the long oak entry table, then stopped in her tracks. She smelled something burning and – was that the smoke alarm? She ran into the kitchen and, when she saw the oil rising madly from the skillet, quickly turned the stove off and threw the skillet into the sink. Bad move – the water from the sink seemed to make the oil even angrier, and some of it splashed up onto her. "Ouch!" she yelped, then opened the window above the sink and started waving a towel at the protesting smoke alarm.

"Peter?" She called. Where was he?

She found him in the bedroom, hurriedly throwing clothes into a suitcase.

"Remember that trip we had planned for the end of this month? To go to Nebraska together?" He asked drily, his eyes on his suitcase still, his hands moving faster every second.

"Ye-es," she stood in the doorway, her heart even more still than her feet.

"Well, there's been a change of plans. I'm going alone." He reached up to the top of their shared closet and pulled down a sweater. A coat. Did he need all that in June?

The *alone* part didn't register yet. His crazed method of packing did. "Now?" she asked stupidly.

"Yes. Now." He shut the lid on his suitcase and finally looked at her. On his face she saw – pain. Fear.

She followed him down the hall. Now that her feet were moving and her heart had started back up again, a million questions flooded her mind. What about her birthday date? When would he be back? Why the sudden change in plans? Why couldn't she go with him? She had to stop his race to the car so she could ask him...

But he turned suddenly at the door, planted a firm kiss on the top of her head, and was gone. She left the door open and watched him go, weeping silently.

She was always staring at his back these days.

chapter eight

Hope wandered around the house, idle. She couldn't study, couldn't clean, couldn't cook. Couldn't think.

24 hours had passed since Peter had left in a hurry. She'd told Anna, but not Papa. Papa didn't need a reason to dislike Peter even more.

But should she tell Papa anyway? Keep him in the loop? Or should she try getting a hold of Peter's family?

She hurried across the cold tile floor, to the entry table where she'd left her phone. Maybe Peter had called since she'd last checked it.

She turned the phone over. No messages. Not since the one he'd sent at 3am that said, *Finally got a flight to Denver. Call you tomorrow.* She sighed and began to step away, but her eyes caught her own reflection in the large, gilded mirror that hung over the entry table. *You really should cover up those dark circles under your eyes, Hope.* Her mom's voice echoed in her head.

Enough of this. Enough of looking in mirrors and being reminded that she'd never be good enough. She ran to the kitchen junk drawer where she kept a dry erase marker or two.

She pulled out the black marker – so it would show up better – and went first to the bathroom mirror. Before she could even remove the cap, she was assaulted by her own reflection again. *I do like your curly hair,* Peter had said to her the week after their wedding. *But do you think you should get some new clothes? Something more modern?* She looked down at the outfit she had on that day. Jeans were her favorite, after riding breeches. And she liked simple tops, fitted with solid colors. Whenever she'd needed a special out-fit, like for her Bat Mitzvah, Mom had gone with her to pick it out. But for the everyday, Hope liked to be comfortable.

Cap off the marker, she began drawing furiously. She had to sit upon the sink to reach the mirror properly. A little girl began to take shape, sitting in a field of flowers. It was a simple drawing, but it was the best she could expect for a bathroom mirror. Over the top she scrawled in loopy cursive letters, *You Are Loved.*

Next came the entryway mirror. She was moving too fast to bother checking her phone now. But she needed a stool to draw on this mirror properly. She ran to the kitchen to get it, then stood for a moment, wondering what to draw here. Remembering that the same God who formed the stars in the sky had also formed her, bit by bit, she drew what she hoped looked like a starry night. It would be better if she'd had color; then she could draw the light that bathed each star. She was about to run back to the kitchen to see if there was a yellow marker when her phone rang.

"Hi," Peter's voice said quietly.

"Hey." She was unable to keep the rudeness from her voice. He had gone so suddenly – and on the trip they were supposed to take together – without any explanation.

"So – my dad died," he burst out.

"What?!" She was as hard to convince as he had been. But within a few minutes he'd explained the whole story to her.

She sat on the paisley blue sofa now, absently holding the mug of tea she'd forgotten earlier. Nodding and smiling sadly, though he couldn't see her, and trying to understand.

"How's your Mom?" She asked after Peter had laid out the details for the funeral.

"Not good. She really needs us here now." By *us,* Hope rightly assumed he meant himself and his brother, Rob.

"Well, can I come? I can help with cooking. Or just be there for your Mom. Or –"

"No, no," he interrupted. "You wait there. I'll only be a few days. There's no use you rushing out here." His voice sounded prac-ticed, rehearsed. She wondered if he had another reason for keep-ing her away.

"Okay," she said slowly. "But Peter – why didn't you tell me all this earlier? When you first found out? I am your wife, you know."

He sighed heavily. "I don't know. I guess I had all this adrenaline after Rob called me. I just didn't think. I had to get here… But you're right. I should've told you." After a moment's pause he said, in the sweet voice he used only for Hope, "Hey, can we FaceTime? I want to see my beautiful wife."

She giggled and agreed. They talked for another hour, about her horses and his lost cows and what Papa would say if he ever set foot on Nebraska soil. About anything but Peter's parents.

She hung up the phone, sighed happily, and finished her now-cold tea. Then she stepped out into the sunshine of the backyard. She and Mom had always said they'd plant a garden here – roses up by the back porch, and a vegetable patch further on, in that open area. But life had always gotten in the way. Maybe this would be the year.

On impulse she decided to head to the lawn and garden store, mentally making her list as she went. *Shovel. 2x4s. Rosebushes. Seeds.*

chapter nine

"Something on your mind?" Anna peered at Hope over the glasses that Jake called librarian-glasses. Anna never failed to tease him and say that that just meant he thought they were sexy.

"Oh. You know. Peter." Hope answered. "Wondering why doesn't he want me there. Missing him and hating him at the same time. You know. That's all." Hope tried but failed to keep the bitterness out of her tone as she folded a dress and added it to the pile. She could let down her walls here, folding laundry with Anna on the couch.

"Hey – why don't you spend the night?" Anna asked quickly. "You shouldn't be in that house all alone. I know your Papa's close by. But still, it's too quiet out there."

Hope smiled, then teased – "Definitely not too quiet here," with raised eyebrows towards Anna's daughters who were wildly taking turns jumping off an armchair and onto a little indoor trampoline.

"See? Problem solved." Anna gestured towards the two little monkeys.

Hope glanced towards her cousin's newly rounded belly. The third addition to their family would be coming in November. Family time was so important. She might as well put to good use this time that Peter was gone. "All right. But only because you insisted."

"Whoop!" Anna rejoiced. "Slumber party!" Then she stood to lightly toss one of the couch pillows towards her four year-old, Cora.

The girls erupted in fits of giggles, too.

"You know, Jake's a jerk to me too sometimes. And guess what. So am I. To him." Hope looked at her, not believing. So Anna went on. "No, it's true. We get tired or stressed because of the kids. It sounds like Peter's under a lot of stress. And none of that makes it ok to treat your spouse like a jerk." She stood up to heat her decaf in the microwave and grab a brownie for Hope. "But you know… it's just like anything. Like the horses."

She sat back down and took a deep breath. "When you first started riding, they didn't just put you on a horse and say, *Ok, go!* Somebody held the bridle. And you started slow."

Anna handed Hope her brownie. She saw the tears prickling in Hope's eyes and took them as a good sign. "Relationships are like that." She said softly, pressing her young cousin's hand. "It helps to walk before you run. But you two took off running." She took a sip of her hot drink and made big eyes at Hope. "I mean seriously! Who dates for only six months?"

"Lots of people." Hope was laughing but serious. She was right. In different cultures, and in different times, it wasn't so weird.

"Yeah. But I mean… maybe now it's time to remember the basics."

"Like what?" Hope asked her softly, forgotten mismatched socks resting in her lap.

Anna shrugged. "Remember why you got married in the first place. Think about the fun things you'll do together when he gets home. That kind of stuff." Then she stood. "Okay girls! Come help Mommy set the table."

Hope stayed put, determined to at least finish sorting the socks before dinner. Her eyes fell on a card that stood on the end table. It was written in gold letters with pink and red flowers around it – a friend must have given it to Anna. The words read, "*The wise woman builds her house, but with her own hands the foolish one tears hers down. ~Proverbs 14:1.*"

She let the words sink in as she listened to the laughter that came from the kitchen. Anna seemed like such a natural when it came to marriage and motherhood. But then, Anna had a mother who stayed.

"Oh Lord," she prayed quietly, "I want to build up a home. I want to bless my own little family. But I don't know how. Please show me how."

That night, in the twin bed that took up most of Anna's hundred year-old attic guest bedroom, a low, quiet, nighttime breeze blew in through the open window and teased at Hope's toes. In her dream, Hope saw herself and Peter standing next to an empty brown box. It looked a lot like the box of girls' clothes that Hope had helped Anna empty earlier that day. But the box in her dream grew bigger and bigger until it stood taller than herself, and even Peter. She stood in its shadow until it grew so tall that it toppled over and fell on top of them both.

Hope jolted upright in bed. Heart pounding, palms sweaty. She half expected to find herself buried inside four dark walls. But in the moonlight she saw it: the brown cardboard box in the corner of her bedroom. It was empty and silent, right where she had left it.

Next morning, Hope awoke to the sound of shouts. Fear gripped her throat for a moment. But she wasn't twelve years old, in her bed at home. She took a deep breath and looked around just to prove it. Sloped ceilings, morning light gently falling in and landing on banana-yellow walls, and the rocking horse in the corner, were all signs that she was in Anna's attic bedroom. Her little house in one of the older suburbs of San Diego had its own quirky personality. To Hope, it felt like home. Maybe more like home than the one she'd left yesterday.

She dressed quickly, but instead of leaving the attic, she pulled out the sketch pad she always kept with her. She wanted to draw the box from her dream before she forgot it. There was a message in that dream, even if she didn't understand it.

Her pencil flew across the paper – it only took a moment to draw four walls, two flaps. Simple. She put her sketchpad away and sighed. What were those kiddos hollering about? Must be pancakes. The smell had wafted up to her bedroom now. It tempted Hope's stomach, too, and she was surprised by how hungry she was. She eased her way down the creaky stairs, then stopped in the doorway that led to the kitchen when she heard what sounded like a heated discussion between Anna and Jake. She didn't want to interrupt – but if she headed back upstairs, surely the creaky stairs would make more noise and distract them from their conversation.

Before she could decide what to do, Anna was saying, "I had to. I just had to find out."

Jake: "But was that wise? I mean, if she wanted to be found, she would've left an address or something."

"I know that's what everybody's saying. But sometimes when you care about somebody, you pursue them. That's what my mom used to say." A clatter of a spatula.

"Ok, but couldn't you have told me? Or waited for me? I would've gone with you." Jake's voice was softer now, reasoning, and Hope thought it sounded like he'd taken a few steps closer to Anna.

"You know I can't be responsible for making logical decisions like that when I'm pregnant." This was Anna's teasing voice. Hope had never heard her best friend joke about pregnancy being a get-out-of-jail free card. But it worked. Jake didn't say anything more; instead, Hope heard him opening and closing the coffee cupboard.

"Who're we pursuing?" Hope stepped into the kitchen, deciding it was hopeless to pretend like she hadn't heard. But both of them just stood there, Anna mid-pancake-flip and Jake with the coffee pot in his hand, poised to refill his cup. They both stared at her.

"What?" Hope asked quickly. Had she forgotten to put on pants or something? Anna looked at Jake, and he nodded.

"Come here," Anna sat down on the bench at the sunny breakfast nook and motioned for Hope to sit beside her. It was an old-fashioned galley kitchen, and the breakfast nook was a little distance away from where Anna had been working at the stove; Hope wondered if Anna just wanted to sit down while they talked, or if this was the kind of talk that warranted a little privacy. She decided it must be the latter when Jake brought her a mug of coffee – only half filled, so it would stay hot, with cream, no sugar – then went to the stove to assume Anna's pancake-flipping duties. Hope took a sip of her coffee – strong, hot and perfect – and waited for Anna to speak. Her cousin was only serious when she had to be. This would be interesting.

"Hope," Anna started, taking one of her hands, "We found your Mom."

"What?" Hope almost spat out her coffee.

"We... I mean I... found your Mom." Anna exhaled and folded her hands in her lap, looking at Hope straight on. She was serious.

"How... where..." Hope settled on the most important question. "How did you find her? Dad and I checked everywhere."

Anna shrugged like it had been easy. "I called some of her friends at her bunco club. I figured if she hadn't talked to family, maybe she talked to a friend. Maybe that was safer." Anna craned her neck back towards the middle of the kitchen to make sure breakfast wasn't burning. But Jake was as dutiful in pancake-flipping as he was in providing for his family.

"Anyway, one of her friends did have her new phone number. So I called her."

"You called her?" Had it been that easy? Had Anna really just picked up the phone and called her mom?

"Yeah. And then I went to go see her."

This time Hope was glad she didn't have coffee in her mouth, because she definitely would've spit it out. "Well... where is she?" She managed to sputter.

"On Catalina Island. She's sharing the cutest little house with that old friend from high school..." but Anna stopped when she saw the dark look in Hope's eyes. "You can go see her too, you know. In fact, you *should* go see her. She wants to show you something... I mean, she wants to talk to you."

The old feeling of numbness that came whenever anyone brought up Mom washed over Hope. She stared down at her hands; they looked like someone else's. "If she wanted to talk to me... why didn't she leave her number with Dad and I? Or why doesn't she call *me?* I didn't change *my* phone."

"I think it's something to do with not wanting your Dad to find out... about her whereabouts. They went through something really hard, Hope."

"Yeah, I know, I was there for all of it. I was a witness to all their fights, remember?" Hope put down her coffee cup and stood. She wasn't ready to leave; but she couldn't sit still, either.

Anna knitted her brows together, trying to understand. She cocked her head and looked at Hope as if trying to see right through her. "Are you still angry with her?"

"Angry?" No, she wasn't angry. She stared out the window at Anna's little front yard with the wagon and the bikes strewn about. They were a family. They stuck together.

There was no anger in Hope's heart. What was there was something else, something deeper… something that ached and made her throat burn. She couldn't name it. But it had something to do with the fact that Anna had been able to reach her mom, while Hope hadn't. She stared out the window a moment longer, then recovered enough to think of a few basic questions. Like, how was Mom's health? And did she have friends on the island? And, was she safe? But before she could open her mouth again, first one niece and then the other catapulted into her. She didn't realize she'd locked her knees until the niece-attack almost knocked her into the wall. Anna was used to interruptions; it was almost like she'd forgotten their conversation as she knelt down to kiss her babies, then headed back to the stove to check on the pancakes. Hope squatted down to exclaim over the princess-pajama-clad girls with hugs and kisses, then took each one by a hand and brought them over to the spread that Jake had laid out on the kitchen island. He refilled her coffee cup, though she hadn't drank much. Hope perched on one of the reupholstered red barstools that hung out around the kitchen island and watched the parents fill plates for their girls. Fruit, eggs, *and* pancakes. "You must have been up early to accomplish all this."

Jake plopped a sound kiss on his wife's cheek. "My wife is always accomplishing amazing things. Wow, I'm alliterate this morning. I mean, not illiterate. I'm alliterating. You know what I mean." Anna laughed and swatted him with the spatula. Hope just watched them over her coffee… a little wistfully… as Jake gathered his things, gave Anna another kiss, and headed off to a job site.

Even when Peter was here, he never treated her like that. Never gave affection just because. Never teased her in the kitchen.

Anna stood by the griddle, flipping still more pancakes. "I'm up early most mornings. This little one already won't let mama sleep." She cradled her barely-rounding belly affectionately. "They do that, ya know. They start disturbing your slumber as soon as they can." Anna put her spatula down and came and sat by Hope. "You know, I read somewhere, that when Mama is walking around, the movement of the fluid in the belly rocks the baby to sleep. Just like we rock them in a rocking chair. Then, when Mama lies down at night, the stillness wakes them up. Isn't that wild?"

Hope smiled thoughtfully. "Yeah. This little one has a schedule already. And it's already opposite to yours." She poked Anna playfully, then went for more pancakes. "Hey, how about you let me take both girls this morning? Jojo can watch Cora do her gymnastics. I bet it'll entertain her. Then you can get some real rest. If their little sister will let you." Hope winked. She knew Anna and Jake hadn't found out the baby's sex yet; but she was more than a little excited at the idea of all girls.

"Oh, really? Are you sure you can handle them both? I mean, of course you can handle them both! What am I saying? Girls, come get your shoes on! Auntie Hope's taking you both to gymnastics!"

This time the squeals were louder even than pre-pancake squeals. Cora ran to obey. Josephine stopped short and looked up at Hope with milky-brown eyes. "Can I bring my unicorn?" the toddler almost whispered.

"Actually, unicorns are required," Hope smiled at the little girl.

A short car ride later, and Hope was pulling shoes off again so the little girls could run and play on the mats. Anna had warned her that technically "Mommy and Me" meant "you are responsible for your own kid." She was ready. She watched how the other moms followed their little ones around the room, some holding a toddler on a hip, others wearing a baby in front, and one mama huffing around with her big baby bump. These mamas got as much of a workout in as their kids did.

Finally it was time for everybody's favorite station: the trampoline. Hope followed to help with spotting. Another mom who came up to spot cradled her infant in her arms; Hope helped her up the steps and they laughed together at how awkwardly positioned this activity was.

Each child took their turn. Somersault, bounce with legs apart, bounce with legs together. Then land on your bottom for the grand finale, and move off to the side so the next kid could take a turn. Jen, their kind and patient teacher, instructed each one with a practiced tone of voice. Four children took their turns, trying their best to follow her directions, and eagerly receiving the praise of their enthusiastic little audience.

Then came Cora's turn. But when the little girl made it to the center of the trampoline, she went deaf to the sound of her teacher's voice and started dancing. Her smile was brighter than the sun that trickled down on her through the tall open windows.

Jen tried to bring Cora back to earth. "No, sweetie, like this," she urged.

Normally Hope would apologize. She'd say something like, "Okay, Cora, time to listen to your teacher now." Normally she would be so terrified of breaking the rules that she would try to help her niece fit in. But today wasn't a normal day. Today, she was thinking about Peter. Jake. Mom. And the box she'd been trying to fit into her whole life.

Were her expectations biblical, or were they cultural?

So Hope sat on the trampoline and studied the curly-headed little girl... how pretty she was. How happy she was. How the rays of sun seemed to laugh, to bubble, to almost dance with Cora, as they slowly trickled down to the trampoline. How even the floating particles of dust looked like fairy magic in the light. And she remembered her dream.

So she bit her tongue. She took a deep breath. She gave a humble smile to the now-slightly-irritated teacher. And she watched her little niece dance.

Peter's tall frame leaned against the window. Almost a year had passed since the fire. If it wasn't for the blackened hills beyond the barn, he'd think it had never happened.

There was the new barn at the bottom of the hill. Bigger and sturdier than the last one. And there were sprinklers installed; Dad had seen to that. Inside, it housed corn seed and a newer, bigger tractor. Dad had gotten into farming, and his plan had been to use the profits from selling corn – which was easier and cheaper to grow than cattle were to feed – to buy cattle, slowly increasing the herd each year; within ten years, the ranch should be back to its former glory. Until then, he and Mom had planned to live on little – Peter hadn't realized how little until he'd sat with Dad's lawyer last night. Rob and Gina, too – if it weren't for Gina's job at the 10-room hospital the town had been able to jerry rig, and for their free rent at Gina's parents' place, Rob, Gina and their baby son would be destitute.

He turned from the window and picked up his phone. Time to call Hope and try to bring her around to the plan.

She picked up on the second ring. "Peter?" Her voice sounded kind of desperate. Wasn't she stronger than that? He hadn't expected her to be such a basket case – he'd only been gone two weeks, after all.

He listened to her ramble about the horses and Anna's kids for a few minutes – then he got to the point. "So, I inherited the ranch. I mean, Rob and I did."

She paused. "Inherited? Like, you'll be able to sell it and split the earnings?"

He puffed out his chest at her comment. Sell it? Why would she think that? "No," he replied, exasperated. "We're going to run it. At least, Rob is. I've gotta help him, though."

"Run the ranch?" She asked, rather stupidly, he thought.

He sighed and sat down at Mom's long kitchen table. "Listen," his voice lowered though no one else was around. He spoke quickly. "I thought my calling was to become a firefighter. I thought that was how I'd make everything right. But now I know – my calling is here. Helping Rob. Taking care of Mom. That's how I'll make things right. I'll help rebuild the ranch." He stood now, and paced the length of the remodeled kitchen – Mom and Dad had added on to the 1920's farmhouse as their family had grown. "I didn't realize how bad their finances were, Hope. If this corn crop doesn't turn a profit, Rob'll lose the farm." He and Rob had walked the fields just that morning, dividing the chores between them. It was better than he'd expected to be with his family again – but a man still needed his wife. "But I can't do it without you. Please, Hope."

"Are you asking me to come there?" He heard the clatter of dishes. Then silence.

"Yes." Maybe he should give her a minute to catch up.

"I can do that. For how long?"

"Just three or four months. Until the harvest. Rob should have some profits coming in by then, and I can sign off my half to him."

"Oh Peter. Of course I want to be there with you, and meet your family, and help if I can... but Anna and the horses and Papa –" Her voice rose to that desperate tone again. He didn't know it, but his voice rose too.

"At least come for a little while. Please. I need you." He thought back to the last time he'd felt her touch. It had been too long.

Only a moment's pause, then – "Okay."

He exhaled and felt a weight lift off his chest. "And I promise to have you home before the first blizzard hits. That is one thing you do *not* need to see."

"Well – when are you coming back? You know, to pack up your stuff?" That was one thing he loved about Hope. She thought about everybody's needs, just like his mom.

"I thought maybe you could do it for me. Or maybe your Dad could help. There's so much work to do here..."

She paused again. Then, "Let me think about it. But listen, I have to go now. I'm at Papa's." Peter winced. Hope would have to break the news about moving to her dad. He didn't envy that job. "Call you later, ok?" Before she hung up, she added, "Love you."

Hope shimmied the phone down from where it was cradled on her shoulder; her hands were submerged in a bowl of meat. She bent low and let the phone plop onto the counter. She went over to the sink to wash her hands, then untied her apron. She needed to think about this.

"Are you happy, Hope?" She jumped a little at the sound of Papa's voice. She'd forgotten he was even there.

He was looking at her from the oversized blue couch while she made dinner for him. She'd gotten sick of staying in her little cottage all alone, and it felt good, but not good, to be back in the big house for a little while. Wanting to busy herself so he wouldn't see the look that must be on her face, she plunged into the fridge for the rest of her ingredients. But he'd asked a question. Face sufficiently cooled, she popped back to the counter and asked in a distracted way, "Hmm?"

"I said, are you happy? Are you happy with him?"

She paused, hands buried now in ground beef, bell pepper and bread crumbs. An extra egg, instead of milk. Grandma Leah's trick. She realized that to Papa, her end of the conversation had only been *"okay"s* and *"Mm-hmm"s.* Tears pricked at her eyes. No, she wasn't happy. She wasn't happy with the way he'd left her here alone to go deal with his family. She wasn't happy that apparently he was planning to drop out of paramedic school, which had been the plan they'd agreed on. She wasn't happy that he was trying to take her thousands of miles away from everything she knew and loved to some forgotten, burned-down Nebraska town. Most of all, she wasn't happy about the way he stomped around and slammed doors when he was angry. It reminded her too much of her parents. But she couldn't say all that to Papa. So instead, she wiped away the tears on her shoulder. And said softly, "I don't think that's a valid question."

Papa just *harrumphed* and got up from the couch to put away his newspaper. He wouldn't understand.

It wasn't that her happiness wasn't important, she thought as she finished mixing the meat and plopped it into the pan. It was just... that wasn't the question on which you should base a marriage. A promise was a promise – and she'd promised to be there for Peter. She went to wash her hands again, then put a hand over her mouth. All the stress was making her sick to her stomach.

She slid the meatloaf into the oven and made herself a cup of tea. She might as well deliver her news now. For a moment, she wished Peter were here with her. But she could soften things better than he could.

"Papa? Can you sit with me a minute?" She beckoned to the empty seat at the little round breakfast table. He sat down and crossed his elbows tightly over his chest, raised eyebrows informing her that he'd listen, but not for long.

"Peter and his brother Rob inherited the ranch," she began. That much wasn't surprising. Somebody had to take care of the property. No one would expect Peter's mom to handle it all alone. "And he wants me to... to..." somehow saying *move there till the harvest* didn't feel quite right. "He wants me to pack up his stuff. And come visit him." That felt better. She held her cup of tea tighter.

Papa *harrumphed* again. It seemed to be his favorite way of expressing himself. "Well, what about school? What about his job here?"

"He says he... might try running the ranch with Rob for a while..." At the look on his face, she added quickly, "Just till the fall."

Papa looked at her with raised eyebrows. "Give up a good job at the hospital! You can't be serious."

"Papa! It's only till the harvest."

"Well, when does that happen?" Dr. Rosenberg crossed his arms over his chest and eyed her as if she were responsible for the whole debacle.

"I think ... September?"

Papa sighed a heavy sigh. But then he responded, "Well, he may still be able to keep his position. And I don't see why he shouldn't be able to return to school in the fall. As long as he communicates with his bosses, and with his instructors. They often make allowances for family emergencies like this."

Hope felt her shoulders straighten like Papa's had done. She hadn't thought of that. Being able to slide back into their plans at home made a temporary move feel better. She'd talk to Peter about it.

"Yeah. And I'm kind of proud of him that he wants to be there for his mom." Hope was going to do everything she could to bring Papa around to the plan. If nothing else, Papa should be able to respect Peter's decision to honor his parents. "If the ranch doesn't start earning an income soon, they won't be able to make payments and Teresa will lose everything." Hope's voice grew quieter. She felt a pang that the woman had still never come out to meet her. Or called, even.

"Didn't Mr. Bailey leave her some insurance money? Can't they use that to take care of Peter's mom?" Papa was sitting back, one leg crossed over the other, and using his doctor voice. The one that said he had all the answers.

Hope looked down at her hands and the ring she was fiddling with. "Apparently Jim cancelled his life insurance policy a couple months after the fire happened. To have more money every month to put into rebuilding the ranch." She knew what Papa would have to say about this before he said it.

"Foolishness. *Complete* foolishness."

"It kind of makes sense if you think about it. He didn't have any health issues at the time. Maybe he planned to start a new policy once they got the ranch solvent again."

"Hmmph." Papa looked at her for a moment before he spoke again. "I looked into it. Called a couple of lawyer friends of mine yesterday," Papa told her, looking down his nose in his doctor-way. "You can still annul the marriage."

"Papa!" She had never shouted at him but felt like doing so now. "His Dad just died!"

"I'm not saying you should. I would never presume to give you such advice. I'm just saying I will support you if you do. He's not who he said he was... just last week you told me he's gotten into debt while living out here. He couldn't even get his family out here to meet you." Papa's face was screwed up with uncharacteristic emotion. "Now he's giving up his career. And leaving your life here to run some farm? He's not who he said he was, Hope."

"It's not a farm, Papa. It's a ranch."

"Just tell me you'll think about it. Please." Papa had never entreated her like this. Not once. She got the chills and put down her mug of tea before her shaking hands could spill it. Did he know something she didn't know?

"Ok, Papa. I will." She lied and stood over the table, leaning down to give him a kiss on the cheek. When the meat and potatoes were done, they ate their meal in peace.

The captain's voice came over the loudspeaker. "Buckle your seatbelts, ladies and gentlemen," he boomed. "We're getting ready for takeoff."

Hope grabbed Esther's hand instinctively. It was only the second time she'd been on a plane. The first had been with Peter, to Maui, just a few months ago. It was funny how she'd led such a privileged life as a doctor's only daughter, and yet such a sheltered life too.

"You ready?" Esther asked, squeezing her hand.

"Ready as I'll ever be." Hope offered a weak smile. When she'd told her mentor about the move, Esther had announced that she'd been meaning to visit her sister in Denver, and wouldn't it be just perfect if they could fly together? Hope knew her mentor well enough to know that she would use this time to pray for her, encourage her. She didn't mind one bit.

"How was your father this morning?" Esther asked, maybe trying to distract her from the sound of the engines warming up. How *did* a plane stay aloft, anyway?

"Oh, you know. Pretty stoic." But she had noticed her Papa's eyes turning red, and he had just stood there, still as a statue, when she went through baggage claim. Kind of like he had on the day she told him she'd booked her ticket – a one-way ticket.

"But you're coming back, aren't you?" He'd asked hopefully.

She'd just shrugged and offered him a half-smile. She didn't want to stay away long; but neither was she ready to give up on her marriage yet. Not till she'd tried everything. "I'll come back to visit, Papa. And you'll come see me soon. Right?"

He'd nodded, but couldn't even muster a fake smile before she left.

Hope leaned her head back against the seat and groaned. The plane was taxiing down the runway now. Esther squeezed her hand a little tighter. "You can do it," she spoke loudly in Hope's ear over the roar of the engines. "There is no place that's foreign to *Yeshua*. He's right here with you." Hope wondered if Esther meant that He was here in the plane with them – or that He'd be with her in the town that she'd learned was called "The Armpit of the Midwest." Hopefully both.

Her goodbyes had been harder than she'd thought. Anna, this

morning, at the airport – she'd held her tightly and wept. "Pregnancy hormones," Anna had wiped her tears and made fun of herself.

"No... I'll miss you too." Hope took a good long look at her cousin. Anna had brought up the mom thing last week when she'd come over to help Hope pack. But when the conversation had gone nowhere, she'd dropped it.

Today she just tried to be brave for Hope. "I will miss you. But I know you are doing the right thing. We'll come visit." Anna said that in her determined way; but Hope wondered how it would be possible. She knew how much finagling it took for Anna to schedule an evening out... how would she ever schedule the few days it would take to get halfway across the country and back? And how much would it cost if ever she wanted to bring her family with her? Hope wondered briefly how long it might be until she saw her best friend again; then shuddered and pushed the thought away.

But if she'd thought Anna's hug had been tight, it had been nothing compared to Ben's. Jake's brother had come to the airport that morning. He'd never hugged her that long, or that close, before; then he'd pulled away quickly, just as surprised as she, and looking a little guilty. Hope had thought nothing of it at the time; everyone was tearful and emotional at airports. But now she wondered. He was so gentle and calm, not like Peter... she shut off the thoughts as the plane suddenly lifted into the air and the ground fell away from them.

Maybe even harder than her friends and family had been her goodbye with the horses. She'd hugged Pirate's neck until her tears mingled with the scent of his sweat and mane. He'd stood stock still, knowing, as he always did, when she needed him. She'd walked through the barn slowly, wishing she could bottle every scent, every sound. This place had always been her therapy. How would she live without it? And Heidi had surprised her as she'd turned left out of the barn aisle that day, wiping her tears hastily on her sleeve. "Take this," Heidi had urged, pressing a key into her hand. Hope had looked down at it. It was Heidi's master key: the one that opened the gate at the end of the drive and both tack-rooms. "You're still taking over this place when I'm done." Heidi had held up a hand to stop Hope's protests. "Now, just take it. I'm excited for you. Going on an adventure and all that. But when you come home, you have a job here." Heidi had given her a quick hug and sent her on her way.

She pressed her back pocket now, where the key lay snug. She hadn't wanted it to get lost in her suitcase. Heidi's promise felt like a safety net. Her life would be waiting for her when she and Peter came back home. In a moment of bravery, she peeked out the window, then drew a sharp breath as the plane bumped and jiggled a little. "Do you think I can do it?"

Esther smiled without looking up from the book she was reading. "You'd be surprised what a woman can do for her family." She reached over to pat Hope's hand.

"I want to. I want to show the love of Jesus to my family," Hope said emphatically. Then quietly, as she looked down at her lap – "But maybe I'm too broken."

"What do you mean?"

Hope sighed. "You know. I've spent so much of my life training. Training horses. Studying for school. I wish somebody would've trained me for this."

Esther looked up this time. "For Nebraska?"

Hope's sigh came from a deeper place. "For marriage." She wiggled in her seat a little. "Did you know Peter didn't even tell me that his dad had died until he was already on a plane that night? I just keep wondering why. Doesn't he want to confide in me? I'm his wife." She fiddled with the ring on her finger, then looked back at Esther. "I just wish I was better prepared for this."

Esther looked up from her book now and resumed her grip on Hope's hand. "Darling, what you need isn't training. What you need is trust. He's already given you everything you need."

Hope smiled at her friend, then reached in her bag for her own book. But she put it back after merely looking at the cover. Her mental checklist wouldn't let her read right now. "You'll check on Papa, won't you?" She pleaded again in Esther's direction, though they'd already had this conversation.

"You know I will." Esther reached down in her purse for a lipstick. She was so glamorous. Even on a plane.

"I know." Hope lay her head back as the exhaustion of the last two weeks caught up with her. Since the phone call from Peter that started this adventure, each day had been packed – cleaning out the little cottage, transferring classes to an online university, changing their address with the bank, not to mention sorting, boxing and shipping Peter's stuff for him. She'd stood before her closet, trying to think through what she would need for the rest of the summer – then, in a moment of triumph, emptied everything she'd ever worn in warm weather and stuffed it into one suitcase. *There. Done,* she'd said to herself as she'd pressed one foot on it to zip it up.

But here on the plane, there was no to-do list to stand in the way of exhaustion. Twenty minutes later she woke up, cramped, parched. "I think I need to get up," she said drowsily to Esther. Esther stood to let her out, and she wobbled down the aisle and back just to stretch.

When she sat down again, she looked out the window without remembering to be frightened. The sky was clear; the land lay below her like a patchwork quilt. "Ohhh," she breathed out a sigh. San Diego had always been beautiful, and of course Hawaii had been a treat; but this was different. This was new.

This was the way to what she was beginning to think of as her summer home: the town of Orion, Nebraska. Maybe it would be good for them to be out in the middle of nowhere together. Maybe he would forget all his worries he'd had about work; the weird competition he seemed to have going with Papa; all the things Hope had done to annoy him at their little cottage. Maybe they'd be able to get back to the way things used to be when they were dating.

As the plane touched down, she felt a little surge of pride go through her. Esther was right; she could do it. Hope was finally starting over with a little family of her own. Nothing could make her mess this up.

part two

NEBRASKA

"When the man saw that he could not overpower him, he touched the socket of Jacob's hip so that his hip was wrenched as he wrestled with the man. Then the man said, 'Let me go, for it is daybreak.' But Jacob replied, 'I will not let you go unless you bless me.'"

Genesis 32:25-26

chapter ten

The flowers Peter had picked up from the grocery store back home only looked a little worse for the wear as he bounced lightly on the balls of his feet. A few daisy petals fell to the floor, but he didn't notice. He was too busy watching for Hope.

The Denver airport wasn't so bad, once you got used to it. But it would be a lot for Hope, who'd hardly flown at all. He was proud of her – proud of her for coming. Proud that he'd chosen her. He'd needed this time with family, but he was ready to have his wife back. She belonged with him.

He thought back to the time he'd caught Mom praying she'd come – just two weeks ago. He'd hung up the phone with Hope and walked into the kitchen. There Mom had been sitting at the table, head bent over her hands, praying. *"Dio Mio,"* he'd heard her say from her place at the doorway – her prayers had never been quiet – *"Dio Mio,* bring my daughter to me. Give me a chance to love her, as you have loved me. Preserve their union, God."

Peter had interrupted then. Just as much as Mom had never worried about keeping the thoughts of her heart quiet, she'd never tried to keep them private, either. "I think she'll come, Mom," he said confidently, sitting down in the chair next to her.

She'd jumped a little since she hadn't heard him come in. Then she'd said, just as confidently, "Good. She should come." And she'd gotten up to finish making dinner.

And they'd both been right, because here she was – tight curls bouncing under her chin as she ran the last few steps to him. She dropped her backpack and jumped into his arms; he swung her around gladly and didn't let go.

"You cut your hair," he noticed as he cupped a hand behind her head.

"New life, new haircut," she said as she turned her head so that he could admire her better. Then her face grew serious. "I'm so sorry. About your dad. I mean, I know we've talked about it, but… this is the first time I've seen you since it happened." She slipped her hand in his. "I wish I could've met him," she added with a sad smile.

With one hand, he squeezed the one she'd given him, and with his other hand, he waved her comment away as if it didn't matter. As they walked towards the baggage claim, he shuddered without knowing it. "I'm kinda glad you didn't," he responded, and kissed her on the cheek.

Hope kept her face pressed to the window. She couldn't believe land could be so flat. Not a mountain, and barely a hill, in sight. Only a few trees worth looking at. It was so different, it took her breath away.

"We're almost there," Peter smiled at her, one hand on the wheel, the other on her shoulder.

"Home?" She'd thought Orion was four hours from the airport, not two.

He chuckled. "The Nebraska border," he clarified.

She could see it up ahead: the bright green state sign. As they drew nearer, she read it: "Nebraska: The Good Life."

"Stop!" she screeched, scaring him. "I'm sorry," she laughed at his frightened face as he pulled over on the side of the freeway. "I just want to take a picture." She hopped out of the beat-up Camry Peter had borrowed from Rob and went to snap a picture of the sign.

"Wait," Peter hollered, joining her. He clutched his chest. "Now that I've recovered from the scare of my life, thanks to you… let's do this together." He put an arm around her, then leaned back for the selfie. She spread her arms wide as if to take in all of the bright blue Midwest sky, like one of the eagles she'd spotted on the drive.

She fell asleep briefly during the next two hours home, waking when a loud clunk from ahead caused Peter to change gears rapidly and swerve to the shoulder.

"Traffic?" She rubbed her eyes, sitting up straight.

"Tractor," he answered. She looked again. It was true; they were stuck behind a bright green tractor on a two-lane highway. She burst out laughing and took another picture; she couldn't wait to tell Anna about this. "What town is this?" She asked while she looked out the window hopefully. It must be Orion. They were passing some stores, a few restaurants, plenty of pretty houses and lots of trees.

"Red Bluffs." He shifted uncomfortably in his seat.

"Oh." Her voice fell. "How much farther to Orion?"

"Fifty miles." He pulled his hand from her shoulder and tightened both on the wheel.

"I hope we won't be stuck behind the tractor the whole way!" She laughed, then reached to massage his shoulders. But he didn't relax under her hand like he usually did.

Hope was thankful when the farmer turned off the main road after only ten miles. But it was another forty till they saw the sign to Orion: forty miles of nothing. The further they drove, the deeper Hope's heart sank into her chest. How isolated would she be out here?

She stretched and yawned when Peter pulled off the freeway. There was a box store on the corner. At least she'd be able to go there for household supplies. Driving down the main street took less than minute. Her eyes widened as they passed the hospital. She was familiar enough with the layout of a typical hospital to notice that this one looked as if half of it had been scooped away. A construction crew was working on the other side of the parking lot, where a frame had been raised. That must be for the new building.

"Where are the nurses and doctors working now?" She asked, confused. If a hospital burned down in San Diego, there would be countless other choices for healthcare workers and patients. But here, this was the only place.

"In the ER. It's the only wing that didn't burn down." He shrugged his shoulders. "It did have smoke damage. But they did their best to clean it up." His voice was lower again, his words clipped. Why did he clam up whenever she asked about the fire?

"Why is it taking so long to rebuild? Hasn't it been a year?"

"They're doing the best they can. Our mayor keeps writing to the governor to ask for funds. You're not in San Diego anymore, Hope." His voice dripped with more than a little sarcasm. "We don't have enough tax dollars to build a whole hospital. We're hard-working, but we all make modest incomes."

"Oh." She didn't know what else to say.

After taking them through Main Street and past the hospital, the main road led them straight out into open fields again. She waited for him to turn off. And waited. Five more miles; five miles of nothing. Blackened land and a few abandoned, burned-down buildings. No construction out here. And she wondered where all the cattle were; didn't this state boast more cows than people? When he finally turned off, she spotted the big white farmhouse he'd told her about and exhaled. She hadn't realized she'd been holding her breath. Her mother-in-law would be here. For the first time since marrying Peter, she felt eager to meet his mom. It would be nice to have another woman around; nice to know she wouldn't be alone.

Peter grabbed her two bags and led the way up the porch stairs. The house was tall but comforted her even as she stood in the entryway. Shoes scattered about, family pictures on the walls; it looked lived in. Like home. Peter dropped the bags and motioned for her to follow him around the corner. When she did, and he called, "Mama! We're home!" Hope was a little surprised at the woman who embraced Peter tightly. She hadn't expected a tall woman with long dark hair. For some reason she'd pictured someone short and a little... frumpier. But this woman was beautiful. Why hadn't she asked Peter to show her pictures?

Hope was surprised again when the woman wrapped her in the same tight embrace she'd given Peter and didn't let go. "My daughter, my daughter," she said again and again. Hot tears stung Hope's eyes; she blinked them back as quickly as she could. She didn't pull away, but she didn't hug back, either. When she was finally released, she distracted herself by trying to take everything in. The kitchen was a small one, but she supposed this was the way with Nebraska homes. The sink was full as if an army had just eaten here. A smell that reminded Hope of Peter's favorite Italian restaurant permeated the air and tickled her nose.

"What's cooking?" She asked, hands in her back pockets, subtly trying to protect herself from another hug.

"Tomato sauce. For the pasta. We are going to feed you a real dinner tonight! Peter, why are you standing there? Take your wife's bags upstairs and show her your room." Teresa made a move as if to whack him with the wooden spoon. He laughed and dodged out of the way.

Upstairs, Hope smiled at the bright blue walls of the little room they'd be sharing. The quilt on the queen-sized bed looked homemade. She'd have to ask her mother-in-law about it later. The one large window looked over the fields. There was a good expanse of green grass encircling the house; but as she looked up the hill she could see where the charred fields began. She knew from what Peter told her that the black extended to the rest of the two hundred acres his family owned. Replanting was slow work.

Back downstairs, she asked Peter, "Is there time before dinner? I mean, could I run to the store in town?"

"Run to the store? What do you need? I have everything you could possibly need." Teresa didn't turn from her spot at the stove as she hollered her question, but she did wave her wooden spoon in the air for emphasis.

"I just… need to get something." Hope said lamely. She wasn't used to being questioned by a gesticulating wooden spoon.

Peter shrugged. "Sure. Rob won't mind. He gave me that car for us to use."

"Oh." She hadn't really given much thought to the fact that she wouldn't have her own car here. "Thank you."

"Do you think you know the way?"

"There's only one road. I think I can manage." She smiled and gave him a kiss on the cheek. Then she grabbed her purse and the keys Peter offered and stepped out the door.

As she stood on the threshhold, she heard Teresa exclaiming, "Why is she going to the store? Did she tell you what she needs? *Tsk.* Such a waste, to go all that way, when I have supper almost ready…" Hope closed the door quietly. She didn't need to hear anymore.

Five miles seemed a little longer by herself. But when she turned into the pharmacy parking lot, her heart thumped along with more than anxiety over driving in unfamiliar places.

She was over a month late. She'd checked the calendar again this morning to be sure. Life had been so busy at home, she'd put off, and put off again, buying a pregnancy test. But now it was time. She had to know.

She sighed and unbuckled her seat belt, then closed her eyes and sat back a moment. Then opened the door resolutely. It was now or never.

As she walked in, she was struck again by how unassuming and far apart the town's buildings were. Like scattered, grey moving boxes. And how few trees. And how the horizon stretched, and stretched, and stretched, never changing. It would take some getting used to.

She walked the aisles aimlessly for a moment, orienting herself. She stopped short when she came upon a supply of guns and ammunition. At the pharmacy? Peter was right – she wasn't in San Diego anymore. She snapped another photo, chuckling a little as she typed in Anna's number and pressed *send*.

She ventured a little further; past pots and pans, vacuums and gardening supplies. This store must be kind of like a catch-all. She found what she needed, and her hands shook a little when she picked it up. She'd never bought a pregnancy test before.

She felt odd buying it alone, so she grabbed a pack of gum and some candy at the checkout line, then smiled a little shyly at the woman next to her. There were four people in line, and no one seemed to be in any hurry.

The checker was chatting with the woman at the head of the line, who was purchasing a bag of chocolate chips and some other baking items. It seemed like the checker's first priority was to find out what kind of cookies her customer was making. And for whom. And when. Her hands sat planted on her hips, not pulling items through the scanner like they should've done. *Come on,* Hope groaned inwardly. Her body ached all over from the long hours of traveling; she just wanted to get back to the house.

When it was finally her turn, she smiled a little weakly, and the checker eyed her suspiciously. "You're new in town." She said definitively, arms crossed over her chest, before even taking Hope's purchases.

Hope didn't know what to say. Did she stand out that much? Was it her clothes? Her hair?

"I know everyone who comes through this store. Now let's see." The checker tapped her chin thoughtfully. "Who was due to come in this week... ope! I got it, you're Peter's wife." Satisfied now that she'd solved the riddle, the checker finally picked up Hope's purchases. She raised her eyebrows over the pregnancy test but said nothing.

When Hope finally escaped, clutching her purchases tightly, she stood a moment in the parking lot and took a deep breath. The sun was setting now. Eyes towards the west, she watched, unable to exhale. You could see everything here. The sun was a bright orange ball, and its flames licked the sky everywhere... around her, above her, behind her. The few dotted clouds reflected its pink light, the sky itself celebrating.

As she drove home, she kept glancing in her rearview mirror for another glance at that spectacular sunset. Was it like this every night?

The stress of the day drained all her energy by the time she parked in front of the big white house. When she entered the front door, she shut it without a word and headed straight upstairs, ignoring Teresa's cries of, "Well, what was all that about? You find what you needed? Huh?" She didn't feel like giving answers, or talking at all, now.

It had been a long day. Longer even than the day Mom had left. Saying goodbye to everyone, then the four-hour plane ride, then another four-hour car ride... she was tempted to fall upon the bed and shut out the world till morning. But she clutched her little pharmacy bag and headed into the bathroom instead. Now that it was in her hands, she was eager for her answer.

A few minutes later, two little pink lines blinked cheerily back at her. New life was growing inside her. A gift from the Creator Himself. She'd always wanted to be a mom. She clutched the test close to her chest and sat on the bathroom stool, grateful tears filling her eyes.

A heavy knock landed on the door. "Hope?" Peter must be wondering what this all was about. She stood, ready to tell him her happy news; then, when he spoke impatiently, she stopped. "Hope, what's going on? Mom's waiting for you."

What would Peter say when he did find out? Would he be as happy as she? He would be surprised, that was for sure. They hadn't planned this. "I'll be out in a minute," she replied simply, wrapping the test back in its box and tucking it in the bathroom cupboard behind the toilet paper. She could hear him huff, then his heavy footfalls upon the stairs.

When she was sure he was downstairs, she went to their bedroom to change her clothes and think. She just needed a moment alone. "Thank you, God." But how would she tell Peter?

As she rummaged in her suitcase for something more comfortable to wear, it hit her like a ton of bricks. Telling Peter wasn't her only problem. Weren't young, pregnant women supposed to have a mom around? Someone to come over when the baby had a fever, or when Hope got exhausted, or just to ogle over a baby's chubby cheeks? Someone to call when the baby took her first bite of food, someone to call when she needed to know how to get spit up off of a couch? Someone to rejoice with her over a baby's first word and first steps?

First the wedding, now this. Mom had picked quite the time to leave.

Her elation melted away, and the tears she'd been storing up followed. Exhaustion broke down her walls, and she lay there, silent tears falling down her face and soaking the pillow, until the last rays of sun slid behind Peter's field, until the dinner dishes downstairs had been cleared and washed and put away, until Gina had come to say hello and gone, until the morning sun had risen, bright and red and cheerful again.

chapter eleven

Peter sat at Mom's long kitchen table, hot coffee warming his hands, foot tapping the floor. What was taking her so long? He should've been out in the fields an hour ago. But he'd wanted to wait for her, to bring her with him. Then she was coming down the stairs, rubbing her eyes. "What took you so long?" He bolted out of his chair.

She stopped in her tracks and looked at him. She always did that. Peter was loud. He knew it. When would she get used to him?

"I… I guess I overslept. I'm sorry."

"What about last night?"

"Last night?" She cocked her head sleepily.

"Mom was waiting for you. She cooked for you."

She stayed at the bottom of the stairs, in no hurry to come to him. "Well. I guess maybe I was tired from the day of travelling out here." Her tone said he should understand. "Sometimes your body needs sleep more than it needs food." She shrugged her shoulders like it didn't matter.

"You offended her. She's Italian; food is love." Peter held out both hands, palms up; why wasn't she getting it?

"Excuse me?" She poured herself a cup of coffee, then placed it back on the counter with a thoughtful look. "Is there any decaf?"

"Decaf? No. Listen. You offended her, because she cooked a special meal for you, and invited Gina over, and you didn't even come." He was leaning towards her now, in earnest.

"What? Peter, I don't really care right now, ok?" She gave an exhausted sigh and continued rummaging through the cupboards.

Not care? *Not care?* After all he'd done for her? He turned on his heel, stomped out of the kitchen, and didn't slow down till he reached Dad's new barn. His new barn.

Absently, Peter dug his hand into a sack of leftover corn seed, noticing how the kernels left a thin layer of dust on his skin. The corn had been part of Dad's rebuilding plan. Rob had explained it all to him after they met with the lawyer. Corn was easier, and cheaper, than buying a bunch of new cattle. It grew fast and had plenty of buyers. Dad had already contracted with a company, and the money that came from selling the corn this fall was supposed to go into the pot for purchasing a small herd of cattle. Thanks to the ever-changing Nebraska weather, there was no way to know exactly how much corn there would be, or how much money they would earn; but Dad had figured it should be enough to purchase 50 to 100 head of cattle. They'd make sure to include a bull or two in the mix; a breeding protocol was part of the rebuilding plan, so they'd have calves next year to sell and to further grow the ranch.

The graphs and charts and projections were Rob's job; hard work was Peter's job. He was grateful for the opportunity. At first, he'd thought becoming a firefighter would make things right. Helping stop fires like the one that had devastated this town. But now he knew God had given him a different path to make things right. It was all clear when Dad died. He'd follow Dad's plan, and rebuild the ranch, and a few years from now, everyone would forget about the fire.

But corn growing in a field doesn't support a family. Inspired by his older brother's getting a side job, Peter had found work too. He'd resisted it at first; working at the local Kmart was too boring for him. It wasn't his dream job. But when he'd heard the news that Hope was coming, Rob had urged him to take a side job, any job, if he wanted to be able to take care of a family.

Thinking of Hope, Peter remembered how she'd gone to the store yesterday. Maybe she'd need to run an errand again. At any rate, he didn't want to leave her here without a vehicle on her first day. He went back to the house and found his old bicycle in the garage. After putting air in the tires and making sure the brakes worked, he headed out to town.

⁓

Hope would have to approach her mother-in-law sometime.

The woman was in the garden behind the house, bent over something. She looked like she was working hard; arms moving fast, head turning this way and that as she surveyed her plot.

Hope took a deep breath and grabbed the mug of decaf tea she'd found, along with the mug of coffee she'd made for Teresa. A peace offering. If she couldn't drink it, at least she could smell it.

She stepped through the white picket garden gate; carefully, so the two hot mugs wouldn't spill. Brightly colored flowers, standing guard along the outside of the gate, greeted her, and vegetables – she didn't even know all their names – lined up in tight little rows inside. Some climbed a pole or a trellis, and she noticed that the taller ones were in the back of the garden, facing north. Somebody had put a lot of love into this garden.

"Coffee?" She asked simply, sitting on the edge of a garden bed next to Teresa.

"Oh, thank you, honey." But the woman took one sip of it, puckered her lips, and put it back.

"Does it need sweetener?"

"Oh no, honey, I'm fine." So the woman wasn't even going to tell Hope how she took her coffee. This would be harder than she'd thought. Hope sighed and sat a little more stiffly on her corner of the garden bed. The cornstalks in the field next to them waved gently in the mild July breeze. "How did you sleep last night?" Teresa asked, stopping her work now and looking at Hope.

"Hmm?" Hope had been looking off into the distance, wondering if she could see the edge of the property. Was it down at the bottom of the hill, beyond the sycamores? Or did it stretch even farther?

"Sleep? Last night?"

"Oh. Great. I mean, the bed was great, thank you." Teresa was looking at her like she expected Hope to say something else. "I'm sorry, by the way." Hope continued. "Sorry I missed dinner. It smelled so good. I guess I was just exhausted."

"Oh honey. Don't worry about it. Of course, you were exhausted."

Hope's eyebrows crinkled in confusion. Maybe the missing

dinner thing wasn't as big a deal as Peter had made it out to be. Or maybe Teresa had just gotten over it since last night.

"Do you know where Peter is? I haven't seen him since this morning. I need to talk to him about something."

"He's at work." Teresa bent low again over her own work.

"Out on the ranch?" Hope looked around for any sign of him.

"No, at his other job."

"He has another job?"

"Yes, at the Kmart. He just started last week." Teresa spoke with pride in her voice.

"Oh. I didn't know." Hope wrapped both hands around her mug again.

"There's a lot about Peter you don't know." Teresa dug into the dirt a little harder, and Hope thought she could notice an edge to the woman's voice. A lot she didn't know? She was his wife. Maybe Teresa didn't know that Hope and Peter told each other everything.

She set her mug down on the other side of the garden bed and hunkered down next to Teresa. If she was going to be out here, she might as well start digging, too. "Can I help?"

"Surely. Yes, of course. There's some gloves and another hand shovel in that mailbox over there."

Hope smiled when she saw the mailbox that had been mounted on a pole in the garden. Perfect place for keeping handy little things that needed protection from the elements but also needed to be kept close to the garden. There was a little red bird painted on the side of it. So her mother in law was an artist, too.

"Okay, I'm ready." She came back, pulling her gloves on.

"Let's go to the back. If I have another pair of hands, then I'm going to put you to work."

Hope smiled. If this was acceptance, she'd gladly garden all day.

She filed behind her mother in law, past the beds of tomatoes and another bed of what looked like lettuce. She stopped and jumped when a bright blue something flew at her from a green, leafy bush. "What's that?" She asked, pointing. When she hunkered down, she saw that there were more of the bright blue bugs hanging out in the bush. "Is it a firefly?" She asked, mesmerized. Its wings were beating so fast; almost like a hummingbird. She held out a hand towards it – it was big; longer than Hope's longest finger. The color was the brightest blue she'd ever seen in nature; it was like something out of her paintbox.

"It's a dragonfly." Teresa answered in her businesslike way. Dragonflies were probably as exciting to Midwesterners as squirrels were to a San Diego girl.

"Wow," Hope breathed. "I've never seen one before."

Noticing that Hope was still mesmerized, Teresa hunkered down too. "Do you know," she spoke in a confiding tone, "That Peter can catch them by the tail with his hand? He started doing that when he was just a boy. And his little hand fit in mine." She turned her palm over as if remembering. "And he can do it without hurting them." She stood now, beckoning Hope to follow her. "Let me show you the work we have to do."

Hope followed, still trying to imagine Peter as a five- or six-year-old boy catching dragonflies. Maybe there were some things about him she didn't know. It was good that she was here, with his family, on his turf. He'd invested time in getting to know her life. Now she could do the same for him.

They'd reached the last ten feet or so of the garden, and even to Hope's inexperienced eye, it was a tangled mess. From one end of the fence to the other, she could see nothing but low, weedy grass.

"Let's start pulling," her mother in law said as she started in vigorously. Hope decided right then and there that she liked the woman. Anyone with that much determination was worth getting to know. And this from a woman whose husband had just died two weeks ago. "This used to be a strawberry patch," Teresa *tsked* as she pulled. "Until the goosegrass took over."

"Goosegrass?" Hope didn't know the name of all the vegetables in the garden, let alone the weeds.

"Yes, goosegrass. See?" Teresa lifted up one plant to show Hope the strong, thick root that ran underneath. Then she pulled it up, which took all her strength – but still the root did not break. Just when the root should have ended, it led to another plant. Another weed. Teresa pulled that one out, too, and showed them both to Hope. "And this is why I forgive you."

"Huh?" Had Hope misheard her?

"I forgive you. For not showing up to supper last night. Because of this weed."

"Um... I don't understand." Hope chuckled a little, confused.

"You see how one plant leads to another. And another, and another." Teresa gestured to the patch they were sitting on; nothing but goosegrass all the way up to the walls of the garden beds, and even beyond the fence that should've been the border of the garden. "I learned long ago that bitterness is like this. If I let myself be bitter towards you, then before I know it, that bitter seed takes root. It infects my whole heart." She worked while she spoke. "*Tsk*. It takes over. Like a disease. Like this weed." She sat back on her heels, picked up her coffee cup, then seemed to think better of it and put it back down. "I have learned that I cannot just pick and choose who to be angry with. If I let myself be angry with you, soon enough I am angry with Peter, with the dogs, with the stranger in the grocery store." Teresa pointed in the direction of the town with her last example. "I am an angry person. Do you understand?" Her voice quieted. "And I don't want that. I want to be a forgiving person. Like my Jesus."

Hope nodded. This was a new way to look at forgiveness. Give in to Jesus, or give in to bitterness – all or nothing. A painting was already forming itself in her mind. And speaking of forgiveness, she had a question for her new mother-in-law.

"I wanted to ask you," she began quietly, while her nimble fingers obeyed and dug up weeds, "Why you weren't at the wedding."

"Didn't Peter tell you?" Teresa was distracted, not looking at her. "We couldn't afford it. Not after the fire."

Hope sat back on her haunches, determined at least to look her mother-in-law in the face, even if the woman couldn't be bothered to return the favor. "He did tell me you were too busy after the fire. But he didn't tell me it was a financial thing. I wish you would've told me, Papa would've helped –"

"Aah, shush. We don't need any help from anybody." Teresa waved the arm that held the trowel as if Hope's question were a pesky fly.

Hope hadn't meant to offer help. She'd meant to do some digging. "I just meant," she tried again, "That it would've meant a lot to me if you had been there."

"Oh, *tsk*. We are here together now. What does it matter?" And the conversation was over as quickly as it had begun as Teresa went back to her work, strong arms pulling up weeds twice as fast as Hope's did. Hope gave up talking and tried to just be helpful until Teresa broke the silence again.

"You know, I would like a little sugar in my coffee."

"Would you?" Hope was self-appointed coffee maker wherever she went, so she jumped at the chance to do something to serve her mother in law. Teresa wasn't easy to figure out, but she had opened her home to Hope. Given her a bed. Cooked her dinner.

When Hope came back with the coffee, she put the gloves on straightaway. The two women worked without speaking until the sun was high in the sky and the mosquitoes buzzed around them. Being from San Diego, Hope was used to sunshine, but this heat was something else. It shimmered on the horizon; a sight she'd only seen before in movies. She was embarrassed when she grew light-headed and asked to go inside while Teresa was still working. She should be able to work at least as long as the older woman.

"Yes, you go in. What am I thinking, you had such a long day yesterday. Go in and rest. I'll be right there."

Hope nodded her assent, wiped her sweat on the sleeve of her light pink shirt, and headed up the hill to the house, where she collapsed on the couch without even taking her shoes off.

Afternoon light was streaming in the windows when Peter got home from work. He took off his shoes at the door and walked around, looking for Hope; there she was, passed out on the couch. He smiled. She was cute when she slept.

But she'd had all morning, and he'd been working hard – she could've made some lunch for him, at least. He made himself a sandwich, grabbed an apple, and closed the fridge a little louder than necessary. He placed his food on the table, then went to wake Hope. He kissed her lightly on the nose. She stretched, opened her eyes to look at him, and smiled.

Then she sat bolt upright, looking around the room. "You remember where you are?" He teased.

"Yeah." But she put a hand on her head and winced.

"You hungry? Or want some coffee?" Maybe he could serve her. It was her first day here, after all.

"Actually, just water please." She followed him to the kitchen and sat down at the table. He obliged with a tall glass but pulled her back to her feet. He couldn't wait any longer.

"I have something to show you. Come on."

She smiled. "Ok."

"Wait till you see my surprise. Then you'll really be smiling." He half-led, half-pulled her the quarter mile to the new barn, he was so excited. "I wanted to show you last night, but it was too late."

He threw his weight against the heavy sliding barn door and grabbed a lead rope off a hook in the doorway. "To take him out of the stall for you." Peter winked in Hope's direction, wondering if she was catching on yet.

The men had put a few dedicated stalls in the new barn for birthing cattle. Now one of them housed a stocky, dapple grey quarter horse. Peter pulled open the stall door and motioned for Hope to enter ahead of him. "Meet Bandit. Pirate, Bandit, they go together, right? Though you can change his name, of course... after all, he's yours."

"Oh!" Hope exclaimed as she went straight to the animal, holding out her hand in greeting. "Aren't you a beautiful boy," she crooned as the horse lowered his head for her; she stroked his neck obligingly. Then she turned towards Peter. "Babe... did you really buy him for me?"

Peter just nodded, chest swollen with pride. "Anything to make you happy, dear."

But Hope's joy was fleeting. He saw her wrinkle up her brow, the way she did when she was thinking, and she asked, "But Peter... can we afford him? Horses eat a lot, you know."

"Oh, it'll be fine." He hadn't really worked out the budget. But hay and water couldn't be that expensive.

She gave a dejected sigh and stepped back from the animal. "Besides, I don't know if now is the best time for me to be getting on horseback."

"Why not? I know he's not as big as Pirate, or as young, but I thought at least you could have fun with him. I thought he'd help you feel at home."

"Peter, it's very sweet. And I'm very thankful. But..." she looked down at the hands she'd spread across her belly.

"But?" He put a hand on hers affectionately.

"Peter, I'm pregnant."

He heard a soft *thud* and realized the lead rope had fallen from his hand. He looked at her blankly. What had she said?

"Peter?"

An image of his dad on that day, the day he'd left, came into his mind. *You'll never amount to anything,* Jim was saying. *You can't survive on your own! You'll end up working at McDonalds!* He could almost feel the pressure of Dad's finger on his chest again. *You are a fool, leaving like this.* The voice dropped an octave. *You are a disappointment.* Peter knew he should answer Hope, but instead he looked down at his hands, which had crumbled his sandwich to pieces. They were trembling.

"Peter?"

❧

Hope hadn't had time to unpack her paints yet; had it really only been twenty-four hours since she'd arrived? So she sat down at the kitchen table with a mug of tea, the journal she always kept with her, and a pencil she'd found in Teresa's kitchen junk drawer.

She craned her neck to look out the window; her mother-in-law was still hunkered down over the stubborn goosegrass. Peter had gone upstairs after she'd told him her news: not seeing her, not seeing anything. Normally she liked how his face, his whole body even, looked like they'd been chiseled out of stone. But today the hard lines of his jaw and mouth said something else. Something she didn't want to analyze right now.

She'd talk to Peter later. For now, the pencil needed to move across the paper, needed to sketch the image that had formed in her mind when she'd been out in the garden with Teresa. The late afternoon sun turned to a low red ball while tangled weeds formed on her page. She jumped when her mother-in-law's voice called her name. She hadn't heard the woman come in. She covered her book quickly – it wasn't good enough to share yet – and stood, almost stumbling on her left foot, which had fallen asleep.

"Do you think you are going to make it to dinner tonight?" Teresa asked with one raised eyebrow.

"I… yeah, if I'm invited."

"Oh, Hope, I am teasing you. Don't look so startled. Here, help me get started."

Hope had never roasted a chicken before. Whole birds had always intimidated her for some reason. But: "This is how we did things growing up. We did not waste anything," her mother-in-law explained. Hope watched and learned. While it roasted, her mother-in-law stirred something on the stove that she called polenta, but that looked a lot like the corn meal mush Hope had tried in Mexican restaurants back home.

"I'm just gonna go take a shower," Hope pointed towards the stairs – but she was really eager to check on Peter. Was he ready to talk to her? But there was no answer when she knocked lightly at the door.

He finally emerged when the food was ready; like he had some internal clock that told him where to go. But he did not make eye contact with her, even when they sat at the table.

Teresa worried and fussed over her son's quiet mood for a few minutes; then decided he was tired from his new job and served him an extra helping of polenta with cheese. Hope tried to make small talk with her to fill the silence.

"So, how have things changed in the town? Since the fire?"

"Oh… so much has changed." Teresa shook her head while chewing on a bite of chicken. "You saw the hospital on your way here?" She waved her fork for emphasis.

"Yeah. Sounds like the nurses and doctors have had to do with less space." Hope shifted in her seat. She still needed to call Papa. Let him know how things were going.

"Yes. And many people have moved. The other farmers, the friends my husband and I had around here – they have dropped like flies. Leaving their land, it's been in the families for generations, can you imagine? But sometimes, when people are hurting, they do stupid things."

Hope looked at Peter to see if his mother's comment had registered with him, but he still had the same blank stare on his face. Was that why Peter had gotten angry with her this morning? And then gone silent tonight? Because he was hurting over his dad's death? Hope cleared her throat. "So none of the other farmers have stayed?"

"Only Hazel and Roger are left."

"Oh." So the blackened fields that surrounded them – the abandoned buildings – they weren't just temporary. Hope shuddered at the thought.

"And we lost our local produce stand." This seemed to be the thing that upset Teresa the most; the waving fork went higher, almost over her head. "Oh, we used to gather every Saturday morning to fight over all the local vegetables that Farmer Joe could find. Remember, Peter?"

Peter just looked at his plate.

"Can't you get the groceries you need at the Safeway?"

"Yes. Yes, we can. There is a lot to be thankful for." Was Teresa coaching Hope or herself? "But still. I will be glad when Joe gets his place rebuilt and goes back into business again. We ranchers are not the only ones who suffered from the fire."

Teresa's eyes flitted to her son briefly; he made eye contact, shook his head lightly, then went back to eating. What had they just communicated? Before Hope could ask, Teresa went on talking – faster this time. "And remember the hardware store, Peter? He always sold the best candles. Homemade. But Greg will get a new one soon. I am sure he will. He is a pillar of this town, Greg Connor. I am sure that he will buy a new store soon. Yes."

Hope had the sneaky suspicion that her mother in law was trying to cover something up. But she was too tired to pursue it. She took her plate to the sink, turned around, and said, "Well, I think I'll rest a little bit. That jet lag is really getting to me." Though Western Nebraska and California only had a one-hour time difference; and California was behind, not ahead; but neither of her new family members seemed to notice her mistake. "I'll come back down to help with the dishes later." Teresa just nodded in her direction, and Peter chewed silently. What would they talk about when she was upstairs?

She sighed and grabbed her journal on the way up. When she sat down at the pale blue desk that stood under the window, she opened it to the page with the tangled weeds. The roots curved to the right, forming a kind of L. She hadn't done it on purpose; but now it made sense. She scrawled in the best calligraphy she could manage: *Let It Go,* in and among the tangled weeds.

What was that Teresa had said? *"I forgive you, because of the weeds."* Hope sat down on the edge of the bed and lifted her Bible from the bedside table. It took her a moment to find a passage on forgiveness; she was still learning how to navigate this book. When she landed on it, her heart stopped a moment: "Bear with each other and forgive one another if any of you has a grievance against someone. Forgive as the Lord forgave you." She underlined the verse. Colossians 3:13.

"But God – You've forgiven me so much," she said aloud. The sobering thought settled in her stomach and grounded her. It seemed too big for this small room crowded with furniture. She glanced out the window: another clear night. She closed her journal, grabbed a jacket, and headed downstairs quietly. She could hear Peter and Teresa talking at the kitchen table, but they didn't hear her sneak out the back door and through the sunroom.

She walked past the garden, down to Teresa's chicken shed where there was a small bench. She sat down and looked up at the stars; there was Orion's belt again, blinking at her. She heaved a deep sigh. The stars here were brighter, bigger, closer than they'd ever been back home.

"God, I forgive," she whispered. If Teresa was right – if bitterness spilled over itself and took over a heart like goosegrass in a garden – then she wanted to rip out any and all roots. But where to begin?

Begin at the beginning. The golden voice whispered in her heart.

She swallowed hard. "I forgive Mom… I forgive Mom for leaving." A weight lifted off her chest as she said the words. Maybe Mom had been hurting. Maybe she hadn't wanted to leave Hope.

Farther, the golden voice whispered again.

Hope pictured herself, six years old, sitting on a bench at school. Mom never came that day. The school principal had to call Grandma Leah, who apologized and made excuses.

"I forgive her, God…" Hope breathed. "I forgive her for every time she wasn't there." This time, the moment the word *forgive* left her lips, Hope saw in her mind's eye an image, one she knew she would never forget. She saw her mom falling out of the tight grip of someone's hands. And falling straight into the hand of God.

She hadn't known that her heart had felt squeezed until her chest opened in one big, grateful breath. It was in that moment that she knew – the hands in her mind's eye, the ones that had been holding a death grip, had been her own.

She walked back through the sunroom, and this time, she didn't hide from her family, but stopped at the dining table. "Good night. Love you." She hugged them both. Peter looked at her for the first time since that afternoon. Blankly; but he looked at her. She just smiled and went up to bed.

Hope opened her eyes; warm morning sunlight filtered in through the window. The sun must have woken her up. She glanced at the clock. 7 am.

She couldn't remember Peter having come to bed, or leaving in the morning. But his side was rumpled and empty, so he must've been there at some point.

Working on a ranch must involve some pretty early hours; but now, with no cattle to care for? Maybe it was just his habit when he was here.

She stretched and decided not to feel badly about missing him. It was only her second full day here. Tonight, she'd ask him about his morning routine, and see if she could help.

She went downstairs and made coffee for two. Surely a cup of regular brew every now and then wouldn't hurt the baby. She smiled at the thought and placed a loving hand on her still-flat belly. It wasn't too late, she discovered while looking out the kitchen window, to help Teresa. The woman was parked in the same spot as yesterday, working hard again.

"Can I help?" She poked her head out the window while the coffee pot gurgled away.

Teresa beckoned her to come closer.

"First, go down to the chicken shed and gather the eggs, please?" Hope was thrilled to have a job. Any job. "Then I'll make us some breakfast."

"I'll make breakfast." Hope wasn't as good in the kitchen as her mother-in-law, but she could scramble eggs.

Half an hour later, the eggs had been gathered and the chickens fed, breakfast had been prepared and eaten and the dishes cleared by the two women, and they were out in the garden again, energized by a rapidly warming sun.

"I see you got this ground cleared," Hope admired. She'd never appreciated an empty patch of dirt before.

"Yes. I worked out here for two, three hours yesterday after you went to take a nap."

Hope felt a momentary twinge of guilt, then shoved it away. Her mother-in-law probably didn't mean it that way. "Well, what are we planting now?"

"Strawberries."

"Strawberries? This late in the summer?"

"Yes, it is the perfect time to plant them. We will trim off any buds that form, and let them throw their starter shoots all over the place, and their roots will grow over the long, cold winter. Next summer, we will have lovely, sweet strawberries."

"Wow. Sounds amazing."

"Yes. As long as we protect them from the hail. And we have no more fires." Teresa grabbed the wheelbarrow and started heading up the hill as she said it.

Hope picked up a handful of dirt absently and let it sift through her fingers. It was fine, light-colored. They called this area the Sandhills for a reason. It was a far cry from living life as a doctor's daughter in San Diego: coming here to sift through dry dirt. To watch the people of this forgotten old town pull themselves up by their bootstraps and try again.

The two women worked side by side until the sun towered above them and that glimmering heat burned off the horizon again. Hope only went in for water once; determined, this time, to work as long as the older woman did. By one o'clock, they had dragged in all the fresh black dirt that Teresa had bought from the pharmacy and hauled home with a friend's borrowed truck. Hope let her mother-in-law help her load the dirt into the wheelbarrow, but insisted on pushing the wheelbarrow herself. Up the hill to the truck. Then back down again.

"Where's Peter?" She asked once, embarrassed that she didn't know. Her cell phone reception was spotty out here; but even if it were crystal clear, would he have called?

"At work," her mother in law answered while huffing over a bag of dirt.

"Oh." How many hours would he be gone? She'd thought farm life meant doing their days together.

When they finished, they had fifteen rows by twenty starts of strawberries. All neatly spaced two feet apart from each other; "For the shoots," said Teresa. Hope did the math quickly and realized that the size of this one patch of strawberries was roughly the same size as Anna's backyard. There was something to be said for having endless space to grow. Something to be said for the possibilities you could fit under that wide open sky.

She looked at the black grime under her hands; Teresa asked her quietly, "Well, what do you think of our town?" It was the first time she'd asked anything about how Hope was settling in.

"I like it," she said automatically. She wouldn't tell the truth – how different it was from everything she'd ever known.

When the two women headed up to the house, Hope went straight for the mudroom. She watched the black grime loosen from her hands and swirl down in the sink. She closed her eyes and saw, again, the way the fine dust they'd covered had sifted through her hands, the way the light had glinted through it. It was a little bit like sand on the beach. How sad that, like Peter had told her, Rob and Hazel and many other Midwesterners had never even seen the ocean. They worked so hard, they didn't have time to travel, he'd said.

As she loosened the grime from under her fingernails, she prayed the Lord would show her something else she could do for the people of Orion, something even more helpful than gardening.

Peter clocked out at 3 o'clock, but wouldn't go home. He didn't want to face whatever waited for him there.

More questions from Hope. More looks from Mom. He'd had enough.

He texted Rob. *Wanna meet at Shaky's?* Maybe some guy time would help. The pizza place was the only place in town worth meeting in.

I can be there at 8, Rob responded, *After Gina gets off.* He had some time to kill.

He drove around town aimlessly. He hadn't felt like riding his bike today; Hope could manage at home, or ask Mom for a ride if she needed to. He took the long way around town to avoid driving by the hospital; but this way only took him by the burned-down grocery store and the boarded-up old hardware store. He turned his eyes and almost ran into a fire hydrant in his effort not to look at the abandoned buildings. He stopped at the local coffee shop, chatted with a few neighbors who were visiting there, then wandered down Main Street, looking at thrift objects without really seeing.

He found his running shoes in the back of the car and decided to head over to the lake. It was cool and refreshing-looking. If he didn't know how unclean it was for swimming, he'd be tempted to jump right in. The geese who wintered here every year hadn't arrive yet; but by the time the lake was covered in a layer of ice, they'd be here, sitting on it. If Nebraska winters were warm for them, he shuddered to think what "cold" was.

He tied his shoelaces tight, then ran around the lake a few times. After slapping one mosquito, then two, from his neck, he headed back to his car. Why had his grandfather settled here, anyway? What had he seen in this mosquito-eaten, dull, flat town?

At 7, he ran out of things to do, and headed over to the pizza place. It was also the only place in town that served alcohol. He'd made a promise to God and Teresa to give up cigarettes after the fire. But he hadn't said anything about alcohol.

"How's the wife?" Tim, the server on duty today and the class president of Peter's high school class, asked as he poured Peter another beer.

"Pregnant," Peter answered as he took a sip.

Tim looked taken aback; whether by the rapidity of the pregnancy or that of Peter's answer, Peter wasn't sure. And he didn't really care. He took a second sip and went on venting. "I mean, how did that happen? We weren't planning for it. I'm not ready..."

"Ope. I think you know how it happened, P." Tim winked and turned sideways to help another customer.

"Humph." Peter didn't want to be lifted out of his sour mood. Or to take responsibility for the pregnancy. He just wanted to forget about it for a few minutes.

Rob finally walked in. "How's Hope?" He asked after he'd sat down and taken a menu.

"Why does everyone want to know?"

"Whoa, brother. Just asking. She is new in town, after all." Rob raised his eyebrows and went back to looking over the menu.

Peter didn't feel like spilling the more intimate details. Funny how that had been easy to share with Tim, but not so easy with his own brother, who'd just become a dad less than a year ago. So he shared what was easier. "She's not settling in, man. When I got home from work yesterday, she was asleep on the couch. She hasn't even taken a tour of the farm, or sat down to look at the plans with me yet." He looked at his watch. "She's probably sleeping now, too."

"She's not cut out for it," Rob admonished without looking up from the menu. "Shoulda married a Midwestern girl like I did." He smirked a little, then finally put his menu down and looked Peter in the eyes.

"You jerk! That's my WIFE!" Before Peter knew it, he was flying across the table at his brother. He'd landed a punch on Rob's face before Rob could realize it. Then Rob ducked, recovered, and pulled back his arm. Peter lunged at him again, but this time Rob hit him in the shoulder and sent him sprawling. The two were wrestling on the floor, all the pent-up energy of the last two years finally letting loose, when Tim came over to them.

"Hey, guys," he said quietly, embarrassed more for his friends than for his restaurant. "Guys," a little louder. "BAILEY BOYS!" It was the phrase their mom always used when they got too rowdy; and it was loud enough for them to hear this time. Peter sat up, a hand on his head where he'd hit the bench. He looked down at his feet. He'd kicked over another table; the silverware lay on the floor.

"Can we help?" Rob recovered first, dusted off his hands, and looked at Tim.

"No, I'll clean this up," Tim spoke quickly. "Just go." He looked around nervously at the other customers; one of whom was an elderly couple, the Hayneses, who served on the prayer chain at church. "Go, guys."

Peter waved, embarrassed, at Mr. and Mrs. Haynes. He'd dated their granddaughter for a little while in high school. He limped on his way out of the restaurant, following Rob.

"Hey, man, I'm sorry." Rob apologized first when they got to the parking lot. "I didn't mean it. It's not her fault, anyway. You dragged her out here." His first attempt at a joke that day disarmed Peter a little.

"Yeah. I know." He paused and sucked in a deep breath. "And I'm sorry I hit you. That already doesn't look good." He grimaced when he looked at Rob's eye.

Rob touched the eye, growing puffy. "It's all right. A reason for Gina to nurse me back to health. Which isn't so bad." He gave a crooked smile.

"Ha." Peter laughed, then tripped a little on the way to his car.

"Hey man, you all right? How many beers did you have?"

Four? Five? Peter couldn't remember. But he knew enough not to drive like this. He just shrugged.

"All right. You're coming home with me, Slugger."

"To Gina's parents' house? I don't think so."

"It's either that, or sleep in your car. And I'm taking your keys."

Cool sheets and the possibility of Gina's famous biscuits and gravy in the morning sounded better than sleeping in a cramped, hot car all night. "Arrright," he agreed, trying not to sound like he felt.

He grabbed his phone from his car before climbing in beside Rob. Three missed calls from home. He'd call back in the morning.

chapter twelve

Hope sat up on the couch, groggy. Had she fallen asleep in her clothes again? She looked at the clock. 8pm. How long had she been out?

After hauling dirt and planting the strawberries with Teresa, they'd both gone into town for groceries. When they drove by the Kmart, she'd thought of stopping to say hi to Peter; but he'd made it clear that he didn't want to talk to her. Then they'd come back and had a late lunch. She'd unpacked as much as she could, not really knowing what space she could use and not wanting to bother her mother in law; then sat down on the couch while Teresa started dinner.

She looked at the coffee table now where an untouched, cold cup of tea sat next to an open book. She'd fallen asleep while trying to rest.

She stood up, then thought better of it, and sat down before she could fall down, one hand on her head. Why was she so dizzy? And what was with the pounding headache?

She tried to ignore the dizziness as she ran to the bathroom to throw up, just missing the floor. Her stomach cramped even more after vomiting.

She went to the kitchen to drink a cup of water, but had to run back to the bathroom to throw that up, too.

Were the dizziness and the headache and the vomiting pregnancy symptoms? She tried to imagine what her dad would say as she sat down on a kitchen chair and wrapped her arms around her knees. No, she'd been pregnant for almost two months without knowing it, and never felt like this. Something was wrong, she realized as she doubled over and clutched her stomach. This was worse than her monthly cramps. This could be… contractions.

When that word hit her, she panicked. She had to get to a hospital. Now.

Hands shaking and breath coming in short gasps, she ran upstairs, one hand over the other on the rail, to look for someone. Anyone. She called out as loudly as she could without bringing the bile back up her throat: "Peter? Teresa?" but no one answered. Their bed was still made; maybe Peter was outside. She went down on her knees again at the top of the stairs; the headache was too much for her. After a few deep breaths, she forced herself to walk slowly back down the stairs. If she passed out, that wouldn't help anyone.

When she looked out the front door, she noticed that the driveway was empty. Not only Peter's car was gone, but Teresa's too. Where had Hope left her phone? In the kitchen, by the coffeepot. When she picked up the device, there was a note under it. *Gone to town to help prepare for the Ladies' Church Tea. Be back late. ~Teresa.* She vaguely remembered Teresa baking something this afternoon, and how she'd chuckled, saying that when she got together with the church ladies, they could talk till all hours.

She looked at the screen on her phone – it alternated between one and two bars. She picked up the house phone instead and dialed Peter's number – no answer. Her mother in law didn't have a cell phone.

"Oh, God, what should I do?" She murmured as she slumped down in her chair, only to jump up and vomit again. This time she didn't bother to try to make it to a chair, but sat on the floor of the bathroom. As she prayed that the dizziness would go away, another name came to mind. *Gina.* The sister-in-law she hadn't met yet. The sister-in-law that Peter had said was a nurse.

She kept one hand on the wall and the other on her cramping stomach as she made her way to the kitchen like an unsure toddler. She would call for help; it would be ok.

But she didn't have Gina's number in her phone; and looking briefly around the kitchen, she didn't see any list of important phone numbers there. Then she remembered the phone book she'd noticed the other day. She'd had to ask Teresa what it was; it had been so long since she'd seen one. As quickly as she could without tipping over, she dug in the cupboard under the house phone. She tried to remember how to use it; white was residential, yellow was business, right? She flipped to the white pages; but what was Gina's last name? Bailey, of course, she realized – feeling stupider by the minute. Bailey, just like hers.

Bailey, R. and G. She located it, and with one finger on the name, she dialed the number.

"Hello?" A perky female voice picked up.

"Gina?" Hope asked, trying to keep the panic out of her voice. Oh boy. What a great first impression.

"Yes?" The voice was patient, businesslike.

"Gina, it's Hope. Hope Bailey. I'm..." a capable female voice on the other end of the line sent her over the edge; she couldn't keep the tears back anymore. Thankfully, Gina didn't notice.

"Hope! I'm so glad to hear your voice. I came over yesterday, but you were sleeping. Not that I blame you, travelling is so exhausting. Then today I had work. I'm planning on coming over tomorrow, did Mom tell you? How're you settling in?"

"I'm... I'm sick." Hope answered, knowing that she definitely couldn't hide the desperation in her voice anymore. "I was wondering if you could help me. There's no one else here. I don't know where Peter is..." She started crying again. Now her sister-in-law would really be excited to meet her.

But it turned out that desperate calls for help couldn't phase Gina. "Well, I can tell you where Peter is. He's asleep on my couch."

"What?"

"Apparently he and Rob got in some kind of a tussle at the pizza place. They're both fine, but I didn't get all the details. I will in the morning, though, I promise you that. Anyway, let's talk about you. What are your symptoms?" Hope heard a rustling and the closing of a drawer, and imagined that Gina was grabbing a pen and paper.

"I... I'm having some bad stomach cramps. And a horrible headache. And I've been throwing up, and..." Might as well tell the whole truth. "And I'm pregnant."

"Wow! Congratulations! How exciting. Another baby..." Then her sister-in-law was quiet a moment, transitioning to her nurse-voice. "Well, you were right to call for help. How bad is the vomiting? I mean, how many times have you vomited? And how bad are the cramps? Are you bleeding at all…"

Hope answered her questions, and Gina responded with, "I'll be there in fifteen minutes. Let me just tell Rob and get dressed."

With a twinge of guilt, Hope remembered that Gina had said she had already worked today. She must've been winding down for the evening when Hope called. "Oh, you don't have to, I'm feeling a little better now…" she lied.

"Nonsense. I've already got my coat on. See you in ten." Then Gina hung up.

What do you do when you're waiting for someone to come rescue you? Hope thought of brushing her teeth but realized it would probably make her vomit again, so she just rinsed her mouth out instead. She wanted to put on a clean shirt but was loathe to climb the stairs up and back down again. So she grabbed one of Peter's sweaters from the hall closet instead, pulled her wild short hair into a half-ponytail, and waited.

Gina arrived, gave her a disarming, sisterly hug, and helped her to the car. They made a little small talk on the way, but when they arrived at the hospital and Hope woke up, she was embarrassed to realize that meant she'd fallen asleep at some point on the short drive.

Gina clucked her tongue. "Poor thing, you're exhausted. Wait here while I get a wheelchair."

"No, I'm okay, really…" But Hope was slumping down in her seat again. Gina was already running in to the ER. She came back with a helper, a young man, and the promised wheelchair. Hope was too weak now to be embarrassed.

"Did you tell Doc Allen to get the fetal heart rate monitor?" She heard the tech asking.

Gina nodded. "I called him on the way."

Moments later, Hope was lying flat on a hard gurney while Gina checked her blood pressure and listened to her lungs. "You're pressure's a little low. That's not surprising, considering the fluids you've lost. I'll start an IV."

She came back with the IV and the fluids, and was silent while the doctor came in to check on his patient. "So, Nurse Gina here tells me you're pregnant?" He asked without preamble.

Hope nodded.

"We'll do a quick blood test just to confirm. Gina, did you bring lab tubes?" Gina nodded, filling the tubes even as he spoke.

Doc Allen took some more basic information, then headed back to his desk to check on the progress of the other three patients who were visiting the ER tonight. "I'll be back when those labs come in," he promised, patting her on the hand. When Gina was finished setting up the IV, she washed her hands, then wheeled a small cart up to the bedside.

"What's that?" Hope asked.

"Fetal heart monitor. Mind if I check?" Gina smiled, then pulled back the warm blanket she'd brought Hope almost the second they'd walked in the doors. "Sorry, it's a little cold," she apologized as she squeezed lubricant onto Hope's still-flat belly. She expertly guided the monitor – it looked like a small microphone – over Hope's lower stomach, straining her ears for the sound and tuning out the beeping, the voices, and all the other sounds that came from the hospital. "Ooh! I got it!" She said excitedly. "Hear that?" A *thump-thump-thump* which was much faster and quieter than any heartbeat Hope had ever heard caught her ears. Hope's breath stopped in her lungs.

"That's the baby? That's my baby?" She whispered, wonder in her voice.

"Yup. At... 158 beats a minute. Just right," Gina added, putting the monitor away, wiping the lube off Hope's tummy, and replacing the blanket. "I'll go tell Dr. A." She wheeled the monitor out of the room, turning down the lights as she went.

Hope lay, silent, a few hot tears filling her eyes. There was a real baby. Not just two little pink lines... a baby. With a heartbeat. She wished she could tell her mom. She wished Peter could have heard it. But as Gina pulled the curtain back and re-entered the room, she prayed silently, *Thank You, God, for the friend I do have. For the help you did send me tonight.*

Gina sat down with a magazine in the hard plastic chair, looking like she was ready to make herself comfortable. Hope hadn't wanted to ask her to stay; but she was glad not to be alone. "I wish

I could feed you something," Gina was saying, "But our policy here is to wait until tests come back. Just to be safe."

Hope nodded weakly. She understood, and couldn't have eaten anything anyway.

Hope faded in and out of sleep while the IV fluids dripped into her veins. She woke and wondered briefly where she was only once, noting the time: 11pm. At that moment, the doctor pulled back the curtain, clipboard in hand.

"Well," he boomed, "Congratulations! You're pregnant."

Hadn't she been the one who'd told him that? She laughed a little inside… thinking how funny it was that doctors liked to be the ones to break the news. Nebraska, San Diego – they were all the same. It couldn't be helped, so she just nodded and said, "Thank you." Gina squeezed her hand and winked at her.

"Other than that, your tests look totally normal. Your hormones are right where they should be for two months along. Baby's heart beat sounds good," he said, nodding to Gina.

Hope smiled. She would never forget that sound.

Now he sat down next to her. "So, we do worry when there's intense cramping in early pregnancy. But you're not bleeding. That's a good sign." He looked at some notes on the clipboard he held. "Now, Gina tells me you just moved here a couple of days ago? Where'd you move from?"

"San Diego."

"San Diego… elevation, sea level, right?"

"Right."

"Well, young lady, what I think you've got here is a case of altitude sickness. Made worse by the pregnancy."

"Altitude sickness?" Hope thought back from the drive to the airport. Everything was flat, flat, flat. "Isn't that something that happens in the mountains?" She didn't want to question the doctor's intelligence, but he had to be a little off today or something.

"Ope. Or just at higher elevation than what your body's used to. We're at 4,000 feet here, missy."

Oh. She hadn't thought of that. She smiled a little sheepishly.

"Now, what've you been up to since you got in?" He asked, leaning forward, elbows on his knees. "Unpacking? Resting?"

She winced a little. "Gardening."

"Good idea, in this heat." He lifted his eyebrows at her. "Taking lots of breaks? Drinking plenty of water?"

She was embarrassed, and he was having fun teasing her. "Kind of forgetting about breaks and water. My mother-in-law is planting a strawberry bed…"

"Say no more." He raised a hand, feigning surrender. "When Teresa wants something done, she gets it done. Gina, you'll talk to her, won't you?"

Hope's new sister nodded her assent. She looked as pleased – and entertained – by the doctor's assessment as Hope felt.

"We'll hold you hostage till those fluids finish up," he said, pointing his pencil at the bag of saline, "your blood pressure gets back to normal, and you're able to eat something. Then Gina here will take you home. Sounds good?"

"Thank you," Hope smiled, but when he left, she turned to Gina. "I feel so bad, you staying here. Don't you need some sleep?"

"Oh, no, I'm fine. I wanna get to know my new sister-in-law. So, how's the farm treating you?"

They made small talk till it was time to head home, and by the time they made it out to the car, Hope couldn't help but laugh at herself. Altitude sickness. What a way to go.

Peter stretched his arms drowsily over his head as the bright morning sunlight streamed in through the big front windows, warming the couch and the man stretched out upon it.

He stumbled to the kitchen, holding his head, and smiled when he saw Rob and Gina at the table. "What's for breakfast?" He asked, meandering towards the stove. "Mmm, biscuits."

"Your breakfast is at home. Where you should be." Gina moved towards him, her tone unmistakably icy. Rob looked at him from his place at the table, raising his eyebrows apologetically, but smiling a little. Apparently he'd known a storm was coming. And it looked like it was just getting started.

"Do you know where I was last night?" Gina demanded.

"No…" Peter asked with open hands.

"Taking your wife to the hospital." Her hands were on her hips. Now Peter felt a little more awake.

He set down the mug he'd been about to fill with coffee. "What? Is she ok?"

"She is now. But she was throwing up and in intense pain last night. She tried to call you, did you know that? We spent three hours in the ER just to get her fluid levels back to normal. The cramping and dehydration can be very dangerous for the baby."

Peter saw Rob raise his eyebrows even higher. Peter would've liked to tell him about the pregnancy himself. Too late.

"Meanwhile, you're passed out on my couch, after some drunken brawl. You both should be ashamed of yourselves."

"Now, Gina, it wasn't that…" Rob stepped in now.

"Hush. I don't want to hear it. Peter's got one responsibility right now. And that's to take care of your family." She took a step closer to him, rising up to what looked like more than her five feet and two inches. "So I suggest you get home and do it."

Rob stood to get Peter's keys. He knew when he'd been bested; and he always said that was one of the things that had made him fall in love with his wife. She always stood up for what was right.

Peter took the keys from Rob, but pleaded in Gina's direction, "Can't I finish my coffee first? And maybe get some medicine for this headache? It's like needles stabbing my brain…" He cocked one eye and leveled a sly smile at Gina. This was the look that usually got him his way with women.

But she wasn't falling for it. She eyed him like a chicken eyes a worm. "You can take the coffee with you," she relented. "But I don't have any Tylenol." With her arms crossed over her chest, she walked upstairs to check on the baby. "And even if I did," he heard her mumble as he and Rob walked out the door, "I wouldn't give it to you."

Hope was up early that morning; the IV fluids and all the sleep she'd gotten the day before had made her feel better. She wandered around the downstairs, exploring; it didn't feel like home yet, but at least she was starting to learn where everything was.

She went to fix coffee for Teresa, who wasn't up yet, and then made a cup of tea for herself. Armed with tea, Bible, notebook and phone, she headed out to the sunporch. This might be her favorite place on the farm, she thought as she settled into the old green couch and sipped her tea comfortably. Watching the sun rise over the golden fields. Literally watching the grass grow – she laughed, because it reminded her of a country song.

Before she could put her tea down and open her journal, her phone rang. Anna. It was only 5:30 there… Anna was up early, too. In eagerness to talk to her best friend she spilled half the tea down her pants; good thing it wasn't too hot. "Hello?" She said quickly into the phone.

"Hey, how are you?" Hope hadn't realized how much she missed her cousin until the familiar voice brought tears to her eyes.

"Good… how are you guys?" She settled deeper into the couch and watched the way the light warmed the fields.

"We're good. Cora's turning five next week. Five! Can you believe it?"

"Wow! I do remember. What're you guys doing?"

"Well, Jake's insisted on a big party. There's talk of a pony ride. I'll see if I can convince Heidi to bring one of her gentler horses out here. Imma' start baking the cake today… I can freeze the layers ahead of time… anyway, enough about me! How're *you?* How's Nebraska? How's Peter?"

Hope didn't know which to answer first. For some reason, she didn't feel right sharing about the baby. Not till Peter at least acknowledged it. It seemed like something they should share with family together. So she tackled the Peter subject. The one Anna might be able to help her with.

"Peter's not himself out here. I don't know what it is. But he doesn't have time for me… we've hardly talked since he came out here. And when we do talk, he just seems so… frustrated. I don't know." Talking about it made Hope realize how much she missed her husband, the way he had been when they were together in San Diego.

"Hmm." Anna just listened.

"And then... come to find out he got in some drunken fight with his brother last night." Hope was still anxious to hear all the details from Gina. But in the meantime she'd process it as much as she could. "He doesn't have time to help me unpack and get set up... but he has time to get in fights at bars!"

"There's a bar in that town?"

"Oh, I don't know. I think it was the pizza place. Anyway." Hope took a deep breath. "I don't know what to do."

"Well. That sucks. I'm sorry you're going through that." Anna's voice was understanding, like always. She clucked her tongue. "I wish I was there to help." Hope wished so, too. "But maybe... you know, his dad just died."

"Yeah, I know." Hope didn't know why there was a hard edge to her own voice.

"Maybe he just needs a little extra love. Didn't *Yeshua* say something about treating others the way we want to be treated?"

"Yeah, He did... wait. What have you been reading?"

"Oh, a little of this, a little of that." Anna evaded the question. "What I mean is... marriage isn't linear. It's not like one person is always the rock. Jake and I take turns. Sometimes he's the strong one, and he lifts me up when I'm weak. Then it's my turn. Either way, we're better when we work together." She paused a moment. "It's almost like dancing. Remember when we used to go together?"

"Yeah." Hope sighed. It felt like another lifetime.

"Well, when your partner makes a mistake, you don't expose them out there on the dance floor. You just dance a little stronger until they catch up."

Hope took a deep breath as the sun fell on her from the window. "Oh, I gotta go. Peter's car is pulling up." She lifted herself up off the couch to see him better.

"Okay! Love you girl! Call me later."

"I will. Kiss those girls for me." Hope pushed down the twinge she'd felt that she couldn't be there for the birthday party, then started running out the door, not noticing that she knocked over the rest of her tea in the process.

If any part of her had wanted to punish Peter for not being there last night, it was gone the moment she saw him climb out of the car. His slumped shoulders, his tired face, told her that he already felt badly about it. She ran to him; he wrapped her in his strong arms. "I'm sorry," he whispered in her hair.

Then he went down on his knees and spread his arms out wide. "Forgive me?" He asked in a pleading voice, but a teasing smile was on his lips.

She rolled her eyes at his antics; but his words opened her heart again. "Yes, I forgive you." She kissed him on the top of his head. When he stood again, she allowed him to lift her up and swing her around like he used to do when they were dating.

He held her hand as they walked up to the big white farm-house. "And I'm sorry... for clamming up about the baby. I do love babies," he spoke quickly. "I just wasn't ready for it. But it takes two to tango... right? We'll figure this out together."

For the rest of the morning, Peter encouraged Hope to lie low and drink plenty of water. Playing with his nephew last night had warmed him to the idea of becoming a father. The tongue-lashing from Gina had put him in his place... and the drive home had sobered him up even more. As he passed the billowing fields of corn that Hope said reminded her of the ocean, he remembered how much she'd left behind to be here with him. It was the least he could do to make sure she stayed healthy.

He couldn't be late for work, though – news travelled fast in this town. By now, his boss would know about the scene that he and Rob had made in the restaurant the night before. He didn't want the man to think he was hungover – or injured – or didn't want his job. He needed that job. The family needed that job.

"You sure you're all right?" He sat next to Hope, on the couch where she sat drawing.

"Mmm. Yeah. Thanks for all your help." She craned her neck to give him a kiss. "Your mom'll be in soon from gardening. We'll make a little dinner together. I mean, supper." She teased him. "Now get to work!"

"Alright. And I'll see you at the meeting tonight?"

"Meeting?" She crinkled her eyebrows. He'd forgotten to tell her.

"Town Hall meeting. But don't worry about it, if you're not up for it. Mom can fill you in. Gotta go." He kissed her hand like a regular Prince Charming, then scooted out the door.

He pulled on his running shoes by the back door, then headed to the garage for his bike. Just in case Hope ended up needing the car again.

chapter thirteen

"You know, I've never been to a Town Hall meeting before." Hope sat with her hands folded in her lap in the passenger seat as Teresa drove.

"No?" Teresa asked, distracted.

"No, I didn't even know they existed."

"Well, our town is very different. We have to work things out for ourselves."

"Hmm." If everyone in the town was as take-charge as Teresa could be, then Hope could see how a town hall meeting would be very effective. The woman had literally taken charge of Hope's pregnancy the moment she'd walked in the door. All Hope's ideas of telling the family in her own way, in her own time had evaporated the moment her mother-in-law had come in from gardening, dropped the portable phone on the counter, grabbed Hope around the waist and squealed, "Congratulations!" Hope hadn't bothered to ask who she'd been talking to; who had spilled the beans. She'd learned enough about this town in the three days she'd been here to know that it didn't really matter. Everyone knew by now.

Teresa had sat her down, pulled out the calendar, and questioned Hope until she'd repeated three times that the due date would be February 3rd. She'd promised that they'd stop by the store after the meeting for prenatal vitamins, and that she'd get a foam pillow-top for Hope and Peter's mattress before Hope "got big", as she put it.

"Teresa, you don't have to do all that." Hope still wondered if she should call the woman "Mom," but had decided to do what felt comfortable to her.

"Nonsense. This is my grandchild." Something about the way she said *my grandchild* made Hope feel warm inside.

They pulled up in front of the big brick building with a sign on the front that read: "Orion Community Church". When they walked in, Hope wasn't surprised to see a packed house. She found a seat next to Gina. "Is this my little nephew?" She asked, tickling the tot on Gina's lap.

"Yes, you wanna hold him? I gotta go help Rob with something."

"Of course!" Hope settled easily into the role of auntie as the meeting began.

The town's mayor, Joshua Gunderson, stood up and banged a gavel on the table. Everyone paid close attention. "We're here to-night," he began, "To address some issues that have come to our attention. First, the rebuilding of the hospital. Now, I know we've had some complaints – but we're building as fast as we can. For any of you who are able, we still recommend that you head to the hos-pital in Red Bluffs – they're just more fully equipped than we are. For urgent matters, you are welcome to head to our Emergency Room as always, where the staff can stabilize you here, and transfer you to Red Bluffs if need be.

"I also have some good news… we've partnered with Farm-er Joe's in purchasing a new building for their store. That grocery store brought some of the freshest produce –"

"Not as fresh as my tomatoes," Teresa leaned over and whis-pered in Hope's ear…

"And I know a lot of our residents have missed it. We'll be as-sisting Joe and Stephanie in whatever way they need to get it ready. Now, before we go on…"

"And he can go on." This time Hope laughed at Teresa's sarcas-tic whisper.

"We have two gentlemen who'd like to present something to you. Rob? Peter?"

Hope looked at Gina, surprised, as their two husbands jogged up to the podium, Rob carrying a stack of notebooks and Peter carrying a large posterboard and – was that her easel? The one she'd carefully packaged and shipped from home? Her breath caught a little in her throat as she realized he'd taken it without asking her.

"Friends. Neighbors." She was struck by how much Rob looked like Peter. It was fun to watch them interact; even from ten rows back, she could see that Peter was eager to please his older brother, waiting for his nods and instructions on where to place their presentation items. And it was a presentation.

"I would like to take this opportunity to inform you that I'll be running for city council when our votes start up in a couple weeks here."

Hope looked at Gina; her sister in law just smiled at her. Gina had known; of course she'd known. But wasn't Rob busy with the farm?

"Most people who serve on our city council do have two or three jobs," Gina explained in a whisper, as if she'd read Hope's thoughts. "The mayor – he's also a teacher at the local high school. One of the other city council members is a doctor that I work with – the other, Greg Connor, owned the hardware store that burned down."

Hope wondered at the fact that the 7,000-population town even *needed* a council. "You call this a city?" She said under her breath, unable to stop her words before they came out. Then she glanced at the wince on Gina's face, and as quickly as she'd made her mistake, she said, "I'm sorry."

"It's ok." Gina recovered quickly. "I know it's different than where you came from."

Hope turned her attention back on the two strong men at the front of the room, feeling a swell of pride that she was part of their family. "Some things that I would change –" Rob was saying – "We need a full-time Fire Department more than we need to rebuild Farmer Joe's. No offense, Joshua; Joe; Stephanie..." The mayor raised his hands to indicate that none was taken. "But when the fire happened last year – it took so long for the trucks from Red Bluffs to get here, we lost some key structures. Not just structures, but organizations that were important to our community. Homes and businesses were lost; more than half of our hospital; and, of course, Farmer Joe's," he added with a respectful nod in Joe's direction. "Imagine if something like that ever happened again? What would become of our town if we lost *more?*" He paused for emphasis. "And, with a full-time fire department, we'd have EMTs and trucks on hand to help transport patients to Red Bluffs, diverting them from our hospital here when possible – since it's still rather limited." He nodded at his wife. She had been part of the planning, too.

Peter now uncovered the posterboard he'd prepared. Hope could see graphs; projections; numbers. He joined in with his part of the presentation. "The Baileys believe," he spoke in a booming voice over the crowd, "That a full-time fire department is like having insurance for the whole town. Robert here has looked over the town budget – which is available in the public record – and identified key areas where we can save, devoting more money to the fire department. If we clean up the existing building, and all we need to do is purchase more supplies and hire more staff, we should be able to have it up and running this fall."

Hope was surprised, and more than a little impressed, to see the command her husband had over a crowd. She hadn't known he was gifted with public speaking. But there was a thunderous applause before Rob could silence it and turn to Peter again. "My brother here," Rob began, "Is a certified Emergency Medical Technician." Hope couldn't help but smile at how Rob had stretched out the word to make it sound as professional as possible. "He's agreed to help us set up the new Fire Department, and to serve as a temporary staff member until more staff are hired."

Hope cocked her head a little. How would Peter juggle that, with his other full-time job, and his farm duties? Would there be any time left over for her?

"If you vote for the Bailey brothers," Rob projected, sweeping his arm to include his brother, as if Peter were running with him – "We promise to keep this town safe."

Chatter broke out in the audience; Hope could hear some folks murmuring about how much they wanted the new grocery store; others saying what job opportunities a new fire department would bring; others wondering why a town as small as theirs needed more job opportunities.

The meeting broke up and Hope stood, baby Brandon on her hip. "So – is the town growing? Is that why they want to expand the fire department?" She directed her question to Gina.

"Growing?" Gina looked for something in her purse.

"Like, are they building more houses? Are more families moving here?"

"Oh. The town can't grow." Gina saw the confused look on her face and explained further: "The four square miles that we have here is the largest the town will ever be. Because it's surrounded by privately owned farmland. Like the land you all are on." Gina pointed at their mother in law.

"Oh. But I thought… I thought a lot of the other farmers had left."

"Left until they could save up enough money to rebuild their farms, maybe. Or until a few years of weather make the grass grow again." Gina took her son, and said, a little reprovingly but not unkindly, "Just because they can't grow anything on it right now doesn't mean they want to sell it. Most of those families have owned that land since their granddaddies immigrated, or came home from World War II and bought it. They wanna keep it in the family." She softened and winked at Hope; she was a stern but gentle teacher. "Oh, honey, great job!" Gina gave her husband a bright smile. "But I might want to see a little more of that presentation before you get my vote."

Rob put an arm around his pretty wife, and Hope could see now, by his red face, that he had been nervous – though neither he nor Peter had shown it when they were up front.

"We gotta do what this town needs most. Yo, Pete, good job!" Peter sauntered up, grinning. If it irritated him to be called "Pete" by his brother as much as he'd told Hope, he didn't show it. He went to Teresa first and kissed her on the cheek; then he noticed Hope.

"Hey, you made it." His crooked smile told her he was pleased.

"Hey, husband. Nice way to communicate with your wife." She teased Peter with a jab from her elbow.

"What, I can still surprise you, can't I?" He hugged her close.

"Apparently you can."

As they walked out, Hope on Teresa's arm, she was stopped by three older ladies she hadn't met yet. "Congratulations," the first one proclaimed, offering a hand to shake and a wide smile.

"Congratulations?"

"On the baby."

Of course. Everyone knew. Hope suddenly felt tired; she was still adjusting to the idea of a baby herself. She tried to smile as she thanked the women.

But as she looked around the circle, Hope saw a grin on Teresa's face that could've lit up the room. It was worth it, Hope realized, to have the whole town know her intimate details, if it made this woman happy. Teresa was still grieving, yet she'd done so much for her already.

Hope took in the scene for a moment: women who'd known each other most of their lives laughing and talking and giving hugs. Teresa gave herself to her garden and her family. Gina gave at the hospital and at home. Miss Hazel, she'd heard, gave herself daily to her grandchildren who lived in town. Where could Hope give? How could she give?

The ladies lingered a little longer. "I know those boys of yours have a good idea when it comes to the Fire Department," Miss Hazel was saying. Then she sighed, "But I sure am going to miss Farmer Joe's. He always had the best cabbage this time of year. I used to make my sauerkraut with it."

"I have cabbage in my garden!" Her mother in law was exclaiming. "You come over, and we'll make it together."

Miss Hazel nodded. Hope wondered if she was thinking whether she'd have time to stop by. There was so much work to be done, each on her own farm.

"And how about you, Miss Hazel? Peter said you had some dairy cows?" Hope tried to insert herself into the conversation in a way that didn't sound totally unintelligent.

"Yes, I do. Just made some fresh butter this evenin'. Nothing better for the grandbabies than summer butter."

"Oh," Teresa clucked her tongue. "I miss my cows so much. I would have loved to have fresh milk for you, Hope, while you grow this little one."

Hope's mind flashed back to gardening the other day with Teresa. To filtering the sand in her hand and watching the sunlight flicker through it. An idea was nagging at her, but it filtered through her mind like so many grains of sand.

Suddenly, Peter turned around quickly. "Dr. Rosenberg!" He shouted. "Over here!"

Stunned, Hope turned around and saw her Papa. "Papa!" She cried, running to him without thinking. "What are you doing here?" She stopped short of giving him a hug — he'd never been much for affection; but she could see by the look on his face that he was as happy to see her as she was to see him.

"I brought you your car," he said, jangling the keys in front of her.

"You drove here? From San Diego?" He must've left shortly after she had.

"I took some time off." Her papa shrugged modestly.

"Did you know about this?" She turned on Peter, shocked. He gave the same sly shrug.

"Oh... thank you, Papa. Thank you."

Dr. Rosenberg shook hands all around, most firmly with Hope's new mother-in-law; who put on her most gracious airs to meet him. When they walked out to the parking lot and Hope saw her faithful green pickup waiting for her, the idea that had sifted through like grains of sand finally settled in her mind.

She knew what she had to do.

Peter rose proudly the next morning at 5 am, while the house was still asleep. Now he could finally show Dr. Rosenberg that a hospital wasn't the only place where hard work happened.

After dragging the pivots into place with the tractor, he spotted Hope coming up from the chicken coop. She held a basket of eggs in her hands and sported a smudge of dirt on her cheek. He wiped it off playfully. "Feeling farm-ish?" He teased her.

"It's the least I can do to help. And, I'm doing research for my project." She raised her eyebrows sneakily. She'd mentioned a project last night after the meeting, and even pulled Gina aside to whisper about it, but had refused to let him in on it. It was fun to see her acclimating. "But I didn't realize how messy those chickens are. I mean, I've scooped horse manure for as long as I can remember... but chicken manure is something else."

Peter wrinkled his nose. He could almost smell it just from the way she talked about it.

"I don't envy that job. But Mom will be thankful. *I'm* thankful you're here." He kissed her clean cheek.

"Really?" She looked up at him in surprise. He should remember to give her kind words more often.

"Really." He hugged her tighter, then ushered her first into the side kitchen door. "Good morning, Dr. Rosenberg." He switched to his formal voice when he spotted Hope's dad at the kitchen table, reading the newspaper.

"Morning." Dr. Rosenberg said. "I didn't get a chance to tell you last night, Peter. But I've spoken with the Director of the ER in San Diego. Your job is secure, so long as you come back by late September." He fluffed out his paper, wearing a satisfied smile.

"Ahh... thank you," Peter uttered nervously, looking up the stairs. No sign of Mom yet.

"What seems to be the problem?" Hope's Papa raised his eyebrows.

"I just... I haven't told my mom yet. About leaving after the harvest."

Papa finally put his paper down, and stared at Peter hard, like he wanted to reprimand him.

Hope returned from the bathroom where she'd gone to wash her face and hands; Peter breathed a sigh of relief that she hadn't heard their exchange. "Okay, boys," she said as she turned around. "I'm off to Gina's. We gotta work on our project. Papa, where are my keys?" She was rummaging through the pile on the end table. "Oh, here they are. 'Bye!" She came around the corner to kiss Peter and pat Papa on the shoulder.

"Have a nice day, Hope. And drink plenty of water! And remember to sit down when you get tired." Dr. Rosenberg beat Peter to issuing Hope's health reminders.

"I will!" The side door slammed, and it was just the two men alone in the kitchen.

Dr. Rosenberg stared at Peter again. "You know, Son, with a family on the way, you really need a steady job. With a steady income." He'd been shocked last night to hear about Hope's pregnancy; but now directing Peter's steps seemed to be his way of coming to terms with it.

"I know that." Peter wasn't backing down from the stare. "And – and I appreciate your help." He tried to keep a tone of respect in his voice. "But... let me tell Mom when she's ready. When we know what the harvest looks like. Then she'll feel more settled."

"Humph." Papa picked up his paper again. "I'm sure she will understand that your education comes first."

Peter looked out the window, and an image came to his mind; Teresa weeping over those fields the morning of the fire. Teresa praying over those fields the night after the funeral. Teresa planting, and weeding, and tending her chickens.

The only education Mom had ever had was the one offered by Life itself. Would she really understand if Peter did decide to leave her here and return to school?

"Oooh, don't forget to call Mrs. Misner. She's got the most gorgeous herb garden you've ever seen. And Mrs. Anderson –" Gina was looking down at her list, ticking off fingers as she spoke. "She's got collard greens. And turnips. Have you ever stewed turnips?" She looked at Hope questioningly.

"No. But I'm excited to try." Hope giggled. This whole thing had her feeling high on life.

"I love your idea, Hope. We can make our own food co-op. We don't need Farmer Joe to do it for us. I'd say that I don't know why we never thought of it before – but I do." She bounced baby Brandon on her lap.

Hope reached out her arms to take him and squeeze him close. "Why's that?"

"Well, you know sometimes it takes a fresh pair of eyes to see what needs to be done. Like, when I look at a patient for the first time, I might see something that the night nurse missed." Hope had a feeling that Gina's discerning eyes didn't miss much when it came to her patients. "But also..." then Gina hesitated, as if she wasn't sure whether she should confide this or not. "Also, Nebraskans are good at being there for each other when a crisis strikes. You should've seen how it was after the fire. Shirt-off-your-back kind of neighborliness. But still… they don't always think of helping each other when it comes to just… daily life. Something like this… swapping produce. I think they're just too busy with their daily duties to see it." She circled some names in the phone book with her highlighter. "It takes two outsiders to start a project like this!"

"Two outsiders? Me and who else? Not you, little Bubbas. Not you," Hope bounced her nephew on her hip and kissed him till he squealed.

"No, not him. Me." Gina took a sip of her coffee.

"You? But I thought you grew up here?"

"Here? No. I'm from Chicago. Headed to Denver to celebrate with my nursing school buddies after graduation. Got a flat tire here in Orion, and while I was changing it, Rob pulled over to ask if I needed help. And that was that. What, you're surprised?"

"It's just… you seem so happy here." The words came out before Hope could realize that it might sound condescending. She tried to backpedal. "I just mean…"

"You mean you're surprised that a city girl can make a life here. Well Hope, I can be happy any place that I have family. And you can too." Gina stood to pull out her phone book. "This food co-op idea of yours is proof right here of what Hope can do. Now come on. Let's see how many of these grandmas are interested."

Hope handed Brandon back to Gina, then scrolled down the phone book to find the first number she needed. *M. Anderson.* "Hello, Mrs. Anderson? This is Hope Bailey calling. Yes, Peter's wife… I'm settling in fine, thank you… Gina and I are setting up a produce swap among the neighbors here in town… yes, Gina, Rob's wife. Anyhow, she mentioned that you have quite the collection of chickens over there? We were wondering if you'd be interested in swapping some of your eggs, for fresh produce? No, no, not donating it. You'd be taking home something, too. Well, like Teresa's tomatoes, or Miss Hazel's cheese…" Hope paused, remembering that she hadn't talked to Miss Hazel *or* her mother-in-law yet, and smiled sheepishly at Gina. "Oh, great. Well, I won't know exactly how much produce until we talk to more people. But for now, how many dozens of eggs can I put you down for next weekend?"

Hope squealed when she got off the phone. "We got our first bite!" She wrote it down on the graph paper Gina had stolen from Rob's office and that they'd labelled at the top with the name of their co-op. After five more phone calls, including one to Anna – who did some research and confirmed that as long as no cash was exchanged, they should be fine without a business license – Hope asked Gina, "Can you make the next few calls for me, please, while I run to the auto store?"

"No problem. Something wrong with your car?"

"Nope. Be right back." She fairly hopped out the front door and felt more elated than ever as she made the drive to the auto store, then the pharmacy. Finally, she would use her art to help someone.

chapter fourteen

Night was falling and the cicadas were chirping when Peter finally heard Hope pull in the drive. He was standing at the sink, washing dishes, wondering with a smile what she was up to.

He walked outside, drying his hands on a towel, and Papa Rosenberg walked up from the little house at the same time. Hope looked different... her short, curly hair dancing in the breeze... and her truck looked different, too.

"Ta-da!" She squealed and struck a pose.

"What have you done to your truck?" Her papa asked, though it was clear from his tone that he was entertained.

"Remember that day before the wedding, when you took me down to the DMV, and you signed the truck over in my name?"

Papa nodded.

"So that means I can do what I want with it, right?"

"I... I guess so. And apparently you have." Papa stood back, arms crossed, eyeing it critically. Peter just went up and put an arm around her.

"It looks great," he whispered in his wife's ear. "Now I think I know what you've been up to..."

Painted on the driver's side door, under the window, was a large wicker basket overflowing with fruits and veggies. Tomatoes, zucchini squash, carrots, collard greens and potatoes tumbled together in and out of the basket. "I had to ask Gina to show me a picture of a collard green," Hope admitted sheepishly. A pile of perfectly painted cheese, butter and eggs sat next to the basket. And painted along the side of the truck bed in bright red calligraphy were the words: *Neighbor's Bounty.*

"So you're bringing back the old food co-op?" He asked as she leaned against him.

"Um, we're starting a new food co-op."

"Oh. And just where will this co-op be gathering?"

"That's just it! We don't have to gather anywhere. It's a travelling co-op. I'll drive around, pick up items from neighbors, and distribute them. There are plenty of people who have extra produce… they just needed somebody to do the organizing and delivering. I can do it." He squeezed her a little tighter and she continued, "I have my first delivery next weekend." She held her clipboard out to show him all the names and numbers. "Wanna see?"

"Hang on. I wanna show you something too." Peter grabbed her hand and pulled her down towards the barn. Hope smiled when she saw where he was taking her.

The barn had felt empty enough with only one horse in it. But now that the family he'd bought Bandit from had been kind enough to take the horse back, it felt *really* empty. Empty enough that he could almost see flames leaping up the walls if he closed his eyes. Soon, he hoped to fill it up with new memories. Memories made with Hope.

"I did something to liven this place up a little. Make it more *ours.*" He jumped up and pointed to a long rope hanging from the ceiling. It had a big knot at the end.

"How did you get that up there?" She asked, craning her neck to try to find the top of the rope. The ceiling was higher than any she'd ever seen.

"I had a little help from Rob. And a ladder from the fire department."

"Ok. But what's it for?"

"For the kids." And grabbing the rope with one hand, he ran with it towards the wall. Then he jumped, kicked off the wall, and sat on top of the knotted end, sailing away on the rope like a giant swing.

"Ohmigoodness." Her laugh was caught between amazement and surprise. "You two think of everything." She shook her head and watched her goofy husband swing from one side of the barn to the other.

"You like it?" He asked, taking one hand off the rope and waving it wildly to show off.

"I love it. It's just like *Charlotte's Web.*"

He jumped off and gave a deep bow, then came over to hug her. "Hey, you look happy. The happiest I've seen you, I think, since the news about the baby."

Hope looked at him in surprise. Didn't he know that she was thrilled about the baby? It wasn't the baby who'd stolen her joy. It was Peter's indifference to the baby. Today was only the second time he'd even spoken the word "baby" to her. But she didn't want to point that out to him. Today was a good day.

While Teresa prepared dinner, half-listening to the plans, Hope pulled out her clipboard and showed Peter and Papa the orders she'd taken and the products she'd been promised. Peter squeezed her and said, "Only you could think of this." Hope was forever creating something. This was what he loved about her.

"I just wish I could be here to see it," Papa was saying, as they sat down to enjoy Teresa's meatballs with garden vegetables.

"Do you really have to go back, Papa?"

He nodded. "Tomorrow. We've got quite the ride to make it to the airport."

The next day, the three of them piled into Peter's borrowed Camry. "This car doesn't look suitable for a farmer," Dr. Rosenberg commented as they climbed in.

"Well, I had an F350 before." Peter had been proud of that car.

"What happened to it?"

"It was singed. Totally ruined. In the fire."

Papa *harumphed*. He was probably thinking about how Peter had been underinsured. They'd already had that conversation.

On the way to Denver, Papa mentioned, "You know, Hope, there's a Messianic Jewish Congregation in Denver." Hope hopped in the backseat a little.

"Really, Dad? Would you come?"

Papa winced a little. "Not today. But there's nothing to stop the two of you from going. Why don't you stay overnight – get a hotel? My treat. Enjoy the city a little."

"Oh, I don't know… I've gotta get back. I have work in the morning…"

"Oh, couldn't you call and ask for a day off, Peter? It would be so good to just hang out together… like we used to…"

"No, I can't, Hope. There's too much work to do." Hope looked dejectedly out the window.

Papa checked his watch. "Well, it is Saturday. Most Jewish congregations meet in the afternoon. You could probably still go and make it back tonight. If you're not too tired to drive at night."

"I won't be tired," Peter answered quickly. He didn't know if this was a challenge from his father-in-law, but if it was, he'd accept it.

Hope leaned forward to kiss him from the backseat. "Oh, thank you, Babe."

The parking lot was full when they arrived. Two things surprised Peter: he wasn't surrounded by bearded men in *yarmulkes,* the little head coverings he'd seen in movies, like he'd expected. He passed by security guards at the door and stiffened a little when he noticed that they were fully armed. Hope shrugged as if it was no big deal. When he pointed it out, she said, "They're here for our protection. Anti-Semitism is still alive in America." She said it like it was a simple fact. His insides shivered a little.

"Where are all the beards?"

She giggled, "A lot of people are Jewish, Peter. From a lot of different cultures. And here, at a Messianic congregation, you find a lot of people who are Christians and are just curious about the Jewish roots of our faith. Maybe they read that Jesus celebrated Passover, and they want to know what that looks like. Or maybe they want to hear more about the Old Testament prophecies. They're here to learn."

She pulled Peter over to a seat on the right side, near the big open floor. He was surprised to see a box of multi-colored flags waiting on the floor next to their seating area.

He looked around, waiting for it to start, people-watching.

The man who greeted people at the door had tattoo sleeves up both arms, but a smile that showed everyone he wasn't the tough guy he seemed. A group of grandmas in the middle of the room sat together, chatting and laughing, and some smiled in their direction when they noticed the young couple.

Behind them, a man's voice prayed in Hebrew. Peter turned around to watch him. He leaned against the wall, a prayer shawl that might've come straight from Israel draped over his dark, curly head. The skin that peeked out from under his robe was dark, too. "That's the *shofar,*" Hope explained when she caught Peter staring at the long, curved object held in the man's hand. "The ram's horn. It's a call to worship." The man's body moved in time with his mumbled prayers, and when the *shofar* blew, it was such a powerful sound, Peter felt it in his bones. The whole room quieted.

"Shabbat Shalom, friends." Rabbi David said from the front podium. He prayed, first in Hebrew, then in English. "Before we begin worship, I want to share something with you." Peter was struck by his friendly manner with the congregation. It seemed small enough that they might all know each other. "I was enjoying my quiet time this morning, just giving thanks to the Lord for all He has done."

"Preach, Rabbi," one of the grandmas put in. Others nodded.

"And I was thinking... isn't it wonderful how *Yeshua* is into completing us. He is into restoring us. You know that the number seven, in the Bible, means completion. Well, just think about the woman at the well. She was married to five guys, living with the sixth guy, and who was the seventh guy to come her way? *Yeshua. Yeshua* completes us. Hallelujah."

"Hallelujah." Several others agreed and raised their hands in agreement. Peter had never thought of the woman at the well that way.

Jesus, complete me too, he prayed silently.

The rabbi gave the call to worship, and the dancers came to the front. Peter stiffened, watching. But it wasn't showy or fancy. Just full of joy. Obvious joy. There were children who were part of the congregation, too, and pulled flags from the box. The dancers moved in time to the worship that was sung first in Hebrew, then in English. The children flew their flags erratically. It was funny, but watching their lightheartedness made Peter feel all the heaviness of the last few weeks. A momentary wish – a wish that he could feel so happy he'd get up and dance, too – flitted across his mind. But he pushed it away. He was here for Hope.

"And now we'd like to pray for all the women and children. Come on up."

Peter knew that Hope never said no to prayer, but he was surprised by the way she bolted out of her seat and made a beeline to the front. He was further surprised by the way the men of the congregation went up to encircle the women and children. Suddenly feeling protective, he made his way to the front so he could be the first to put a hand on Hope's shoulder. "Let's form a hedge of protection, men," the rabbi said, but it had already been done. It was their routine. Peter was the only one who prayed silently.

The prayer was short; but Hope was crying at the end of it. Why was she crying? Wasn't she happy here?

As the circle broke up and the people started to disperse, Peter noticed Hope lock eyes with the man who had blown the shofar. "Aahh, a prophetess," the man spoke with a sense of knowing in his deep, gravelly voice. Hope just looked away and turned red.

When they walked out, Peter held Hope's arm tightly, protectively. It was the first time he'd attended any sort of Jewish event with her. It hadn't been as boring as he'd thought.

"Dinner?" He asked as he held her tighter.

"Yeah." She looked up at him contentedly.

"Italian?"

"Italian."

"Peter!" Hope burst from her car and ran up the driveway, slamming her driver's side door in the process.

"Yeah?" He called from the kitchen where he had his hands in a pile of sudsy water.

"Second delivery finished," she hollered with pride in her voice.

He grabbed the red ragged dish towel to dry his hands. "Wow!

Good job," he said as he took the porch steps two at a time to greet her.

"Thank you." She curtsied with a flourish. "What's all this?" She stopped midsentence and lifted her hands to look around her. She stared in amazement at the pinkish-white cotton balls that filled the air.

"Cottonwood fluff."

"What?"

"It's fluff. From the cottonwood trees on the way to the road. You haven't seen it before?"

"No." She turned in a circle a moment, just admiring another unique thing about this place. Then she came back down to earth. "Will you help me unload these?" She pointed to the pile of empty baskets in the back of her truck.

"Yeah. Let's do it quickly. Looks like it might rain." He started unloading as many baskets as he could carry to the garage. He'd bring the wheelbarrow on the way back. "So how does it work anyway? You take their orders, then go around doing pickups?"

"Actually, the opposite. I take inventory when I call – then confirm the numbers when I pick everything up." She handed him three more baskets as he came back with the wheelbarrow. "I sort all the produce evenly – then I deliver. The Bronsons are dairy-free, so I gave them extra eggs. I need to make a note of that." She reached in the cab and came out with a clipboard. "Mrs. Wilson says they don't like pears – but do you think I should factor that in? I mean, that's a preference, not an allergy, and I just don't know if I can accommodate stuff like that for everyone..." She tapped her clipboard thoughtfully.

He looked back at the mountain of baskets in the garage, and the pile yet to be unloaded from her truck. "Where'd you get all these?" He asked suddenly, thinking of the budget he'd worked on this morning, the one that left no wiggle room.

She looked at him with her understanding eyes, knowing just what he was thinking about. "Each participant pays a one-time basket fee. Ten dollars. Then I keep the basket for next week, after we unload the groceries. Sometimes, I even go in and help them unload. If they need it, like Mrs. Anderson..."

"Is that all they pay? Ten dollars?"

"Yup. I mean, I guess you could say they pay each other in food. Everybody gives, and everybody receives something."

"But I mean… no one's paying you?"

She stopped for a moment, a basket in her arms, and cocked her head. "Well… no," she said softly. "But I sort of thought… this was a way I could help the community. While I'm here."

"It's great and all. But have you thought about getting a real job?" He angled back up the hill with the wheelbarrow and left her to think about what he said. When he came back down the driveway and rested with his arms over his chest, she looked like she might cry. He tried to stop himself from rolling his eyes. She was so sensitive.

But then she blinked – like she was trying to recover. "I guess… I guess I could apply at the pharmacy," she said softly. Then she brightened a little and he could see that she was about to tease him. "Maybe they'd even give me a discount on guns and ammo." She smiled, and he felt bad for what he'd said. But before he could apologize, she went on – "If we need more money, you should tell me. We'll figure it out. But I feel like they are paying me – I mean, I know this is volunteer, but I'm getting something back, too. Today, at Mrs. Anderson's –" he nodded. His former, widowed kindergarten teacher. "I went in to help unload and put away the produce." She leaned against the bed of the pickup. "She just had hip surgery – you heard about that? Anyway, her daughter stayed for two weeks, but then she had to go home. So Mrs. Anderson hasn't been able to leave the house for three days. Three days! I'd go crazy." She shook her head. "She said she's been in too much pain. But I think she's afraid of falling again. Anyway," she leaned against the truck, looking at Peter. "You should've seen her face when I brought in the food. It was like a kid on Christmas. Or, what I imagine a kid on Christmas would look like," she added wryly, and he smiled, nodding down towards his feet while he listened to her. "I told her I'd come back on Monday just to check on her. Maybe I can take her to the grocery store or something. See, Peter? I'm here for a reason. Even if I'm not making money."

He turned towards her and wrapped his arms around her waist. "You're right." He knew Hope liked to hear the words "I'm sorry," when they disagreed – but that had never been his strong point.

So instead, he lifted her arms, started humming the tune to Frank Sinatra's *I Get a Kick Out of You,* and trying, but failing, to move his feet in time. Her face lit up with delight, and she took the lead.

For a minute they were the only two people on the planet. The fields of corn stood stock-still behind them. The cicadas in the trees above were silent, watching. The early August heat didn't shimmer on the horizon; it hung about, quiet.

In a final flourishing dance move that looked ridiculous coming from someone who had no idea what he was doing, and was all for Hope's enjoyment, he threw out his arms and flipped his head back. She was clapping and laughing at him, but he stood stock still, staring at the clouds. Those were not ordinary thunder clouds. They were deeper, darker, lower. Something boomed in the distance. "A hailstorm!" He hollered at Hope. "We gotta get inside!" He ran and picked her up, still smiling, and carried her, fireman-style, up to the porch. He deposited her in the swing. "There you are, my lady." She collapsed in giggles and patted the swing next to her. He held up a finger in waiting and ran to move her car under the carport. She had no idea how damaging this hail could be.

He sat down and absently rubbed the worn spot; he'd promised Mom time after time that he'd repaint this old white porch swing. And one day, he would. But today he just wanted to put an arm around his beloved and watch the hail fall.

"My first hailstorm." She snuggled in to him and sighed. "I mean – I've seen hail before." She clarified, a look that looked a little like Dr. Rosenberg's doctor-look on her face.

He laughed. "Just wait. You haven't seen hail like this. If it starts falling sideways, we'll have to go inside."

"Sideways?" Her eyes were wide.

"Yep. Watch – it's starting."

Golf ball-sized balls of ice started falling to the ground – slowly, at first – then in a pummeling sort of way. Like they were angry with the earth. "Wow," Hope breathed. "You weren't kidding."

Now they were the size of oranges, and they were hitting the earth at a slant. "We gotta get inside!" Peter had to holler to be heard over the sound of the great balls of ice banging on the roof above them.

She nodded and went ahead as he opened the door for her. Teresa was downstairs in the kitchen, white-faced.

"What's wrong, Mom? You look as if you haven't seen hail before." Peter asked as he stomped his feet on the rug and motioned for Hope to do the same.

"Hi, Mama T." Hope went to her mother-in-law and kissed her on the cheek. It was the first time Peter had heard Hope use any sort of nickname for Mom. But Teresa didn't seem to notice.

They sat down on the couch to watch the rest of the storm. "It should pass in about ten minutes or so," Peter explained to Hope. "It always does. But it can do a lot of damage in that short time. Good thing I moved your car." He liked being her hero.

"Yeah. I'm actually glad you don't have cows outside right now. They'd be miserable! Or hurt, even." Then she turned to him thoughtfully. "But what about the corn?"

The color drained from his face until he was whiter even than Teresa had been. "The corn!"

He grabbed a jacket and burst out the door.

Peter's jacket was sorry protection for the pelting ice that flew at his face as he ran down the hill towards the fields.

He stopped in his tracks when he saw the damage that had already been done. Acres and acres of corn. Flattened, battered, brought down by the ice. Gone.

"No!" He shouted, and went down on his knees. Not again.

He turned when he heard a sobbing noise beside him. Mom had followed him. Now she knelt, praying. Her hands were on the earth and she was saying, "Oh Lord, heal this land. Lord, heal us." She rocked back and forth on her heels. Peter stared at her a moment. He'd failed again.

The hail was stronger, faster now even than it had been. "Mom! Get inside!" He lifted her to her feet. She resisted only momentarily, then allowed him to lead her into the house.

chapter fifteen

The house was quiet the next morning when Hope came down to make the coffee. Too quiet.

She poured herself half a cup; it had been a rough night. She let Miss Hazel's cream settle down in to it like the memories settled in her mind.

She closed her eyes and Peter's voice reverberated in her mind. "It's gone. It's all gone," he'd pronounced when he'd come in from checking on the corn. His mouth had been set in a stern line and he'd gone off to bed without another word. But he'd tossed and turned all night. She'd tried to wake him up; to talk to him; but he'd just brushed her off. Eventually she'd come down to the couch to try to get some sleep. Just because he was torturing himself didn't mean she had to.

She picked up her phone, found Anna's number, and pressed "Call," just to pass the time. She knew Anna worked on her business early in the morning.

"Hey!" Anna answered cheerily. Her familiar voice was comforting.

"Hey." Hope kept her own voice quiet, even though the family was upstairs. Peter and his mom needed their sleep. She didn't want to risk waking anyone.

"Guess what I'm doing, right now, as we speak?" Anna's voice elevated with excitement.

"What?" Now Hope had trouble keeping her own voice to a whisper.

"Packing up baby clothes. To send to my dear cousin!"

"Girl clothes?"

"Yes, girl clothes, of course. Why do you ask?" Hope imagined that Anna had the phone cradled on one ear and was folding pretty, soft pink-and-white onesies as she spoke.

"Oh, I just have this feeling it'll be a boy. That's all."

"Well, I've got a few neutral things in here. And you'll use the girl stuff eventually – if not this time, maybe next time." Hope could hear Anna's smile in her voice.

Steps creaked down the hallway and she said a quick good-bye to Anna, then went to refill her own mug and fill one for Peter. "G'morning," she said quietly when his groggy face appeared in the kitchen doorway. "Get any sleep?"

He didn't respond; didn't even look at her. Just started rummaging through the cupboards. Opening doors, closing them, looking for something but not finding it.

"I'm sorry – about the corn." She said from her spot at the counter.

He scoffed. "As if you even understand."

She blinked, confused, then went to him to put her arms around his waist. "At least we still have each other, right?" She whispered.

"What?" He wriggled free of her hug. "No. Not *at least* anything. We have nothing."

She leaned back against the kitchen island, and caught herself before she started clicking her fingernails. That annoying habit that Mom had hated. Peter would probably hate it too. She clasped her hands together, instead, and waited for him to go on. Maybe he just needed time to process what had happened.

"That corn," his voice rose as he turned on his heels, "That corn was supposed to be our livelihood! It was supposed to support the farm! It was supposed to fix things!" His face screwed up; and for a moment she thought he might cry. She'd never seen him cry before, not even the day his dad had died.

"Well... if you wanna talk about it..." she said softly. "Or pray together... I'm here." She shrugged her shoulders humbly. She wanted to be here for him when stuff like this happened. This was part of marriage... right?

"Talk about it?" He looked at her, as if confused. "Not with you. I need to talk to Rob." He clattered the cupboards closed, making her jump at the sound; then thundered up the stairs.

She sat at the table in numb silence until ten minutes later, when he came pounding back down the stairs, fully dressed. He came into the kitchen, grabbing a travel mug and slamming it down on the counter this time.

"Never shoulda gone to San Diego." He was shaking his head, adding cream to his coffee.

But then you wouldn't have met me, Hope thought, but the words didn't quite make it to her lips.

The old kitchen walls reverberated as he slammed the front door; and Hope reverberated, too. Her head went down on her lap; she couldn't stop the sobs from coming.

It only took Hope a few moments to gather her thoughts; she knew what she had to do. She felt better when she had a plan.

She climbed the stairs slowly and dug her suitcase out from under their bed. The thought of going home early had flitted through her mind, but she couldn't leave Peter, not in the middle of a crisis like this. She could, however, move down to the little blue house. She'd only been there once, when Papa was staying; it was quaint, clean. Two bedrooms, 900 square feet, with a little basement for storage. If Peter wanted to apologize, he could find her there.

She was rummaging through drawers, stuffing items in her suitcase when she heard the front door slam. She braced herself for another barrage from Peter; but it was Gina who ascended the stairs, huffing, her son in her arms. "Hope," she spoke quickly, "Thank goodness you're here." Then she looked around, taking in the mess Hope had made. "You goin' somewhere?"

"Just down to the little blue house." Hope spoke quietly. Once her mind was made up, her mind was made up. "I need some space to think." She kept folding clothes, but more slowly now. "Peter and I... we had a fight." Was that true? *Peter* had conjured that fight all by himself. She hadn't fought back.

Gina clucked her tongue and shifted Brandon to her other

hip. He pulled at her hair and she turned her head the other way, trying to keep her bun in place. "Yeah, he can be kind of a jerk sometimes." Hope looked at her sideways. Why was being a jerk simply accepted as fact? "Don't worry, whatever it is, he'll get over it." Then Gina set her son down on the bed so she could re-tie the scrub pants that he'd almost pulled down in his death-grip on Mama. He squealed and crawled back to her. She picked him up again and sighed. "Hey, can you watch Brandon for me? Please? Just until Rob gets home? He and Peter are off somewhere... he was supposed to watch him for me today. But I think he forgot. And my folks are in Red Bluffs shopping today or I'd ask them... I have to be at work in twenty minutes."

Hope looked at the pile of clothes on the floor. It wasn't that she had so much work to do; it was that mentally she was in another place. Caring for Gina's active son seemed overwhelming right now.

"Please? I'll pay you."

"It's not that." At her sister-in-law's plea, Hope relented. "All right. Come here, little dude. Maybe you can help me pack."

"*I'll* help you when I get off. If you're not finished by then. Thank you. You're a goddess." Gina kissed both Hope and her son on the cheek, admonished him to be a good boy, and hustled down the stairs as quickly as she'd come.

"All right. Shall we get to work? Shall we start packing Auntie Hope?" But calling herself Auntie Hope only made her think of Anna... and Anna's girls. Why couldn't she be like Anna: so sure of herself? Or more like Gina: letting things roll off her shoulders? She sighed as Brandon picked the neatly rolled clothes out of the suitcase. It was useless, trying to pack with a toddler in tow. "Ok, buddy. Let's head downstairs. Maybe we can find you a snack."

By the time they'd hung out in the kitchen for a while and Hope had given Brandon some applesauce, she started warming to her auntie duties. The quiet babble of a toddler was actually soothing compared to the yelling that had been going on here lately. She put that thought on hold when he army crawled faster than she would've thought possible, shrieking all the while, and heading for the stairs. "Oh, no you don't," she admonished him. "We are not going back up to unpack all of Auntie's things. You did enough damage already. Yes you did," she teased as she tickled him. "Let's find a book. I think *Nonna* has some books for you over here."

She located the wicker basket full of picture books that Teresa had placed strategically by the couch. The couch where, just yesterday, she'd sat with Peter's arms around her, watching a storm. Her eyes stung, but she brushed the tears away with the back of her hand. This was why she hadn't wanted to babysit. She was too emotional. But reading would be easy.

"Okay, buddy. You pick." Brandon hadn't turned one yet; but he was a smart boy. He reached into the basket and pulled out a book that must have been somebody's favorite; the spine was worn and peeling.

"*The Little Red Bird,*" Hope began. "The little red bird got lost in the snowstorm. Can you find him?" Each page featured a different winter scene, and each page prompted the reader to find the little red bird. It was pretty poorly written, Hope thought. Why did writers think they could get away with that, just because it was a children's book? But she liked the paintings. She actually enjoyed trying to find the little red bird – was it called a cardinal? – on each page. She helped Brandon jab his chubby little finger on the spots of each page where the bird was hidden. "Good!" she exclaimed when he got anywhere close.

On the last page, the bird was hidden in the thickest snow of all. By the picture of whirling snowflakes, you could tell that the artist was depicting a windy day. When Hope and Brandon finally located the little red bird, the words that came out of Hope's trembling mouth were not from the page of the book, but were her own: "You see, buddy. No matter how bad the storm is, there is always, always something beautiful worth finding."

When Peter got home late that night, Hope was nowhere to be found. He called her name upstairs, then down. He was just pulling out his phone to call her when she came in the front door. She looked at his phone, then at his face. "So you do have your phone?" She asked gently.

"Yeah, why wouldn't I?" He replied, knowing his voice was testy, but not caring.

Her shoulders shook a little. "I just thought... maybe you'd misplaced it... when you didn't call me today. After..."

"After what?" He leaned against the counter and rubbed his eyes. It had been a hard day.

"After you yelled at me and left." Her voice was still soft. "I didn't know where you were. And Peter, when you talk to me that way..."

"Yell? I didn't yell at you. What are you talking about?" She stared at him blankly. He went on. "Look, I was a little frustrated this morning. Then you and I weren't getting along. So I thought I should get outta the house. I had some business to talk over with Rob anyway. Come here," he held out his arms, and she came over to join him at the kitchen island, but she stood a couple feet away from him, instead of falling into his embrace like he'd hoped. He huffed a little. Fine. If she was gonna be that way, they didn't have to make up. He could just talk business with her.

"I told Rob about the corn. It's a disappointment, of course; but I think we figured out another plan. If I pick up more hours, and I sell that old Camry... and Rob's gonna sell their quads... and if he gets this city council gig, we should be able to keep making the payments on the farm. I still don't know how we're going to save up to buy cattle in the spring. But we'll figure it out. God will provide." He looked at her and nodded, trying to reassure her. But she wouldn't meet his eyes.

Instead, she looked at her feet, and asked softly, "Well, I thought we were staying through the harvest. Now there won't be a harvest – so how long are you planning to stay?"

He'd thought about that too. "I'm gonna stay till the fire department gets set up. It's the least I can do to help the town. And Rob." He'd thought she would be happy that he had a plan. But she still wouldn't look at him. "Hey, where were you anyway?" He remembered that he hadn't seen her on the porch, or anywhere, when he'd gotten home. "Were you out... for a walk or something? Playing with the chickens?" Maybe teasing would work. He knew cleaning out the chicken manure was her least favorite chore.

A smile tickled the corner of her mouth, then disappeared. Was she trying to drive him crazy?

"I was just having some quiet time down at the blue house. I needed some space to think. I set up a little art room in the basement. I hope Mom doesn't mind."

"Oh." He stiffened a little. "Well... you're gonna come back tonight... I mean, to sleep, right?"

Finally she looked at him. "I might stay there for a few days. Peter... when you talk to me the way you did this morning..." she turned to face him. "It makes me feel like you don't love me. And it reminds me of my parents... the way they used to fight..." she covered her face in her hands as if she were about to cry.

He rolled his eyes. Not this again. "I am *not* like that," he said, turning to rummage through the fridge. Had no one cooked anything? Where was Teresa? He slammed the fridge and looked at her, arms crossed across his chest. "Now you just wanna pile on the guilt, huh?"

She looked at him again, blinking. "I'm just gonna go back down to the little house tonight. I don't wanna fight anymore."

"Fine! Fine." He shrugged his shoulders as if he didn't care. But when he watched her back retreating through the side kitchen door, he just had to ask her – "You'll stay here... won't you? Till we get the fire department open?"

She nodded, but her face was still sad. Her going to the little house, he could handle. Back to San Diego, no.

"Promise?"

"Promise." And she shut the door quietly.

chapter sixteen

Hope didn't plan to stay up till 2am painting. But once she started, she just couldn't stop. Normally she didn't love being alone, but something had changed once *Yeshua* came into her life. "This will be the place where I'll have some real good quiet time with You, Lord," she whispered into the stillness.

She had Bach playing in the background; that was one good habit she'd picked up from being around the Baileys. She'd traded some of the country music for classical. At least when she was painting. But when driving down those country roads, still nothing sounded better than Tim McGraw.

She'd dipped her brush in the red paint first. How had the artist in the children's book done it? Had he painted the bird first, or the snowstorm? She decided to start with the bird. She placed him in the upper left corner of her paper, clinging to a twig.

Having never seen a snowstorm, she decided to paint an autumn scene instead. *Paint what you know,* her teacher had said. That was one good thing about being here, in the armpit of the Midwest; it was so different. She could expand the boundaries of what she knew.

The tree that the bird sat perched upon and the swirling, fall-colored leaves began to take shape. Whenever she thought she got to the middle of her work on a painting, Hope always stepped back a few paces to take in the big picture. The tree and its three strongest branches had taken on the shape of an *E*. When she'd closed the little book with Brandon, she'd felt the Lord's still, small voice whisper to her heart one word: *Encourage.*

"Is that what this picture is about, Lord?" She decided to write it out on the top of the painting, so she wouldn't forget: *Encourage.* This was new for her, combining words with art. But maybe words were art too.

Painted words... spoken words... written words, she thought as she gathered up her brushes to wash them. Maybe the words she spoke to her family could be like art.

She thought she'd better start with her baby. She decided to write a little note to him in the sketch pad. Maybe she'd give all her drawings to him one day.

Dear Baby,
I am excited to meet you. I can't wait to see what color eyes you have, to hear your little voice, to hold you in my arms.
Love, Mommy.

She dated it and sat back, satisfied. But as she read it again, at the word *Mommy,* a lump caught in her throat. When would that word ever stop hurting?

She sighed and closed her sketchpad. Then she took Brandon's book and displayed it proudly on a windowsill in the living room. There was one more thing to do.

She went to the box that she'd brought in from the garage. It held a picture from their wedding that Peter had sent to Teresa before they'd moved here, and Teresa had had printed and framed. It was a photo of the two of them dancing together, Hope's dress swirling around her feet, Peter looking straight at her with shining eyes. She hung it up above the guest bed, every drive of the nail driving determination into her heart.

She would fight for her marriage. She would fight to speak words of life. She would fight for this family.

Hope woke up to a pounding on the door early the next morning. Too early. "Hmm?" she mumbled as she rolled over in her makeshift bed on the couch.

Peter opened the door. "Hope," he said, exasperated. "Time for church."

"Oh, right…" she sat up and put a hand to her head, not surprised to find a dull ache there. "We talked about that, didn't we? But, I was up really late last night, Peter…"

"You haven't been with me since we got here. Come on, let's go."

It was true. The first weekend, she'd rested up, trying to get over her altitude sickness and the shock of the pregnancy. The second weekend, Papa had been here, and she'd enjoyed the *Shabbat* service so much that she'd declined Peter's invitation to church on Sunday. And last weekend, she'd been so busy with the co-op…

"Alright," she said, swinging her feet onto the floor. "But Mama T better have some breakfast ready."

Peter smiled. "Crepes, tomatoes and coffee at your service, my dear."

When they pulled up to the parking lot, Hope wasn't surprised to see it filled with trucks; some of them lifted on tires that seemed as tall as her; some of them splattered with mud from hunting or off-roading or other hare-brained adventures; some of them unassuming, hard-working but not showing off. There was even a tractor or two in the parking lot.

When she walked in, she wasn't prepared for the formality. A lot of the men and women she'd seen in town were there; but they looked different in their Sunday best. Hands were shaken, greetings exchanged; then, when the pastor took the podium, everyone sat down quietly.

She sat stiff in her seat, not knowing what to expect. "Church," the pastor began, "I'd like to begin by praying for our farmers. A lot of people in this area were hit by this week's hailstorm. Let's bow our heads together."

Hope obeyed, quietly, like everyone around her, and listened to the prayer: "Dear Lord, we know that You are sovereign over the weather and all things. We also know you love and care for each farmer in our area, and for his family. Some of them are struggling to make ends meet, Lord. We pray that you provide for them, and give them strength to take care of their land and animals. In Jesus' mighty name, amen."

"Amen," everyone repeated. Hope exhaled. She had never heard a rabbi pray for local farmers before. It was funny at first —

but when she'd realized he was serious, it was kind of refreshing –
the way everyone here cared for each other.

On the way out, Jackie stopped her. She'd only met the young
woman once, on her co-op route; but the woman didn't just greet
her, she wrapped her in a warm hug. Something about her new
friend's sincerity brought tears to Hope's eyes.

"Hey, I heard you're pregnant!" Jackie exclaimed. "You gotta
come to our mom's group. Here, I've got the information all written down." Jackie pulled a little card out of her purse; Hope took it
and thanked her.

"Hey. You wanna go for a drive?" Peter came up and smiled
at Jackie, then put his arm around Hope. This time she didn't
pull away.

"Sure."

It only took them five minutes to make it over to Long Lake.
Hope breathed in the atmosphere. It was nice to see the trees. The
water. It reminded her of home.

"Here?" Peter gestured to a bench that looked out over
the water.

"Sure." She shrugged and sat down beside him. She was short
on words today.

"Hey. I'm sorry… that I yelled at you yesterday. You're right. I
shouldn't have blown up at you." He nudged her with his elbow. "I
told Mom about it, and she… well, she reminded me that I have to
treat you different. Because you're not like us."

Hope wrinkled her brow. She wasn't sure how she felt about
Peter discussing their marriage problems with his mom. Or how
she felt about being the "different" one. But at this point, she'd
take all the help she could get. She thought for a moment, then
nudged him back. "Ok. I forgive you."

They both looked out over the water. "I know it's not an excuse," Peter said after a moment, "But I've been worked up.
About Dad's heart attack. I guess… I sort of feel responsible." He
shifted in his seat and looked down at his boots. "Like I shoulda
been here…"

"You mean… he might not have worked so hard, if you'd
been here?"

He nodded, his mouth set in a thin line.

Her first instinct was to brush it off and say something practical, like *it wasn't your fault* or *he was responsible for his own choices.* But instead, she just watched the water for a moment. Underneath the surface, somewhere beyond what she could see, there were little fishes swimming around. They were hidden, like Peter's goodness sometimes was, but they were there. She took a deep breath and said, "I can see how that would burden you." He looked right at her for the first time that day. She turned to face him, too. "But I've watched you with your Mom. And I've watched you with my Dad. And I think you should know that you're a good Son."

She watched him as he thought for a moment. His shoulders straightened up a little. And the darkness that she'd seen descend upon his face after the hailstorm was suddenly no more.

When they pulled up the drive in Hope's green truck, Peter wasn't surprised to see Teresa hunched over her work in the garden. He knew from experience that his mother never stopped working; not even to grieve. "Let me go see if I can help her," he said to Hope as he turned off the engine and jogged over to the garden. She nodded and headed inside.

"Mom? What are you doing?"

"I'm trying to rescue the last of these vegetables. Whatever wasn't ruined by the hail. *Tsk.* Such a waste. Such a waste." She threw down a handful of greens and looked at him, her face red but determined.

"Let me go change. Then I'll come back to help." She looked relieved at this idea, and he trotted off towards the house. He didn't like to see his mom working alone.

When he'd changed and come back downstairs, Hope was waiting for him in the kitchen and ready to help. "Let me start by bringing water for everyone." She raised her eyebrows and showed him the tray she'd made; a pitcher of cool water with lemons, and three tall glasses.

"Thanks." He filled a glass and downed it before they headed outside.

"Where should we start, Mom?" Hope asked Teresa as she hunkered down beside her.

"Here. At the tomatoes. Some of them were protected by the leaves of the plant and by this cottonwood here." Teresa gestured to the tall tree that stood guard over her garden, but didn't look at Hope as she spoke. She was working too hard to pause for eye contact. "Even if they are bruised... we can cut off the bruised bits and can them. Such a waste." She made a *tsk*ing sound again and finally turned to Hope. "You have to understand where I came from. In the village... where I grew up, as a child... we did not waste *anything.*"

Peter inspected tomatoes and handed any salvageable fruits to Hope, who presided over the garden basket. "You're right, Mom. It is a waste." He checked another tomato, and discarded this one, then mumbled under his breath, "Dad would be crushed if he were here to see this."

Hope looked at him then, a little funnily.

Hope and Peter went back up to the kitchen, before Teresa – though her work clothes were drenched in sweat, she wasn't ready to quit yet. They'd start preparing lunch and boiling water to peel the tomatoes. "So – you comin' back up here tonight? You want me to help you move your stuff?" He asked her, coming up behind and putting a hand on her back.

She turned towards him, a slight smile on her face. "I was thinking. What if we moved to the little house together?"

He stared at her blankly. "The little house?"

"The little blue house."

"I know which one you mean. But why would we do that?"

"Well... no one's using it, right? Do you think your mom would mind?"

"No... but why?"

"I just thought... it could be a good place for us to start being our own family. You know," she patted her belly protectively. For the first time, he noticed that it was softly starting to round under her shirt.

He tapped a finger on his chin. "Are you... are you nesting, Mrs. Bailey?" He asked, giving her his most charming look.

She looked around as if confused. "Mrs. Bailey... huh? Who, me?" She pointed a finger to her chest in mock surprise.

"Yes, you." He pulled her closer to him. "All right, Mrs. Bailey, if you want to move to the little house, then we'll move to the little house. Anything for you."

She turned back to the sink where she was rinsing tomatoes. "And I mean... it's only two months." She looked around the corner at the hanging wall calendar. "Rob said the Fire Department should be up and running in October, right? But I'd rather make a home with you for two months in the little blue house, than be stepping over other people all the time."

Peter jumped when his mom came in the side door. What would she think about them moving to the little house? And if he was this jumpy about moving 100 yards away, how would it feel when the time came to take Hope back to San Diego?

The first stop on their co-op route that Saturday was Rob and Gina's. Gina helped Hope with the organization part of the job; but deliveries were up to Hope. It felt good today to have Peter beside her. It felt right. "Thanks for coming with me, Babe," she turned her eyes from the road to smile at him a moment. He was tired from work; but he was here.

"Is it just me... or are the fields around the farm getting greener?" Hope asked as she set the basket of overflowing vegetables on Gina's kitchen island.

"Maybe," Gina leaned against the counter, her baby on one hip and a cup of coffee in her hand. She tipped her head and thought for a moment. "Could be that hailstorm was actually good for the surrounding fields. When the ice melted, it would have watered any grass that was there."

"Hmm." That made sense. Whatever had caused it, it had been nice to spot some blades of green among the blackened fields on the way over here. She absently stirred cream into her coffee – just a small cup – while she watched Peter bouncing baby Brandon on his lap. He was going to be such a good dad. "Where did the fire start, anyway?" As she asked the question, she realized: she should know this already. She should know more about Peter's town, about Peter's life before she'd come into it.

Rob gave Peter a strange look. Something passed between them. "Well... it started in our barn."

"In your barn?" Hope asked, shocked. She'd had no idea.

Gina gave a sad nod in assent.

"But if it started there... then what happened? What started it?"

"Well... we don't really know." Rob took over the conversation as he unloaded Gina's produce. Hope didn't notice Peter walking out until she heard him slam the door. Rob went on, unphased by Peter's sudden exit. "It was an older building. Probably it was electrical."

Hope wrinkled her nose. She wasn't a firefighter, but she knew that back home, a fire this big would've warranted an investigation.

Analytical Gina read her mind. "If there'd been any casualties, experts would've come from one of the bigger cities to find out what caused it."

"Yeah. Thank God there were no casualties." Rob agreed, storing broccoli and salad greens in the fridge.

"Hey, where do you think Peter went?" Hope asked, gesturing towards the door.

"He's been exhausted from work lately. Here, sit down, finish your coffee. Let's give him a minute to chill."

"I would... if I didn't have Miss Hazel's fresh milk in my car. Thanks, guys." Hope hurried out; when she got to the car, she found Peter asleep in the passenger seat. He must be exhausted from work, like Rob had said. She'd let him rest.

After she'd made all but one delivery, she turned around and started to head back out of town. Peter was still sleeping. She spotted a yard sale and pulled over. Maybe she'd find a crib or a rocking chair for the baby. The thought made her put a hand on her belly instinctively. As excited as she was that this baby was coming, she didn't feel ready for him at all.

The sun was high in the sky now; she wanted to let Peter keep sleeping, so she pulled under a tree for shade. "Be right back," she whispered, just in case he could hear her.

She had a little cash in her pocket that Mrs. Anderson had

given her as a tip. She'd refused and refused; but the older woman had insisted. "If you're going to be delivering my groceries," she'd said, "the least I can do is give you a little gas money." Hope hadn't wanted to admit how badly they needed it, and had just given the woman a little kiss on the cheek, thanked her, and pocketed the ten-dollar bill.

Now, as she looked around at the homemade goods, it was burning a hole in her pocket. She nodded to the homeowner, a woman she hadn't seen before, and made her way to a pile of paintings. One painting stood out to her: a field of corn waving in the breeze with a windmill standing tall. The sunset behind it. Over the top were scrawled these words: *"The boundary lines have fallen for me in pleasant places; surely I have a delightful inheritance."* ~Psalm 16:6. It was so perfect. So Nebraska.

"So *Peter*," the woman said as Hope brought up the painting to purchase it. She tipped it back and clucked her tongue. "You know, he was in such a fit to shake the dust of this town off his feet. He was bound and determined to take his guitar and make a different path. A different life. A different everything."

Something the woman had said stuck in Hope's mind. "Peter plays guitar?" She asked, surprised.

But the woman was making change for Hope and hadn't heard her. "I'm sure glad that inheritance brought him back. Brought the Baileys back together. And it brought you here, too, I understand."

Hope nodded and took her painting. As she stared at it, she could imagine a young woman running across that field under the wide open sky. Was that how Teresa had felt when she'd first met Peter's dad and come here? Grateful just to have a piece of land, grateful to have a home? She went back to the car, eager to show Peter her find.

Peter woke up suddenly as Hope tried, unsuccessfully, to be quiet about sliding the painting into the seat behind him. "Wha – what are you doing?" He asked, disoriented.

"Putting my painting in the car," she answered simply. "I didn't want to lay it in the bed of the truck. It might blow away on those gravel roads. There. Is that ok?"

She'd tilted his seat forward gently. He grimaced a little but nodded. "You painted something while I was asleep?" He was still disoriented. Late-night shifts at the Kmart did that to him.

"No, silly. This is a yard sale," she gestured around her as she pulled the car out of the drive.

Their last stop was Miss Hazel's. Hope always saved it for last; partly because it was close to home, and partly because she loved the view. Miss Hazel's insurance had paid for her to rebuild her ranch. It wasn't what it used to be, she'd told Hope. But Hope still liked to walk through the lush green pasture that she'd been able to grow for her dairy cows. She liked to nuzzle the cows' soft noses, at least the ones who would indulge her. It gave her a glimpse of what Peter's life had been like – and what Teresa's could be like, again, if they could ever get ahead on their bills and actually start saving.

The sun was setting when she pulled up Miss Hazel's drive. She would never get over these sunsets. "Hi, Hazel," she crooned as she slammed her pickup's door and Peter flinched. He climbed out of the car to help her with the basket.

"Well? What did they say about my cheese and butter?" Miss Hazel wanted to know, as she grabbed the cooler she'd given to Hope to haul her dairy products in, and led the way back up to the house.

"Oh, they were so impressed. You should've seen Mrs. Anderson freaking out over the butter. 'This looks just like June butter,' she kept saying, and she turned it over and over. It was the cutest thing."

"Oh. I don't need any thanks." Hazel waved her hand over her shoulder as if to brush off the compliment. "It is kinda nice, though," she admitted sideways to Hope.

"I know! It is! Everybody's so thankful. I'm glad we can do this. Thank you… for helping." Hope set the basket down on the kitchen counter and folded her hands, waiting for instructions.

"Tell you what," Miss Hazel said, hands on hips, "Why don't you two set out on my front porch a minute. I'll bring some iced tea. It's hot out, but the sun'll be setting… it'll be worth it."

"Ok. Thanks." Hope turned to put a hand on Peter's arm, but he was already outside.

She sat down next to him. "What do you think? About the sunset?" She asked as she settled into a pillow, trying to rest her back. It was starting to get a little achy lately.

"It's nice," he spoke quietly, and took a deep breath. Then, for the first time that day, he smiled in her direction and took her hand.

When Miss Hazel returned with her lemonade, her husband held the door for her. Peter stood to shake Roger's hand. That was one thing she loved about him; the respect he always showed for his elders, for his community.

Something more than respect was growing in Hope's heart for the community of Orion. As she watched the warm sunlight bathe the faces of her new friends, she knew what it was. Love.

Hope heard Gina's voice hollering about something from outside the front door. She gathered up her paintbrushes and headed upstairs; she could let Gina in, then wash them in the kitchen sink. When Gina came in the door, Hope finally deciphered what the hollering was about; Gina was singing, "Peach Day!" at the top of her lungs.

"What's all this?" She asked over her shoulder, brushes in water, as Gina carted in a huge box.

"Hang on. There's more." After Gina had set down the second one, then the third, she straightened and huffed with the effort. "Peaches," she exclaimed. "Three bushels of peaches."

"Bushels?" Hope was still distracted, drying her brushes.

"40 pounds each, so 120 total. Give or take a few."

"Wow, where did you get all this?" Hope asked, taking off her smock and coming over, picking up a ripe full fruit and turning it in her hands. It was heavy, firm but not too firm, and sweet-smelling. "Wow, they're perfect," she breathed, eager to take a bite.

"I know. I pick them up in Red Bluffs every August. There's nothing like summer peaches."

Gina went out to her car; when she came back with a huge pot and a bag of supplies, Hope asked, "Wow. But what are you going to do with all of them?"

"*We* are going to can them."

"Okay. What do you need?"

A few minutes later, both girls' hands washed and the countertops sanitized, they had a pot of water boiling, ready to blanche the peaches. "Now watch," Gina explained as she dropped five or six of them into the bath of ice water. She waited a moment, then lifted them expertly with a slotted spoon, then showed Hope how easily the skin slipped off.

"Wow. It's like… like when your skin peels off after a sunburn."

Gina made a face. "Gross."

"Where's your dishwasher?" Gina asked when they had a pile of peaches ready to go.

"I don't have one."

"Shoot. I forgot. We'll have to sterilize the jars by hand."

Once the jars were boiling lightly on the stove, Gina walked around a little, taking inventory of the house, drying her hands on a red dish towel as she went. "I like what you've done with the place," she said, touching the painting of the wheat field and the windmill that Hope had brought home that weekend. "Did you know we stayed here after the fire?"

"No. No, I didn't."

"Well, we did. But I never decorated. Guess I was exhausted from the pregnancy, and from working… But you, you just seem to get even more creative juices flowing when you're pregnant, don't you?" Hope smiled modestly; Gina just nodded approvingly at her. "That's good. Oh, you've got Brandon's little handprint on the fridge! How cute. And what's this? '*The tongue has the power of life and death, and those who love it will eat its fruit.' Proverbs 18:21.'* Hmm. Don't know if I've ever heard that one before. What made you put it up?"

Hope turned from where she was making coffee and sighed. "I guess… I've always known that words can destroy. I've spent so much of my life trying to forget the stuff that people have said to me." Gina sobered a little when Hope said this, and she realized that she hadn't really gotten this serious with Gina before. She tried to lighten up and said cheerfully, "So, it's good to realize that words can bring *life,* too. I guess that's why I put it up. I wanna remember to speak encouragement. To speak life."

"Speak life. I like that. Ooh, our jars are ready." Gina went to lift them out of the boiling water as the timer beeped.

Two hours later, they had their jars packed and resting on the counter beside the cookbooks; 20 quart-jars for each of them. "They're so pretty," Hope said, pausing to take a picture of all their hard work. Her fingers were scalded from lifting peaches out of boiling water and her back ached from leaning over the counter so long; but both pains were forgotten for a moment as she gazed at the sunset-colored globes that filled each jar.

"I like to ration them," Gina confided. "I open up a jar every Sunday starting in November. Anyone who tries to sneak peaches before that suffers serious consequences." She winked at Hope. "That way they last through March, and by then, we usually have fresh local fruit again at Farmer Joe's." She brightened. "Oh! Only this year, we'll have your co-op to look forward to."

Hope flinched inside. "Maybe you'd like to run it... after I go home?" She asked quietly.

"That's right." Gina's shoulders slumped a little. "You still planning to leave after the boys finish their work with the Fire Department?" She asked, even more quietly than Hope.

"That's the plan." Hope noticed her sister-in-law looked a little sad. "You ok?"

"Oh. It was nice to have a sister around for a while. Guess you can't blame me for hoping you'd change your mind." She stood quickly. "Well? Shall we clean up?"

Hope looked around the kitchen and groaned; the pot, counters, and Gina's tools were all covered with peach juice. The sink was full of the dirty water that had come off the peaches. She rolled up her sleeves and the two of them got to work.

Late-afternoon light filtered in through the cottonwood outside and fell on to the kitchen counter. Hope made a vow right then and there to always have a kitchen where the light filtered in. The few scattered clouds were turning pink; when she opened the window, she could hear the cicadas summoning the night.

"So. How're things with Peter?" Gina asked her as she handed her another tool to hand-wash.

"Oh. You know." Hope scrubbed her ladle a little harder. "One minute I'm the best thing since sliced bread; the next minute, everything I do is wrong. Do you ever feel that way?"

Gina nodded slowly. "Sometimes. But I think Peter is still struggling over his Dad-stuff. Rob had a better relationship with Jim, you should know."

Sometimes Hope wished Peter could just get over those issues; couldn't he let the past be the past? This was now. She was here. This was their new family.

She sighed and tried to remember why they'd fallen in love in the first place. "The funny thing is... I felt like he really loved me. Before, in San Diego. Now... I don't know. I can't remember the last time he took me on a date, or bought me flowers. I guess he just doesn't feel the need to pursue me anymore." She let the hurt show on her face; Gina was a safe place. "I really don't know if he even still loves me."

"Oh honey. I've seen the way he looks at you. He loves you." Gina looked at her sideways and clucked her tongue as she watched a few tears roll down Hope's cheeks. "Anyway, that's one thing the Bailey brothers *do* have in common. We could drop hints till the cows come home about flowers, and wine, and date nights... and they *still* wouldn't get it." Gina smiled while she said it.

Hope paused her drying and asked, confused, "Till the cows come home?"

"It's an expression. Haven't you heard it before?"

"No."

"I thought you were a horse person?"

"Yeah, horses, not cows!"

"Oh. Well then," Gina laughed a little. "'Till the cows come home,' is an expression. It means, 'For a really long time.' As in, it takes a really long time for the cows to come home. Does that make sense?"

Hope sighed. "If you're saying, it's going to take a really long time for Peter to start acting like the guy I fell in love with again, then yes, it makes sense, but no, I don't like hearing it."

Gina just chuckled and turned off the sink. Both girls stood back and admired their work. The kitchen sparkled; it was cleaner than it'd been this morning.

Hope went over to the boxes; each still had one layer of peaches left in the bottom. "What'll we do with these?" She asked, picking one up, thoroughly tired of the sight of them.

Gina smiled, putting her apron back on. "Pie."

Orion's kids were filing down Main Street in their costumes, covered with snow coats and ready to visit the local businesses for their yearly candy supply, as Peter turned Hope's pickup down the street. Whether they were cute or not, and who was there, Peter didn't notice. His eyes were only on the section of road in front of him, his knuckles white on the steering wheel.

He'd failed yet again. How was he going to tell her? She was so anxious to get back to San Diego. It wasn't his fault that the Fire Department opening was going to be delayed again. But she would see it that way. She would blame him. At least she was good at something. Blaming him.

"Hope!" He hollered in the direction of the house after he slammed the door on her truck. She came out the door, her smock still on. Couldn't she find something more productive to do than painting all the time?

He propped open the hood to reveal the truck's engine. "Could you get my tools from the garage at the big house?"

She looked at him and the car, questions in her eyes, but didn't say anything. When she came back with the toolbox, she asked quietly, "What's wrong?"

"Car wouldn't start. I had to get a jump just to get home. The guy who helped me said I could clean out the battery plugs..." He grunted over the engine, not knowing what he was pulling.

"Do you know how to do that?" She asked, wide-eyed.

"No." He slumped against the truck. "No, I don't."

Hope cocked her head, like she was thinking. "But your dad... I thought he worked on all the cars and tractors. Didn't he know how to do this stuff?"

Peter scoffed. "Yeah. But he didn't have time to teach me. He wouldn't even let me watch. There was always more work to do."

A look of knowing came on Hope's face; then she stepped over to him and put a hand on his arm. "We can fix the truck later," she suggested. "I don't have anywhere to go today. Let's go inside and get a cup of coffee first."

He followed her; but not before he'd landed a well-aimed kick at the front tire, and thrown some choice words at it too. He saw Hope wince; he knew she was sentimental about this old truck.

Once they were in the kitchen and the coffee pot was gurgling, he decided this was as good a time as any to tell her about the delay. "You might as well know," he spoke as if he were talking about the weather, not their future. "The opening has been delayed again."

She turned around from where she was washing dishes in the sink. Couldn't she do that ahead of time? So that everything would be ready when he got home? "What do you mean?" she asked.

He rolled his eyes. "I mean, the building's not up to code. Actually, the bathrooms aren't up to code, of all things. Before we can get the funding to advertise for staff jobs, we have to get it up to code." He leaned against the counter, watching her reaction.

"How long do you think the delay will be?"

"At least a couple weeks. Maybe more."

She nodded slowly, saying nothing.

"I know you wanna get back to San Diego. But I'm doing the best I can." He slammed a hand on the counter. "It's not my fault the fire department happens to be in a 100-year old building. Like this old house..." he looked around, disgusted.

"Peter." She held up a hand as if to stop his tirade. "I want you to know that I see that you are working very hard. You are trying your best to provide for us, and to help the town. I am really proud of you."

He stared at her, his sails deflated, the wind fully taken out of them.

⁓

"And I'm thankful for you." When Hope had finished what she had to say, she let her hand rest by her side, and walked over to her husband. His shoulders slumped as if he'd been defeated; but his face was softer, somehow. She went to his arms; he wasn't the grumpy bear he'd been a few minutes ago. He was Peter, the man who'd danced with her, again.

"You really think that?" He asked as he ran a hand through her hair.

She looked up at him. "I really do." She put a hand in his and led him to the opposite counter. "Now. Here's your coffee. Let's go see about that battery. I've cleaned out batteries before."

He stopped, mid-sip, stunned. "Your dad taught you?"

"No." She smiled. "Heidi."

"Oh." He downed half his coffee, then set the mug down and rolled up his sleeves. "Well, I am ready to learn from you, sensei." He grabbed coats for both of them from the hook by the door, then before he helped Hope zip hers, he leaned down to kiss her belly. "You've got a smart mama, yes you do," he said.

Hope's shoulders straightened as she blinked back tears. It was the first time he'd addressed the baby directly, or kissed her belly. She kissed him on the top of the head before he stood back up.

"Brrr... it's freezing!" They both hurried up to the truck; somehow, in the last fifteen minutes, it had gotten even colder.

"Shoot," he grumbled. "I shoulda parked it in the garage. Let me see if it starts, and we can work on it there." They were both relieved when the engine rumbled to life, and he headed up to the big garage. But Hope stood rooted to her spot.

"Snow!" She yelled excitedly. She held her hands out to try to catch a flake; she stared up at the sky, watching them fall.

He sauntered down to see what all the fuss was about. "You act like you've never seen snow before, Mrs. Bailey."

"That's because I haven't!"

He whistled under a breath. "Well, let me tell you. Nebraska snow is no ordinary snow. They're predicting three feet by morning."

She twirled slowly under the dancing flakes. She remembered a time when she was a kid; the first time she'd noticed the way the sunlight dappled as it filtered through the leaves of the big tree in her parents' front yard. She was four years old; and she'd lain down on the grass, just to watch the light trickle down and tickle her belly, her face, her toes. "Three feet? Is that enough to make snow angels?!" She'd always wanted to make a snow angel.

"Yeah. It'll be enough to make snow angels." He seemed like he was laughing at her. But she didn't care.

The next morning, Hope woke up to a world of white. She didn't rush out to make snow angels, but sat by the window instead, savoring her tea and the view.

This had been the last week of her food co-op. She'd delivered kale, butternut squash, and a last heap of potatoes; and that had been it for the year. She'd wondered what she would do with herself now that it was done. Looking out the window, she knew the answer: she would enjoy the snow.

Everything was so quiet; the world seemed hushed under the blanket of snow. Like even the squirrels and birds were afraid to disturb the beauty. Nothing else was visible – not the dirt, not the potholes in the driveway. Every imperfection was perfectly covered in white.

Peter got off work at 10pm and went out to Hope's old truck. He was sick of driving it; sick of his job; sick of all the delays with the fire department. He was ready to take Hope home, where she belonged.

He checked his phone. *Do you think we can hang out when I get home?* He'd asked. No answer. He threw the phone down on the front seat in dismay. She couldn't even take the time to respond to his texts.

On second thought, he picked it up again and looked at the screen. He had a missed call from Sheldon. "You call me anytime you need me," Pastor Sheldon had told him after his hasty move. So the two men had set up a standing weekly phone chat; every Tuesday at 9:00 Peter's time, 8:00 Sheldon's time. He was an hour late. But if ever he needed help, it was now.

Sheldon picked up on the second ring. "Hello?" Good. He didn't sound tired at all.

"Sheldon? It's Peter."

"Pete!" Somehow the nickname didn't bother him so much coming from this man. This guy who'd been there for him. "The wife and I were just talking about you guys. How's everything?"

"Not so good." Peter had learnt to be honest with this man. Even if he wasn't, Sheldon would see right through him. Saved time this way. "Aah, man." He rubbed his forehead with the heel of his hand. "I feel like all I do is work. Then when I get home... Hope's always exhausted. This pregnancy just sucks out all her energy." He got up from his seat and leaned against the side of the truck. The cold, bitter air suited his mood better than the stuffy confines of the car.

"Hmm," Sheldon just listened. Even though he was a good speaker and a wise man, he was a good listener, too.

"I just wanna spend some time with my wife. But with all her projects, and the pregnancy, she doesn't save any time for me. I don't know what's happened to her. I just want things back to the way they used to be. I feel like I lost my wife! I get *no* respect in my own home... no respect!"

"Peter," Sheldon interrupted. "Listen to how many times you just said the word *I.*"

Peter stood up straight against the car and thought about it. Three, four times?

"A godly husband doesn't think only of himself. A godly husband puts his wife first. Like Jesus would do."

Conviction started to settle in Peter's gut like a heavy stone; but he shook it off before it could make its home there. He had one more question.

"How is that gonna work – how will that make her respect me?" Peter exploded. "She belongs to *me*, not to her paintbrush, not to the co-op, not to her friends."

"That's where you're wrong." Sheldon's voice took on the tone of a parent correcting a rebellious child; normally a tone like that would have Peter hanging up the phone. But tonight he clung to the device like it was a life raft. "You're right that you both belong *with* each other; marriage does that to a couple. But you don't belong *to* each other. You each belong to Jesus. So I only have one question for you: how would Jesus love her?"

~

Hope slowly picked her way down the winding steps. But these weren't the steps to her basement, or to her sunroom. She knew because of the cold gray stone under her feet. She knew by the feel of the swirling fog around her that this could not be home. She knew by the feel of the silk swishing around her legs that this must be a dream. But she kept walking, down, down, down. There must be some reason why she was here. In one hand she held a candle. With the other she gripped the rail, and descended.

At the middle of the staircase she saw an outline. As the fog cleared, she could see that it was a stone wall, built high and thick around the castle. She was in a fortress.

Inside the castle wall was a garden. And in the garden was a family playing.

She kept walking closer, until she could see that the members of a family, playing with a big red ball, were a willowy woman and a curly-headed little girl.

She was still high enough that she could see beyond the walls of the fortress. And out there were wolves. A pack of wolves circling the walls. She heard a few of them baying out to each other, and saw others coming close enough to sniff the stones that held the walls. They kept trying, but they had no way to get in.

The woman and the little girl went on playing and laughing, oblivious to the danger outside.

When she came out to the courtyard, green and growing, alive with flowers and pretty benches and sporting a little table where maybe tea would be served later… the fog cleared completely and the sun shone through. The girl lifted up her hand towards the rays, as if to catch a drop of sunshine for her mother.

Should she warn them? Before she could decide, one of the big, gray wolves jumped up in front of her face and growled a terrifying growl.

She sat bolt upright in her bed, sweating and shaking. She must've been in a really, really deep sleep – the dream had felt so real. She lifted the alarm clock beside her bed – 10:30 pm.

She'd never be able to sleep again after that. So she pushed back the covers, pulled a hoodie over her head, and went out to the kitchen. She'd make herself some tea and toast. Maybe plan a new drawing.

She was just dunking her tea bag up and down, up and down – when the door slammed and Peter came in.

"You didn't respond to my text," he accused without preamble.

She blinked. "I was sleeping."

He grunted. "You look awake to me."

"Peter... I'm sorry if you texted me and I didn't see it... but that's no reason to get so upset." Peter had been like an over-stretched rubber band lately. Waiting for him to snap made her want to snap.

"I'm not upset!" He threw up his hands. "I just wanna spend a little time with my wife."

She'd been thinking this too, lately. About how long it'd been since they went dancing or just out to dinner together. He never asked her to do any of those things; she'd felt empty inside whenever she thought about Peter. She took a deep breath and wrapped both hands around her mug. Maybe this was a good time to share what had been on her mind. "I was talking to Anna..." she started, thinking if she made it about someone else's advice instead of all the troubles brewing right here at home, he might listen. "I was talking to Anna, and she said it's normal for couples to have a little slump when the baby's coming. But if you could just show me a little more love, then I would –"

"More love!" He exploded. "All I do is take care of you. And don't tell me what Anna says." He looked at her, that hard line back in his jaw. "She never had to live with you, did she?"

Hope stood up quickly. In a moment, all the hurtful words Peter had spoken in the last months collided together and fueled a fire in her belly. Though she trembled, she felt her spine straighten. Like it was suddenly made of steel. She took a deep breath. "I am a child of God," she said, louder than she'd ever spoken to Peter before. "And you will *not* talk to me that way." She turned on her heel and walked out of the room. She grabbed a blanket from the pile in the corner and headed down the hallway.

"Hey! Don't you walk away from me when I'm talking to you!"

She heard Peter yell from the kitchen. But she ignored him, closing the door to the sunporch firmly behind her.

She picked up, without really seeing, a few magazines with names like *Country Living* and *Country Woman*. She flipped through pages with pictures of lemon trees and pecan pies and advice on how to set up a proper picnic; all with trembling fingers. She'd never let herself feel angry with Peter before.

She pulled a pencil and paper out of the blue refinished coffee table-turned desk that sat in front of her. She drew a rough outline of the fortress she'd seen in her dream. She'd paint it tomorrow.

As she sketched, she wrote the word *Security* over the top, blending the letters in with the turrets of the castle. She deserved to feel secure. Too many times she'd let Peter storm her gates with his anger. Well, no more. As she sketched the stairs of her castle, she realized: all the words she'd told Peter before, words like *please don't talk to me that way* or *you're hurting my feelings right now*, had been like the mist around the castle. All those words had been so softly spoken that he hadn't even heard them. Tonight was the first time she'd spoken his language: the language of action, not words.

And it was the first time they'd ever go to bed without making up. She finished her sketch, then grabbed another blanket and hunkered down on the sofa, cold but determined. She prayed for him, but wasn't ready to talk to him. Not yet.

The next morning, she woke up to the sound of Peter slumping down on the sofa beside her and his whispered "I'm sorry."

The look on his face melted her. The clarity in his eyes told her he'd finally heard her. She rubbed her eyes, took the peace-offering coffee he'd brought, and leaned against his shoulder. "I forgive you," she whispered.

The entire east wall of the sunroom was windows. No wonder she'd been so cold all night. She shivered a little; but it was worth it, now, to watch the fields turn golden, then orange. "Wow," she breathed. "We should come out here every morning."

A moment passed before either of them spoke again. "Sheldon was right," he said, staring at the sunrise absently. "I've expected too much. I've *thingified* you."

"Thingified?"

"It's a word I just made up." He shrugged his shoulders. "It means I've turned you into a thing, in my mind. A thing that was made for my pleasure."

"Oh. You mean objectified."

"I like *thingified* better." He turned to kiss her. "Anyway... can we be friends again?"

"Peter, Peter, Peter." She rolled her eyes for dramatic effect. "I want you to kick a soccer ball in the garden with me. But you have to leave your wolves outside, ok?"

"What?"

"Never mind." She slid last night's sketch underneath the pile of magazines. "I need a refill." She stood to take her mug into the kitchen. "You want some?"

~

"Okay. Sure. We'll be there." Peter nodded into his phone, hung up, and turned towards Hope, "Well, there's some kind of announcement at the fire department. Rob says to meet him there in an hour. Can you come?"

She paused where she was layering tomatoes on top of mozzarella and fresh basil from Teresa's herb garden. Thanksgiving was just two days away. In the Bailey house, pre-Thanksgiving meals were just as big a deal as the actual show. She had never prepared an elaborate pre-Thanksgiving meal, let alone one with *caprese* involved. Her hand hovered over the table, trying to decide where this last slice of tomato should fit. "Can you go without me? I'm trying to help Teresa with dinner."

Peter shrugged and put away his phone. "Rob said to bring you."

She cocked her head. "I wonder why. They can't be finished early, can they?" The last delay had led to more delays; when they'd pulled apart the old bathroom, they'd discovered mold hiding there, and had had to replace the subfloor. Neighbors and friends had showed to help out with the painting stage; next week would come furniture. Rob had lost no time, after securing the city council position, in advertising jobs and interviewing applicants. It was all supposed to be finished at the end of next week; in fact, it better be. Hope looked at the calendar, where the last Saturday of November was circled in red. Inside the circle was written: *Ribbon-cutting ceremony at the Fire Department.*

"Definitely not finished early." Peter came to the table to help her place the last tomato. "I was just there this morning. There. Perfect. Like you." He placed a kiss on top of her head. He'd been a little more careful with her. Ever since the talk they'd had in the sunroom a few weeks back. She could tell he was trying to give her more space to paint. There had still been no flowers or date nights; but she knew he was busy. And as she told herself, she didn't need gifts or fancy dinners as long as she had Peter, himself – Peter, the happy-go-lucky guy she'd dated.

"Well... I wonder what it could be?" She wondered vaguely as she covered the caprese in plastic and put it in the fridge; as she breaded the chicken to cook it later; and finally, as she removed her apron to reveal the floral-print maternity dress Gina had handed down. It was a cold night; she grabbed a jean jacket from the hall closet and pulled on her old riding boots. She'd dug them out of the garage when the weather had gotten colder; just because she wasn't riding out here didn't mean she couldn't make good use of them. They came in handy when she had to go out to clean the chicken coop. She wiped them clean for tonight's occasion.

What could it be? Maybe they had a new applicant for the fire station that they wanted Peter to meet? But no, she wouldn't need to be there for that. Maybe there was some sort of problem that Rob needed help with? But again – why would he have asked Hope to come?

As she headed out the door to meet Peter at the car, she decided it must be that Rob needed Peter's help, and Gina needed Hope to watch the baby. That was the only logical explanation. She doubled back to the house and went down to the basement for her sketch pad and pencils. If they were going to be there for a while, she would need something to do; and little Brandon had been amused lately by gripping her pencils and scrubbing them across sheets of paper. She chuckled as she remembered how last week he'd gripped and scrubbed so hard he'd broken a few.

Grabbing her oversized tote from the hall closet, she stuffed everything inside, then finally went out to meet Peter in the driveway.

"Wow." Peter whistled as Hope walked down the driveway. "You look very... Nebraska."

"Why thank you," she ducked her head in a false show of modesty. "I'll take that as a compliment."

They chatted on the drive over – about how he'd been promoted to a shift lead at work, about how Rob had high hopes for a better corn crop next year, about how things were looking up for the farm in general. "Thank God," Peter said, "for Mom's sake. This farm is all she has."

"She has you guys." Hope looked over at him and smoothed her skirt.

"It's not the same." Peter shook his head. "When she came here from Italy – this was the place Dad took her. It's the only place in the States she's ever really been able to call home."

Hope nodded, trying to understand. She liked to imagine that she could call anyplace home. On those quiet sunset nights, she'd even entertained thoughts of staying in Nebraska – those nights when she could picture a curly-headed little girl or boy running across the open fields and into her arms. Yes, she could make any place home. But maybe it was different for Teresa. Different when you got older.

"I'm glad she'll be on a better path – you know, to rebuilding the farm – before you and I go home." She hadn't confided in Peter those fleeting thoughts of staying on the ranch. She didn't want to get his hopes up. Her heart ached whenever she talked to Anna on the phone, just as it had ached when they'd dropped off Papa at the airport. She longed to feel the snuffle of Pirate's nose on her hand again, and to walk down the barn aisle, surrounded by all the horses. Still, though – she thought as she looked out the window – there was something about these sunsets.

Peter whistled as he parked. Not only was Rob standing outside the Fire Department waiting for them; the mayor was there too. Not to mention a whole crowd of folks from the town. Hope looked around the parking lot, filled with cars, and noticed Miss Hazel, Jackie, her mother in law and Gina, even baby Brandon, among many others. She and Peter climbed out of the car slowly, hand in hand. "What's all this?" Peter hollered at his brother and Mayor Gunderson, who stood side by side, holding a gigantic pair of scissors between them. Hope noticed fleetingly that there was a big black truck behind them, a huge red ribbon tied around it.

"If you could just stand right here next to me, Peter. Hope." Mayor Gunderson commanded them with a ridiculous grin on his face. Then he held a megaphone to his lips. This town didn't have fancy equipment like outdoor microphones; they used what they had and they didn't want for any more. He cleared his throat before he began speaking.

"Peter. We have a surprise for you." Then he turned towards the crowd. "Fire departments are nice; but they are nothing without the hard work and dedication of our local everyday heroes." He lowered the megaphone and whispered, "That's you, Peter." Then lifting it again, he added, "As some of you may know, Peter was one of the most instrumental heroes of the fire that hit our town just over a year ago." Here, Mayor Josh got choked up. "He, Rob and their father, Jim – God rest his soul – risked life and limb to get patients out of our hospital. They were the ones who first spotted the fire, gave a valiant effort to put it out, called emergency services. Without them we might not have much of a town left at all." He cleared his throat again. "As you may further know, Peter's personal vehicle was destroyed beyond recognition in the fire. That beat-up old Camry you were driving – that was no car for a farmer. No offense, Pete."

For the first time in this whole exchange, Hope turned her surprised eyes from the Mayor to Peter. He was white as a sheet, and his mouth was set in that thin line that came when he was angry. "Did you know about this?" He hissed at her.

"No," she whispered back, answering honestly. What was the matter with him? Couldn't he see they were trying to bless him?

"We're sorry it took us so long, Peter. But we are finally able to replace your vehicle."

Hope's brother-in-law nudged her in the ribs, and whispered with one hand covering the side of his face – "That's why we had such a delay fixing up the fire department. We were diverting some of those funds to buy Peter this truck."

Hope felt hot tears coming to the surface and covered her face with her hands. Was this how kind these people were? How selfless? They'd bought him a *truck?*

Mayor Gunderson handed Peter the ridiculously huge pair of scissors. "Go on, Peter, you cut the ribbon. It's your truck."

Peter, arms still crossed over his chest, did not take the scissors. "No."

The mayor looked confused. "Aw, come on, Peter. This is no time to play modest." He laughed. "We just want to say thank you."

A few people from the crowd spoke up. Hope heard one young woman say, "Yes! He saved my mother that day."

Another man in a wheelchair came forward and added, "You young men saved *me* that day."

The mayor lifted the megaphone to his mouth again; he was determined not to take no for an answer. "Peter and Rob, you were both heroes that day. We are trying to take care of you as your dad surely would've done." A few in the crowd started clapping; then suddenly all joined in.

Hope watched Peter nervously. He was even whiter than he'd been before. He took a few steps backward, stumbling and almost falling in the process. She started in his direction to ask him what was wrong, but he held up a hand and roared over the noises of the crowd: "Stop it! Stop it, all of you." He waved his hands in a shushing motion. He didn't need a megaphone; his booming voice was heard by everyone.

"I wasn't a hero. Rob was a hero. My dad was a hero." He leaned forward, hands on his knees, as if he were trying to catch his breath. Hope stayed back, giving him his space. He recovered and stood. "I *started* the fire. Okay? I started it." His thumbs pointed to his chest and his voice, still shouting, cracked.

Hope looked at Rob. He looked as confused as she felt. But he was the first one to speak. "What are you talking about, Peter?"

"I was smoking, Rob. *Smoking.* That day, while I was stacking the hay. I dropped my cigarette." He spread out his arms as if playing at surrender. "So I started it. Go ahead. Cuff me. Take me to jail. I give up."

The crowd was silent now. Mayor Gunderson was the first to recover. "You're not making sense, Son. Slow down." He put a hand on Peter's shoulder. "And whatever did cause the fire that day doesn't cancel the fact that you risked your life to get people out of that hospital. You are still a hero, Peter."

"Do *not* call me Son! We went to *high school* together, Josh!" Peter wrenched free from his old friend's hand on his shoulder; then with equal force he wrenched the scissors out of Josh's hands. "And *I...*" he gave the tire of the truck a good whack with the scissors, "am *not...*" another whack, this time denting the bumper, "a *HERO!*" the third and final whack was aimed at the window, and it fell right where he'd aimed it, breaking the glass with a loud shatter.

Hope didn't notice that her own jaw had dropped a few inches, just like several others among the crowd that day. So it hadn't been her imagination. He had been hiding something from her.

Slowly, she turned to look out at the crowd. Teresa was watching her son, sobbing. Gina had an arm around their mother-in-law, and she was crying, too. She looked back to Rob, whose face now had a look of knowing on it. A horrible thought occurred to Hope. Had they all known? Had they been in on the lie?

She stared back at her husband, the man with the ridiculous scissors in his hand and the pile of glass around him, heaving from the effort and from the emotion of his speech. Another thing wasn't her imagination; he *did* have an angry streak. He had an angry, lying, cheating streak.

She stared at him and her life, her marriage, flashed before her eyes in a split second. Horrified, she ran, not looking back, to the car they did have, *her* car, where thankfully, Peter had left the keys in the ignition.

Promise or no promise, she had to get outta that town.

part three

HOME

"I am the vine, you are the branches.

If you remain in me and I in you,
you will bear much fruit;

apart from me you can do nothing."

John 15:5

chapter seventeen

The skies slowly darkened as Hope gripped the steering wheel and made her way towards Denver. She knew the route, at least for the first two or three hours, which would get her to Cheyenne. She glanced down for a moment at her phone. Three missed calls from Peter and two from Gina. Tears threatened to burn her eyes, but she huffed them away and turned the device off with one hand. She'd stay on the 500 freeway till the cows and cornfields gave way to buildings and civilization. Then she'd turn on her phone and her GPS.

She looked around at the expanse of nothing that surrounded her, where the light was slowly fading. Field after field after field. She allowed herself to feel excited about heading home. Home, where one cigarette couldn't burn down a family, where there were more people than cows, where her daily life wasn't dependent on the weather. Where the pharmacy sold medicine and little else… and where "Ope" wasn't some catch-all word that meant *excuse me, oops, no, don't do that,* and who knew what else.

When she crossed into the city, her pride melted into fatigue, and she had to stop to use the restroom. Her vow to give up coffee for the rest of the pregnancy was quickly broken.

~

Hope's heavy belly pulled on her aching back muscles, making her sure that her walk looked more like a waddle, as she carried her coffee back to the car. She turned on her phone; she needed the map now. More missed calls. She'd wait till she got to the airport to check them.

When she finally found the airport and parked her car, she hesitated a moment. A feeling of guilt wrapped around her — what if Peter needed the car? Then she realized that his feelings were the last thing she should be worrying about. He was the one who'd lied. He was the one who should be feeling guilty right now. Still, she took a picture of the parking spot under which her oddly-painted truck sat. Maybe she'd send the picture to Peter later. Or maybe she would stay in San Diego, and Papa would come get her car for her.

When she finally made it inside, she discovered that the earliest flight home would leave in two hours. Perfect. She had plenty to do to distract herself till then. She could draw, read, and people-watch.

But before she sat down to get comfortable, she decided to call Gina back. Somebody in the family should know where she was.

"Hope," Gina's voice scolded over the phone the second the line picked up. "Where are you?" Then her tone softened and she asked the question Hope wanted most to hear: "Are you okay?"

Hope's voice trembled a little. "No. No, I'm not. I'm going home. He lied to me, Gina. He lied to the whole town. I can't be around him anymore. I just can't."

The line was quiet for a moment. Then Gina spoke, her voice reprimanding again. "Don't you think that if you leave like this — you're just reacting the same way he would? You're not thinking. Get a hold of yourself, Hope."

Hope shut her mouth in shock. Gina went on. "You can't just leave him like this, when he needs you most. That's not what a farmer's wife does."

"But I'm not." Hope recovered and gripped her phone a little tighter. "I'm not a farmer's wife. At least, I didn't sign up for this."

"Fine, then. Go home. Running away runs in the family, doesn't it, Hope?"

Silence.

"Hope, I'm —"

But Hope was too stunned to listen anymore. She hung up

the phone before the woman she'd come to think of as *sister* could apologize.

Maybe Gina was right. Maybe she was running away. But then the voice called her gate over the loudspeaker, and it was too late to change her mind. Hope boarded her plane without looking back.

～

Peter pushed the heavy broom around and around, making circles in the dirt. It didn't make sense to sweep out an empty barn. He should be baling hay for cattle. Or better yet, slinging a guitar in California. He shouldn't even be here.

All because of one stupid mistake. His dreams had all gone up in smoke with the barn that night.

He should've known it wouldn't work to bring Hope out here. She didn't belong here. She'd stayed as long as she could... but she belonged in San Diego.

She'd been gone a week already. She'd called Gina once, apparently; Gina wouldn't tell him anything about that conversation except that Hope had been at the airport. Then she'd called the house to let them know she'd arrived home safely, but only Teresa had been there to talk to her.

She couldn't be bothered, apparently, to answer her husband's calls. What was he supposed to do, just wait? He pushed the broom harder.

"Whoa," the voice that sounded so much like Dad's it made Peter jump came from the open doorway. Rob coughed. "So much dirt in the air it looks like smoke. For a minute it looked like you picked up your old habit again."

"I thought about it."

Rob eyed him sideways. "Here. Let me help you." He grabbed the push broom and swept out the rest of the fall leaves that had snuck into the barn: Peter's excuse for sweeping. "Should we windex the windows, too?" He joked, pointing to the open-air windows.

"Ha." Peter was in no mood for laughing. He sat down in the corner, in the only stool in the place.

Rob leaned against the wall next to him. "Hey. I wanna apologize to you."

Peter didn't look up, didn't move.

"I shoulda been here that day." Rob spoke slowly. "I was out on a date with Gina. We were talking, and... and I knew you were here stacking hay. But I didn't want to leave."

"Rob..."

"Let me finish. I didn't want to leave. Even though something in my gut said I should be here to help you. Maybe it was my conscience. Maybe it was some kind of warning. I don't know. But I do know that, if I'd been here helping you that day, maybe you wouldn't have smoked in the barn. There. So I'm sorry."

Now it was Peter's turn to look at his brother sideways, and he noticed that Rob's shoulders were slumped. He looked gentler, somehow. Peter said nothing but offered a hand, and the two brothers gave each other a firm shake.

Rob went on. "And you know... so you were smoking. But how do we know that's what started the fire? It could've been faulty electrical, like the fire chief suggested. We just don't know."

"Fat chance." Peter shifted in his seat.

"The point is, there's no way of knowing." Rob extended a hand again to pull his brother up from his seat. "Now come on, Mom told me you haven't left the farm at all in a week. Dinner's at my house tonight."

Hope stopped in the San Diego airport only to rent a car, then decided to call Anna before heading over there. She'd see Papa, too — everyone, she hoped — but if she needed to clear her head, the place to start was with Anna.

Her cousin was surprised but thrilled to hear that Hope was in San Diego. She commanded her best friend to come over immediately — no detours allowed. But Hope couldn't bear coming empty-handed, even though her pregnant body was crying out for rest.

She pulled into the Safeway by Anna's house. She stopped and looked around when she entered; they'd reorganized everything.

She picked up a fall bouquet, pressed the flowers to her face, and inhaled deeply; the scent was nice in this sterile, changed environment. "Excuse me," she asked a worker who was passing by. "Do you know where I can find animal cookies?"

He turned around without looking at her directly. "With all the packaged cookies. Aisle Nineteen."

"Thank you. They're my nieces' favorite. They used to make a beeline for it when I brought them here, but it looks like you've changed things around..." Her voice trailed off as he walked away.

Suddenly she stood, alone with her flowers, and felt even more alone than she had in the airport. So small-town Nebraska had rubbed off on her after all. She had forgotten how impersonal people could be in Southern California. They were living life on a hamster wheel, as Peter had put it whenever they'd gone out and about together. They didn't take time to chat about the weather, or the grocery aisles, or animal cookies, with strangers.

She wiped stubborn tears from her eyes. She wouldn't cry in the garden aisle, not at Safeway, no matter how tired and lonely and pregnant she was. Instead, she marched over to Aisle Nineteen to pick up her nieces' favorite cookies.

When she walked in the door, Anna wrapped her in the hug she needed. Then, after all the necessary auntie hugs and the cookies were dispersed, she sent the girls outside to play. She directed Hope to the kitchen table where she poured tea for both of them. "You look so beautiful!" She gushed as she sat down next to Hope. "I mean, I knew you were seven months along now. But it's different seeing your baby bump in person."

"And you." Anna was due in just one more month. She put a hand on her lower back and shifted in her seat. It was another girl, Hope knew from their conversations earlier. "Do you guys have a name for this kid yet?" Hope raised her mug of tea to her lips and settled in her comfy chair. The last time they'd talked, Anna had been tight-lipped about it. She always did that till the decision was final.

Anna's look was full of meaning. "We're naming her Hope."

"Oh gosh." Hope hadn't meant to cry this early in the conversation, but found herself wiping determined tears from her eyes. "I don't know what to say."

"You don't have to say anything. It's a good name." Anna stood to refill both tea mugs. "Now. Tell me what you're doing here. Is Peter here too?" Anna craned her neck to look around the hallway as if looking for him to appear. "Did you want to surprise me?"

"Peter's not here." Hope took a sip of tea, knowing her tone of voice alerted Anna to the fact that more than tea was brewing.

"Uh-oh. Hang on." Anna got up to check on her girls, then sat back down. "Okay. What's going on?"

Hope sighed. "He lied, Anna. You know the fire that happened in Orion? In Peter's town?"

Anna nodded.

"He started it."

Anna's eyes were wide. "Whoa. On *purpose?*" She asked, wide-eyed.

"No." Hope held her mug a little tighter. "It was an accident. But still... he shoulda told me." Hope lowered her voice as if Peter were listening. She'd thought she was all cried out, but more tears came as she talked.

"Yeah. Why didn't he?"

"I don't know." Hope then spilled the story about the meeting that had happened outside the fire station; was it really just yesterday? When she got to the part about how Peter had yelled and smashed the window, Hope's shoulders hunched over and she could barely talk. "It was like... he was somebody else. And it's not just yesterday. He's been so angry lately."

Anna didn't say anything; just put a hand on Hope's arm. When she did speak, she said quietly, "Has he been angry with you?"

"Yeah. Just with words." Hope grabbed a napkin and blew her nose.

"Words can be destructive too," Anna asserted. "Remember that old saying we used to have in school? 'Sticks and stones will break my bones, but words will never hurt me'? I always hated it. Because words... they become part of you. They stick with you forever."

Hope nodded, and traced her finger on the design of her napkin.

Anna squeezed Hope's hand, then stood up to start breakfast. "Maybe it's a good thing you came. Show him where the boundaries are." She squatted down to take a small pot out from a bottom shelf. "I mean, first of all, I'm glad to see you, of course. But I'm also glad you're showing him he can't treat you like that if he wants to keep you."

"I didn't come here to teach him a lesson," Hope explained as she went to the sink to help her cousin. "The more I think about it... maybe I came home to stay."

Anna raised her eyebrows but said nothing.

"Seriously. I thought about it a lot. I don't belong there. Maybe I don't even belong with him." Her voice choked a little.

But that night, a feeling Hope hadn't expected tugged at her heart a little bit. She was missing Peter. She pushed aside the urge to call him. Instead, when she woke up the next morning, Thanksgiving morning, she thought about all the people she had to catch up with.

First was Esther. Her mentor would understand why she'd come, and be able to help her make sense of the pieces that seemed to be her life. Hope called the number she'd been calling weekly since she met the woman.

"Oh, you're here?" Esther exclaimed on the other end of the line when Hope shared her news.

"Yes, can I come visit this weekend?"

"Well, you can come help me pack."

"Pack? Where you going?"

"I'm moving. To Denver."

Hope let the shock settle into her chest. The woman who'd stepped in, in so many ways, to Hope's life was going to be moving just four hours from the ranch? She couldn't believe it. "Why... why are you moving?"

"I'm moving in with my sister. There's no sense in two widows living alone. Got a job lined up already. I'll be expecting to see you there, too, you know."

Hope didn't confide that she wasn't sure she'd be going back. Only made some brief plans to come over and help her friend pack that weekend. She hung up with Esther and went to bring her nieces into the kitchen to make cranberry sauce together. One of their favorite traditions.

"Ohh... he's kicking!" Cora and JoJo followed Hope's lead and each put a loving hand on her belly. Hope tried to freeze the moment in her memory, and silently prayed that she'd always remember how it felt – this little life moving inside her. "Somebody's anxious to come meet you all."

∼

When the meal was ready and the family was gathered around the table, Jake blessed the food, then turned to Hope and asked, "So, what brings you home?"

Hope looked around the table at the multitude of cousins and nieces and nephews, then answered, "I just missed you guys." She couldn't bear the whole family knowing the truth about the fire.

But later, while they were watching the kids play games in Anna's living room, Hope decided to spill the beans to Jake. Maybe he would have some insight. She started by telling him about the rebuilding of the fire department, then when she mentioned Peter's confession, Jake almost spilled his cup of coffee. "And they didn't arrest him on the spot?" He was shocked.

"No – no," she stammered. "I don't think it works like that." She thought for a moment. "I mean… there were no fatalities in that fire. A lot of property damage… does that translate to jail time?" The possibility of Peter's being arrested hadn't even crossed her mind.

"Whether it does or not… he could still face an alarming number of civil suits." Papa, who'd been listening off to the side, joined in the conversation now.

Hope thought for a moment about the way the people of Orion were. A dozen scenes flashed through her mind as she gazed into the fireplace. She pictured the story Peter had told her of the men who'd come to raise a new barn for the Baileys after the fire. The way Gina had dropped everything to take her to the hospital. The way that Farmer Joe and his wife had put off their plans for re-opening their market in order to help back the new fire department. Somehow, she didn't think suing a neighbor would be high on the list of priorities of anyone who lived in Orion, Nebraska.

~

"Spaghetti, huh?" Peter asked Gina when he ducked his head to enter through the low door of their war-era house.

"Don't worry. Mama T made the sauce." Gina spoke in her bossiest nurse-voice and commanded him to butter the garlic bread and set the table. "Your nephew's been waiting for you," she added when they heard Brandon catapulting down the stairs.

They sat down together, said grace, and dug in. "Sorry for cramping your style like a third wheel," Peter mumbled under his breath.

Gina set down her fork and looked at her husband, then responded to Peter: "Have you heard from Hope at all?"

"Nope." He didn't try to keep the bitter tone out of his voice.

Gina took another bite and chewed for a minute before she spoke again. "I think you scared her, Peter."

"What do you mean?" He asked defensively.

"When you smashed that window at the fire station. You seemed really angry."

"But I wasn't angry at her! I was angry at them, for making me a hero."

"Or maybe you were angry at the fire. Or at yourself." Rob chimed in.

"I don't think it matters what you were angry *at.*" Gina cut in, putting a hand on Rob's arm. "You still scared her. Your wife deserves better than that. She's worthy of a little more self-control from you."

Peter cringed at those words and went back to his dinner.

"Hey, what about custody?" Rob, ever the practical one, thought of it even before Peter had. "She's due in like, two, three months, right? She can't just leave like that."

Gina raised her eyebrows and ticked off her fingers. "Nine weeks. And technically, she can, during pregnancy." She thought a minute. "Once the baby's born, they'll have to share. But Rob, it's too soon to talk about that. I'm sure they'll work it out." She gave Peter a look that was meant to be encouraging, but only served to remind him of Hope when she was trying to teach him something.

"You know what, I'm tired of working stuff out." He stood from the table and placed his plate on the counter a little more noisily than necessary. "C'mon, Brand-o, let's go play." He lifted the tot from his high chair.

"He's not even done with his —" Gina started, but this time Rob put a hand on his wife's arm to let her know this was not the time to worry about Brandon finishing his dinner.

Gina sighed as if she were letting it go. But when Peter carried Brandon to the living room, he could hear her say through the open doorway, "When is your brother ever going to grow up?"

Hope soaked up every pleasure she could all that first week and into the next; she played with her nieces, took them to gymnastics, visited the horses and resisted the temptation to lift her huge bulge of a belly up for a ride. She argued with Papa, helped Esther pack, even visited a couple old high school friends, until finally there was only one person left to see.

That Wednesday morning two weeks after she'd arrived, she waited till she'd helped Anna make breakfast and sent Cora up to get ready for school. Before Anna could take out her computer and start her work day, Hope asked, "Can you take me to the Island today?"

chapter eighteen

Anna drove; Hope looked out the window. So much had changed since she'd come here as a kid. Or maybe she'd changed. The palm trees still graced the sides of every street. The soft breeze still tickled in through the window. But its salty scent felt foreign.

"Have you called Peter yet?" Anna asked without turning towards her.

"I texted him. Just to let him know I'm seeing my mom today. He didn't respond." Hope looked down at her phone again just to be sure.

"Can't say I blame him," Anna spoke under her breath.

"Excuse me?" Hope shot back quicker than she'd meant to. She was tired; she was achy; she'd been excited about the idea of seeing the Island, seeing Mom, last night; but now that it was here, she just wanted to get it over with.

"I'm just saying. You're still a family with him. You guys are about to have a child together. You'll always be tied to him, whether you like it or not." Anna flipped on the turn signal and made a sharp left turn. "You can't just undo the choices you've made, Hope."

Hope sat up straighter. "He *lied* to me, Anna. He lied like Mom lied. He never told me the truth about the fire, just like I still don't know the reason why Mom left." Her voice rose like it never had towards Anna before. "Nobody tells me the truth, ever. Do you know how that feels?" She kept her hands clenched in her lap. "What am I saying, of course you don't. If anyone has a perfect family, you do." She was unable to keep the sarcastic tone from her voice.

"Hey now, that's not fair." Anna wrinkled her brow and tightened her grip on the steering wheel. "Just 'cause I still have my mom around doesn't mean everything's perfect. And I know you idolize Jake. Now, I know you do." Anna wagged a finger at Hope when she tried to protest. "But we have our issues too. Everybody has a story, Hope." Anna let her breath out slowly and quieted her voice. "Just because it's different from yours doesn't mean we have it easy."

"Humph," Hope grunted, folding her arms over her big belly. "Anyway, I thought you were on my side," she grumbled.

"I am. That's why I'm being honest with you." This was the closest the two cousins had ever come to a fight. Except for that time they'd fought over Barbie dolls, but that was a million years ago. Anna sighed and seemed to be trying to quiet herself down. "I'm just saying I know Peter hurt you. But God willing, there's a lot of life left to live. Don't you think you should give him a chance to reform? Don't you think you should try to work it out?"

Hope turned her gaze from her cousin to the window, shaking her head. They were coming up on the ferry that would, hopefully, take her to see her mom. She could only tackle one challenge at a time.

Peter had déjà vu standing in front of the fire department. Same town, same people, same old building. Two weeks had passed since the day he'd refused their gift – the truck. It was amazing how everything stayed the same here; Mayor Gunderson stood, again, with the giant scissors. Rob was here with him again. Gina and Mom were watching proudly.

And yet everything had changed. He'd since accepted their gift, knowing that it would change the future of the ranch, that he could leave it with Rob even if he didn't stay here. The mayor had been generous – everyone had – in not blaming him for the fire. The majority had held their tongues about it, and a few people even echoed Rob's sentiments. The truth was out, and he tried to be thankful for their forgiveness.

But it was hard to feel thankful with Hope gone.

He went through the motions; watched Josh proudly cut the ribbon, clapped at all the right times, and allowed himself to be led on a tour of the inside by Rob. This was the place where he'd be working full-time. The place where he'd finally make all the wrongs right. But he was numb inside.

He felt a tugging on his arm as they walked up the stairs to the second floor. "What, Mom?" He whispered distractedly when he turned and saw that she was trying to get his attention.

"She should be here." There was a tone of urgency in Mom's voice.

"Who?" As if he didn't know who she meant.

Mom *tsked*. "Hope. She should be here. Or maybe you should be there." Now it was more than urgency. Her tone was bordering on anger.

They were standing on the second level now, and the rest of the group had moved on to see where the firefighters would sleep. The windows were cracked open to help the new paint dry. Peter saw his mom shiver from the cool breeze and gave her his jacket. "What do you mean?"

"I mean what I said. Maybe you should be there."

"Mom, don't be ridiculous. The fire department is just opening and I've promised to help. And the ranch. I can't leave you all alone in that big house…"

"Oh, hush. I've been alone before. I can do it again. You've done everything you can do for us. There is nothing left to do at the ranch, with winter upon us. Rob can find other people to work here in this fire department. People with more experience than you," she made a show of wagging a finger at him. "Besides, Hope came here to fight for you. Maybe it is time for you to go and fight for her."

He sat down on a stool that had been left by the painters and put his head in his hands. "No. I can't go to San Diego again. I can't leave you guys here."

She did not sit down, but used the opportunity to look down into her son's eyes, like she used to be able to do a lifetime ago

– when he was the smaller one. "There comes a time when you have to trade your old dreams for new ones. Once we had a thriving cattle ranch here. But we do not have that anymore. You have your own family now. And that baby deserves a mother and a father. Go."

He stood now, hands shaking, knowing she was right and amazed that his plans could change as quickly as all that. He wrapped his mom in a hug as she said again, "Go, Son."

～

"You sure you don't want me to come with you?" Anna asked gently from the driver's seat. Both girls were still a little shaken from their disagreement. It was so unusual for them.

"No, I want to do this myself. Thanks, though."

"Okay, I have some shopping to do for a remodel anyway. I'll just hang out here in town. Call me."

Hope smiled weakly. She climbed out of the car, used her credit card to buy her ticket, and boarded the Dana Point ferry. She knew this area well but didn't stop to look at the beauty. Now that she was here, she thought only of her destination.

As the ferry bobbed up and down on the waves, she paced the deck. She laid down – for the moment – the question she'd held inside for over a year – what *had* sent Mom away? What mattered most now was getting to her.

When the ferry docked in the bay of Catalina Island, it was all she could do not to run over the folks in line in front of her. She didn't stop at the row of lockers; she'd rather carry her small leather purse. She didn't stop at the ice cream store where she'd licked mint chip off gigantic cones as a kid. She didn't stop at the glass-bottom submarine ride she'd always wanted to try. In fact, her heart pounded too fast to allow her to even notice these things. When she reached the row of modest houses she remembered, she prayed that God would help her find the right one.

She hadn't seen this place in ten years. But the little house, Molly's little yellow house, was still at the top of the hill, surrounded in front by a colorful garden. The home was smaller than Hope remembered.

Now that she was here, she stopped for a deep breath.

What if Molly wasn't home? What if she *was* home? Would she remember Hope?

Hope walked up the path, through the white picket fence, and fingered the rosebushes. Tiny, pink flowers. She didn't remember roses having been here. Or climbing vines, either.

When Anna had talked to Mara this summer, she'd said she was living here, at her old friend's house. But what if she'd moved? And what if Molly didn't know where she'd gone? Hope would've wasted all this money, and the time it had taken to get here. She pushed the fears aside and strode to the front door, then raised a hand to knock.

But before she could knock, the door opened and a surprised face stared at hers. "Hope," her mother said in shock.

"Mom." Now that the moment was here, Hope didn't know what to do. All the things she'd thought she would say flew from her mind; instead, she just wished that Mom would hold her. But that was out of the question; it had always been out of the question. Her hands tightened, then released. The only words she could find were, "Can I come in?"

"Sure," her mother said, standing up straighter and pulling the door open wide. If Hope had seen a flicker of vulnerability in her mom's eyes the moment she'd opened the door, it was gone now. Mom's old walls were up. Hope knew now how it felt to be safe behind your very own protective walls.

Mara beckoned Hope in to the sparsely furnished, but comfortable living room, where mother sat on one end of a deep blue sofa and daughter sat at the other end. Hope chose a spot where a shaft of light fell through the window. Then she looked at her mother a moment. Her hair was grayer than Hope had remembered.

It was Hope who spoke first. "So, how've you been?" She was unable to keep the sarcasm from her voice. Mara said nothing, just watched her daughter. Hope noticed her hands trembled a little bit. Desperate for something to talk about, Hope asked, "I don't remember that rosebush being there."

"I just planted it. Last year." Mara shifted on her side of the couch.

Hope *harrumphed,* noticing it was a sound not unlike the one Papa made. So Mara had had time to plant a garden, but not to call her daughter.

A sound came from where Hope remembered the back bedrooms being, breaking their awkward silence. Hope strained to hear a little, then she was sure. It was the sound of a baby crying. "What's that?" She asked her mom.

"Hmm?" Mara raised her eyebrows, pretending not to have heard it.

Suddenly, the broken pieces of the puzzle that was last year started coming together. Hope got the same feeling she'd had when she'd sat in a dark room as a kid, someone had lit the candles on her birthday cake, and warmth from the flames leapt up the walls.

Hope stood. "You know, I'd like to see the back bedrooms. Where I used to stay when I was a kid. Reminisce a little. You think Molly would mind?" But she was already walking that direction.

"No… don't," her mom pleaded. But there was no more pretending now.

When Hope stood in the doorway, her heart stopped in her throat. For there, standing up in a crib in the middle of the room, was a baby boy in blue footie pajamas. He was smiling, smiling and happy and perfect. "Ohhh," Hope breathed, then walked over to him.

Mara went to open the window – now that the little boy was awake, she let the light in. She came to stand by the crib with Hope, letting all her pride for her son wash over them both.

"Can I hold him?" Hope asked. Mara nodded.

Hope lifted her little brother out of the crib – he looked and felt as if he were about six months old. He gurgled and grabbed a strand of her curly hair. And pulled. Hard. She looked in his face a little closer. He reminded her of her own baby pictures. Except he was a little lighter. A little more delicate.

"Mom, is – is he the reason why you left?" Hope asked, handing the little boy to Mara when he reached for her.

Mara nodded.

"But Dad – he always wanted a boy. I don't understand why that would make you leave."

Mara sunk into the rocking chair that graced the corner opposite the crib. "I'm sure your Papa would've wanted David. If he had been the father." She let her worry-worn face rest atop her son's head.

"Ohhhh." Hope couldn't think of anything else to say.

"I wanted to protect you from all this. I didn't want you to know what your Papa and I went through, when I got pregnant." Mara's voice choked. It was as if, after being held back all this time, her words were all in a race to get out first. "I didn't know... I didn't think that you would miss me. You were always a daddy's girl." Mara hastily wiped a few tears from her cheek, then gazed at baby David with a look of such love that Hope wished she had her paints and easel with her. She'd capture their image forever. Had Mom ever looked at her like that? Hope felt certain that she had.

"Oh, Mom. I missed you."

Just then, Molly walked into the room. "Oh. Hello, Hope." Molly stood still, then seemed to notice that she'd walked into the middle of a moment. She came over to take the little boy from Mara. Molly was simple but confident, like always. "Come on, David. Let's go for a little walk outside, shall we?"

Mara sat across from Hope, quietly weeping, her face in her hands. For the first time, Hope saw the shame in her mother's face; had that been the real enemy? The reason why she hid?

When the back door closed, Hope's mind flashed back to a scene a few months ago, to when Peter had walked in the door early one morning, seen her crying, and just held her.

She took action before her fear could tell her not to. She crossed the room in three long strides and held her mother till the tears stopped.

This time, on the ferry ride back, Hope allowed herself to look out on the ocean. She allowed her eyes to feast on the way the sun sank down into it. Yellow, then orange. Now a low ball about to be swallowed by the sea.

She wrapped her arms around herself in defense against the cooling breeze. Much the way she'd wrapped her arms around her mother only three hours before.

She'd held Mara till the sobbing stopped. Then her mother had seemed so exhausted; they'd sat on the floor together. Hope had absently started stacking some of David's blocks. Mara had covered her face and quietly said the words Hope had waited so long to hear: "I'm sorry." Only they weren't earth-shattering like Hope had imagined they would be. Maybe she didn't need them anymore, now that forgiveness had already been given.

After they'd sat there on the floor for a few moments, Hope had put an arm around her mom, and noticed a thinness that hadn't been there last year. So she'd suggested dinner. They'd waited for Molly to return with David, invited her to dinner, too – Molly had politely refused – then the three of them, mother, daughter, and son, had headed to the crab shack that Hope remembered from long ago.

She gripped the rail of the ferry tighter now, and closed her eyes to picture the scene. It had felt good to tousle her little brother's hair while he sat there in his high chair. Her mom – their mom – had given him a bottle of milk and ordered him some mashed potatoes. Hope had insisted on paying for everyone.

Hope hadn't wanted to ask about David's father. It just came out over dessert. Was the man paying child support? Was he helping at all? Who *was* he? She had to know. "Where…" she coughed a little. "Where is David's father?"

Mara looked a little deeper down into her plate. "In jail." Her voice was quiet.

Hope just stared, wide-eyed. "Oh."

Mara sighed and put her fork down, but she did not look up. "There was a day when your Papa forgot his lunch, and I took it to him. At work. That day, in the parking lot, a man –" Mara's long, straight bangs hung in front of her eyes like her words hung in the air.

Hope's knuckles went white. She tried to help her mom. "Took advantage of you?" She whispered.

Mara's "yes" was so quiet, Hope wouldn't have been able to hear it if she hadn't already been straining her ears.

Mara was still sinking low in her seat, but she fidgeted as if there were more to tell. Hope guessed that, now she'd begun, she was eager to get the whole story off her chest.

"Do you remember that day, at the hospital? When I left?"

"Of course I remember." Hope almost snorted. It was one of the scariest days of her life. She sat up a little straighter in her chair.

"Well, that day… your Dad had me admitted. He wanted me to… I mean, we had decided… to get rid of the baby." Mara looked up now, but not at Hope. She looked at David, and the sight of the boy seemed to give her courage. Mother and son smiled at each other, and Hope saw the secret sorrow they'd both endured.

"Well, but then what happened? Why did you leave?" Hope covered her mother's hand with her own as if her comfort could tempt the rest of the story out. "Oh, I have to squeeze this little guy." She rose to kiss his chubby cheeks, and as she sat back down, a flame ignited in her belly. "But Papa… he… he really wanted you to have an abortion?" Hope felt dumbstruck. Her parents had always said they were pro-life.

"We both thought that… that the baby would just remind me of my trauma. And that I was too old. But then a man came to my hospital room, and he just sat with me for a while. I was too caught up in my own pain to ask, or to even care, who he was. After a little while he said something." Mara smiled a sad little smile before going on, then spread out her hands as if pleading with Hope. "He said, 'The baby's name is David.'" She sat back in her chair as if exhausted from her tale. "Something about that simple statement… I don't know… I just couldn't do it. Knowing the baby had a name."

"So you left." Hope sighed a little and stared at her plate. Both women spent a few minutes in silence, toying with their dessert but not eating it. "I think I might have seen him." Hope's brow crinkled as she tried to recall that day. "Was he wearing corduroy and… a little bit rumpled?"

Mara's brow matched her daughter's for a moment. Then she shook her head. "I don't remember."

Hope felt sure that the man she'd seen and the man who'd

saved her brother were the same. "Mom, that man was either a prophet, or an angel."

Mara shrugged. "I guess I'll never know."

"Maybe not, but you obeyed. And look at the treasure God gave you for your obedience." Hope gestured to the perfect boy who sipped his milk contentedly.

And a new truth dawned on Hope as her eyes flickered from the graying woman in front of her to the toothy-smiled boy beside her:

"Mom, you're stronger than I ever knew." She blurted out the words before she had time to overthink them.

"I guess I didn't know how strong I could be, until I had to be... for him."

"Write to me?" Hope's mom had held on a little too tightly when it was time for Hope to catch the ferry back. Hope had promised.

Now, under the light of the ferry's lanterns, the memory of her mom's tight embrace faded. Hope put down her things to stand at the rail, rocking one way with the ferry, then another. A dolphin leapt in the water before them. The low ball that was the sun faded into a thin red line on the horizon.

She resolved, right there, looking out on the water, that no matter what happened, she wouldn't keep this baby from Peter. She thought of the little curly-headed wonder she hadn't known about this morning. The beautiful miracle boy who still hadn't met fussy Grandma Leah, or determined Papa, or spunky Anna and her kids. A child deserved to know his whole family.

As she watched the last of the sunlight fade, she knew where she had to be.

Maybe she'd even plant some roses when she got there.

Peter stood in the barn, suitcase in hand. He'd wanted to say goodbye to the place before leaving for good.

Dad would've thought that was weird. Saying goodbye to a dirt floor and four high walls. But Dad didn't have a poet's soul.

If Peter closed his eyes, he could still see flames licking down the walls of the old barn. He indulged himself in the memory one more time, then opened his eyes quickly.

Mom was right. This was one inheritance he wasn't meant to take on. He'd signed his half of the property over to Rob last night, refusing to take a penny for it. "It's not worth anything right now anyhow," he'd insisted. Rob had shook his head and promised that Peter always had a place here.

A car horn honked; that was Rob waiting for him now, to take him to the airport. He turned from the place that held so many memories and got into the truck.

He was going to a new place, to make new memories. He might shirk off his responsibilities at the ranch. But he would never shirk off being a father.

"Hey man, pull over here," Peter urged his brother in Red Bluffs as they approached the parking lot with the old music store. "I've got a stop to make." An idea started to form in his mind. "Something to surprise Hope."

When the ferry finally docked, Hope was one of the last people to disembark. She walked slowly, this time, to Anna's car. "My house?" Asked Anna, munching a burger as she maneuvered out of the ferry's parking lot.

Hope thought for a moment. "Actually, can you drop me at Papa's? I haven't seen him since Thanksgiving."

Anna's eyes widened. "You're not going to tell him, are you?" She meant, of course, about David.

"No." Hope shook her head and stole a few fries from Anna's dinner. "No, I promised."

An hour later, Hope stood in front of the home where so many questions were still unanswered. She took a deep breath and knocked. It felt weird, but right somehow, to knock – instead of going right in. "Hi, Papa." Hope gave him a hug as he pulled open the heavy front door for her. He looked more tired than when she'd left those months ago. More tired, even, than he'd looked just two weeks ago at Thanksgiving. Maybe he was lonely too.

"Hi, Hope." He didn't ask if she was hungry. Didn't offer her a cup of coffee. Just sat down on the couch and waited for whatever she'd come to tell him. But then, he'd never really been the type for small talk.

She took a deep breath and sat down. She'd get right to it. "I wanted to let you know... I saw Mom today." Mom had asked her not to share about baby David. But she hadn't said anything about concealing her whereabouts.

"Excuse me?" Dad's voice remained quiet but his face turned beet red.

"I saw Mom today." Hope's voice rose in confidence. She'd felt nervous when she'd walked through the door, but not anymore. Doing the right thing could do that sometimes.

"Okay." He folded his hands in his lap and leaned forward.

"Well... don't you want to know where she is?"

"Sure." He shrugged his shoulders.

Suddenly there was an ocean of muck to slog through between the two of them. Muck that strangled her words. He didn't care. He truly didn't care. How could she share what mattered so much with someone who didn't care?

"She's on Catalina Island," Hope had to force out her words. "At her friend Molly's house. You remember Molly?"

Dad nodded and looked away. He sniffed. Finally. A show of tenderness. She decided to say what she'd really come to say.

"Mom is lonely, Papa. I think you should check on her."

"Oh. As if you're in the situation to tell me how to conduct my marriage." Papa scoffed.

That was too much. Hope stood to go. Before she headed out the door, she turned to tell him what she'd decided. "I wanted to let you know..." She sighed. This baby seemed to get heavier at the end of every day. "I've decided to go back to Nebraska. To try to work things out with Peter."

Papa eyed her belly, which was larger this week than it had been last week, and stopped grumbling long enough to say, "Hold on." He went into the kitchen, where she could hear him opening and closing drawers. She stood with one hand on the door and waited a moment longer. When he walked toward her, he held out a prescription pad with writing on it.

She read it quickly. "Thank you, Papa," she whispered. "Thank you."

Hope walked slowly to Anna's car, fingering the note. Suddenly she stopped and waved to her cousin to signal her to wait. If there was one thing she didn't want, it was to end up like her parents.

She felt her spine straighten a little as she pulled out her phone to call Peter. He picked up on the first ring.

"How was your visit with your Mom today?" He asked after their brief hello.

"Good. But Peter... I need to know something."

"O-kay."

There could be no secrets with him. No sweeping under the rug like Mom and Papa had done. No hiding her true feelings until it was too late. So she plunged ahead. "I need to know you're working on your anger."

"Yeah, I am."

His quick response took her by surprise. "No, I mean really working on it. Not just apologizing and then yelling again. Like, maybe we could get some help, or..."

"Hope, I know." He interrupted her, and even through the phone, Hope could tell he was exasperated. "God already told me I need to work on it. I joined an accountability group at church."

"Oh." She didn't know what else to say.

"Is that all?"

"Yes... I guess so."

"Ok. I hate to go, but I'm with Rob right now." His voice grew more tender. "Call me later?"

"Yeah. Sure." Hope ended the call and climbed into the car beside Anna.

"Everything ok?" Her cousin asked with a concerned look.

"Yeah." Hope put her phone away and showed Anna the note from Papa. "I'm going home."

chapter nineteen

Peter arrived early at the Denver airport. Eighteen days were too many to go without seeing your wife. His steps lightened at the prospect of holding Hope in his arms, at the idea of how happy she'd be.

But what if she wasn't happy? Or worse, what if she didn't want to be with him anymore? The recurrent fear stopped him in his tracks so suddenly that he sat down on an airport bench to think it over. Now that he had time to kill, there was nothing to distract him from the truth. She hadn't sounded like herself when she'd called to ask him about his anger issues. She'd sounded... distant. He needed help, and fast. He pulled out his phone to dial his mentor.

"You're coming?" Sheldon was delighted with his news. "Well, what a nice surprise! Babe, Peter's on his way to San Diego!"

"Hope's there, too." Peter held the phone close against his ear, trying to drown out the noise of the airport.

"Oh, great. Come over tomorrow!"

Peter paused for a moment. "We're not together." The words hurt. Then he explained that Hope had left him.

Sheldon listened without speaking, until Peter asked him, "How do I get her back?"

"I don't think you do."

It took a minute to register what he had heard. "Um... what?"

"I think... you show her love. Like Jesus would do. Let her decide if she wants to come back to you. Listen... I'd love to keep talking, but… Ruby! You ready? I'm taking my daughter on a date. Prettiest date in town. I'll catch you later, Peter, ok?"

Peter hung up the phone, deflated. He'd wanted a plan, not more waiting. He'd just have to find Hope and do his best.

For now, he reached into his duffel, his new purchase clanging against his back. He pulled out a notebook and pen and prayed for inspiration. Something to show her love.

~

Hope stroked Pirate's long nose. Her flight to Nebraska was scheduled for this afternoon. She didn't know how she felt about seeing Peter. But she'd made a promise.

"It's hard to say goodbye to you," she whispered as she scratched the area behind Pirate's jaw, "when I don't know when I'll be back."

Hope stopped to let one of the gray mares she'd trained snuffle her hand. Her visit to the ranch today was twofold; she needed to say goodbye to the horses, of course – but also, she needed to talk to Heidi. Had she ever thanked Heidi for teaching her all those years? Teaching her to feed, and clean, and brush, and train, and clean again…

She leaned against the tack room doorway and let her gaze roam around all the equipment that hung on the walls. All the work it represented. This was one place where she'd loved every minute, no matter how hard the work was. A picture started to form itself in her mind. She closed her eyes; she could almost see the paintbrush gliding across blank canvas…

She had to capture it before the image fled. She checked her watch. One hour before Heidi finished the lesson she was teaching. Plenty of time. She ran to her borrowed car to grab the sketch pad and pencils she always kept with her. And sat down on a stool by the tack room, where the light wasn't blinding; but just enough filtered in through the open barn doors to illuminate her page.

She drew thoughtfully, slowly, at first. Then she let the pencils go with abandon and formed the head and strong neck muscles of a horse. A girl of about 12 years old stroked the horse's chin, and she held a grooming brush in the other hand. Some hairs of the horse's mane, lifted lightly by an unseen wind, formed an *S*. She looked at it for a minute, then formed the word *Sustain* with the rest of the horse's mane.

Anything worth having was worth the work it took to maintain it. To sustain it. Horses, children, marriage. They were all worth it.

Writing out words with pictures had been helpful lately. Maybe she'd try writing out her prayers, too.

God, I know what I need to do now, she began on the next empty sheet, *but I don't know how to do it. I know I need to go back to Nebraska, to make my home there, alongside Peter and his family, at least for now. Maybe one day we'll come back to San Diego. But wherever we live... I want to take You with me. I want to carry Your presence inside me like a brightly lit lamp. I want to sustain this marriage. I want to bless my own little family, Lord, but I don't know how. I still feel broken inside. Like I'm doomed to keep making the same mistakes, to carry on the patterns. When will You ever show me how to say goodbye to the past and start fresh?*

Then it dawned on her.

Bless. Her heart caught in her throat. Could it be true? The word she'd been asking for... was the answer right here? She leafed through the pages so quickly she nearly tore one of them.

The images she'd sketched so carefully over the last few months confirmed her theory. Relief washed over her – God *had* heard her prayers – and with the relief came weeping. She clapped a hand over her mouth so as to not alarm Heidi's students; but her shoulders shook with silent sobs. She fingered the pictures gently, wanting to memorize each one.

This whole journey, this pictures-into-words art journey, had started with an image of a box. She recalled the day she'd dreamt of the box, and realized she couldn't compare Peter to Papa or Jake or anyone else. Underneath the box she'd written one of her favorite verses, 1 Samuel 16:7: *Man looks at the outward appearance but the Lord looks at the heart.*

Then the tangled weeds, and the *L* that meant *let it go*. At the bottom of the page she'd added, *and let it make you stronger.* She'd vowed to let the hurts and fears of her past be a propeller – one that would drive her straight into the arms of Jesus. She wouldn't be weaker because of her past. She'd be stronger because of it.

Next was the little red bird, the one that meant *encourage*. Then the fortress with the word *security* scrawled across the top. That one had been the hardest to learn, she thought as she sucked in her breath a little and remembered. She wasn't proud of how she'd left Peter. But it had been a necessary evil – even if only for a few weeks – to show him where the boundaries were. Now it was time to help him feel secure in her love, too.

Last came the drawing she'd just added today. *Sustain.*

Box.

Let it go.

Encourage.

Security.

Sustain.

The first letter of each word – together, they spelled out the word *bless*. These pictures she'd poured so much love into over the last few months – they weren't just hers. They were the Lord's. A love letter from Him, especially for her.

She could do this. God would be within her, and she could bless her family.

She was just putting away her sketch pad when Heidi appeared. At the sight of her, Hope forgot to verbalize all her thanks, forgot even to explain her plans – just grabbed her mentor's hand in a tight grip. She'd kept the key to Heidi's tack room in her back pocket all this time – but now she pressed it into the palm of her mentor's hand and whispered through tears – "I've already found the key I needed."

Hope walked through the San Diego airport a few hours later, shoulders back and head high. Her goodbyes hadn't been easy, but she would face head-on whatever challenges awaited her at home.

She flinched a little when she neared her gate and noticed a tall man striding toward her purposefully. She would've thought it was Peter, but he had a beard – and a guitar slung over his back. But when he came closer, she knew.

"Peter!" She hung back a little bit. Would he be happy to see her? Or was he upset over how she'd left? But she needn't have worried. He swooped her up in his arms just like he used to do.

When he set her firmly down on her feet, she asked timidly, "Peter, do you forgive me? For leaving?" She had to be sure.

"Of course." He raised his shoulders a little. "I don't blame you. I would've left me too."

She sighed with relief. Her life, her future – and the life of the little one growing inside her – were tangled up with this man. She clung to him gratefully.

But relief was nothing to the surprise that came next. Peter got down on one knee and opened up the guitar case.

"Peter, what – what are you doing?"

But instead of answering, he started strumming, and singing loud enough for all of gate 32B to hear.

Hope, you taught me to hope
So I'll make a life with you
Whether we're out in the middle o' nowhere
Or here, by your ocean so blue.
In the dryest desert
Or the greenest forest
It'll be a good life – with you.
Hope, you taught me to hope
You're God's gift to me
And I'd go a thousand miles for you.

His voice was a little bit crooner, a little bit country twang. Tears sprang to her eyes at the beauty of it. He put his guitar away and she went into his arms. Applause broke out around them and Hope hid her face in Peter's shoulder – every person sitting outside the gate had heard the serenade, and more than a few of them had risen to their feet to clap their appreciation.

"Peter – I've never heard you sing."

"I can still surprise you, can't I? Now, let's go home." All fears that she wouldn't want to be with him anymore had melted the moment he saw her face light up like it used to do. He shifted his guitar, took her hand, and started walking towards the exit and the San Diego sky.

Hope stopped in her tracks. "No, Peter. Not that home." She

pulled out her boarding pass to show him. It was a one-way ticket to Denver. "See? I can surprise you too."

The look on his face was brighter and cheerier than Mrs. Anderson's had been when Hope had brought the June butter. "But Hope.. are you sure?" He asked. "I meant what I said in the song… I'll live anywhere with you. Your life is here – I can be here too." He held both of her hands in his, entreating her. "Really."

"I know you would." Looking in his eyes, Hope felt certain he really would live anywhere with her. She closed her eyes a moment and took her time answering his question. She pictured the bright green road sign that would welcome her when she crossed the border into Nebraska, and the message it bore – "The Good Life." She pictured the cornfields waving under a big blue sky, she saw herself canning with Gina on a Saturday morning. It was a simple life. But it was a good life.

She squeezed his hand and pulled him towards her gate. Then she leaned in close to his ear and whispered, "Let's see if they have a seat left for you."

chapter twenty

As Hope and Peter stood in line to board their plane, an attendant felt the need to stare at Hope's belly. Why was everyone doing that lately? The flight attendant politely asked the couple to "Wait here, please," directing them off to the side. Hope raised her eyebrows at Peter as they waited, like it was no big deal, but she didn't have a good feeling about this.

The attendant used the phone on the wall to communicate with somebody, turning away as if the conversation were private. The line moved forward as folks boarded the plane; Hope and Peter tried to be patient.

Her conversation finished, the attendant hung up the phone and went on with her business, checking folks in. Hope shook her head when she realized they'd lost their place in line. Suddenly the pilot emerged from the tube of a walkway. He was in a huff, as if he didn't appreciate being summoned. The attendant pointed to Peter and Hope, and the pilot sidled up to them. He, too, took a good look at Hope's protruding belly. But then he politely pulled them a little further from the crowd and said, "I'm sorry, ma'am, but you won't be able to join us on our flight today."

Hope just looked at him with wide eyes. "What?" She laughed a little. Was he joking?

"This airline has a policy that anyone seven months pregnant or more," he raised his eyebrows, waiting for her to confirm – she nodded unwillingly. "Anyone seven months pregnant or more," he continued, "May only fly at the discretion of the pilot. I am the pilot. And I am telling you that I will not take you on our flight today." He crossed his arms over his chest, looking as if he were willing and ready to fight over it.

"But... I... oh, wait a minute." Papa's letter! That would help. Hope reached into her purse, found it, pulled it out, and handed it to him. She'd memorized what Papa had written and knew what Mr. Self-Satisfied Pilot would read as his eyes darted back and forth across the prescription paper:

To Whom It May Concern:
Hope Bailey is a patient under my care. Her pregnancy has been healthy and free of complications thus far. It is my firm belief that she should be allowed to travel up until the day of birth without any fear of risk to her or the baby's health.
Sincerely, Saul Rosenberg, MD.

Hope knew the rest of the prescription paper listed Papa's other qualifications. Like Medical Director, Mt. Cedar hospital, and Hospitalist, Oncology Unit. She smiled with satisfaction and straightened a little as she watched the pilot read. Papa had taken care of this before it was even an issue.

"Who is this doctor? He's an oncologist, not an obstetrician. Besides, I'm the pilot here. And I say no." He handed the note back to Hope and turned away, back down the tube, without a backward glance.

Hope and Peter just stared at each other, open-mouthed. "I'm... I'm sorry," Hope whispered. She didn't know what else to say.

"Not your fault." Peter shook his head. But he looked a little frustrated. He rubbed his forehead with his hands. How would they get home? Then his eyes brightened. "We can drive."

"Drive?"

"Why not, we'll just rent a car."

Hope's worries lightened, too. "Can you make it a convertible? A red one?" She teased.

"Anything for you, my dear." He took her arm in his. "Walk with me to the car rental place?"

"Sure."

First they stopped at the baggage check-in; it was too late to take Hope's suitcase off the plane. But they could pick it up at the Denver airport when they got there. Peter only had a carry-on, anyway. He'd come in such a hurry. He held her hand all the way to the car rental booth.

"So… getting out of Southern California, hmm?" The attendant asked, bored, as he rested his face on one hand and navigated his computer with the other.

Hope smiled and squeezed Peter's hand. "Yup. It's a nice place to visit. But it isn't home."

The attendant didn't look at them, but raised his eyebrows as if in surprise. "Long drive," he added, still entering information into the computer.

Now Peter squeezed Hope's hand. "It'll be good for her. She hasn't seen much of the country."

"I haven't seen anything." She agreed, bouncing lightly on the balls of her feet.

"Just the beach. And the cornfields," Peter explained, looking fondly at Hope.

"That's me. I'm just an ignorant beach bum from Nebraska."

The attendant looked a little confused, but he kept on typing, then printed something out for them. "Ok, sir," he said, handing the paper to Peter, "Here's your new receipt. Have a nice trip."

Hope and Peter headed towards their car. Her heart soared with anticipation at the idea of spending a whole week driving across the country with her husband. It wasn't a red convertible after all; but it would be the most time they'd spent together since their honeymoon.

The sky was all blue; not a cloud to be seen. It was a perfect day to drive. They made it to western Arizona easily. She looked over at Peter, who was driving happily. It didn't matter that his gaze didn't make her melt like it used to. What mattered was that they were a family; she was obeying God; she knew how to be a blessing now. She wouldn't give up.

She thought back to the phone conversation she'd just had with Heidi. Her mentor had asked if she'd changed her mind yet.

"Not yet." Hope had smiled a little sadly at the idea of letting down her childhood hero.

Horsewomen didn't normally use a lot of words to communicate. Heidi must've felt extra rambunctious that day, because she kept talking: "I admire what you're doing. You're a stand-by-your-man kinda girl."

Hope thought about how she'd left Peter in his hour of need. How even when they were together, she didn't always know how to help him. But how Jesus had never left her. "Actually," she confided as she studied the complicated man behind the steering wheel, "I think I'm a stand-by-Jesus kinda girl."

Hope could almost see Heidi nodding through the phone. "That's good too." She'd answered. "These animals are a lotta work besides. You'll come back when you're ready."

Hope turned her gaze now, back to the desert landscape around her. Would she be back? Maybe one day. But right now, Nebraska felt like the right place to build their family.

She pulled her gaze to their first real stop: the Grand Canyon. When they pulled into the parking lot, Peter said, "You've given a lot to move out there with me. I want to make this trip worth your while."

"Wow," she breathed as she stepped out of the car.

"That's what they all say," he agreed, and reached for her. But instead of standing side-by-side with him, she went for her sketch pad and sat immediately at one of the long benches that was situated in front of the canyon. He sighed. Well, she liked to draw, and he liked to take pictures. He stared at the awesomeness for a few moments, then grabbed his phone out of the back of the car. Snapped a few photos and then called Rob to share the news: they were coming home. Together.

Looking at the power that had carved out the Grand Canyon always drew him back to the power of God. How could people deny the existence of a Creator when they stood before something like this? Crags went down deep, deep. To his eye they might as well have gone down to the depths of the earth. Yet it was all held together as if by some invisible force. Light from the fading sun reflected off the many crags and nooks in the canyon. If he wanted to see every square inch of it, it would take days and days.

When Peter read his Bible, he liked to just let it fall open and read what was on the page. He was spontaneous like that. When the page opened to Psalm 81, he read hungrily. Then, satisfied that he'd given Hope enough quiet time, he went to sit beside her.

"How's it coming?" he asked, but she turned her paper to the side in mock shyness. He knew she didn't like him to see her work until it was done. He'd caught a glimpse, though, before she'd turned it away. Already she'd made a rough sketch of the area right in front of them. "You going to do this one in color?" He asked. He was no artist, but even he knew the Grand Canyon wasn't the same in black and white.

"Oh, definitely. I just don't have my paints with me. I'm trying to burn the image into my brain so I can paint it at home." She shifted a little on the bench, then asked him, "What do you have there?"

He held out the passage so he could read it to her. "I removed the burden from their shoulders; their hands were set free from the basket. In your distress you called and I rescued you..." He cleared his throat. He hadn't cried since he was twelve years old, and he wasn't about to start now. "It makes me think – the basket – maybe sometimes we try to carry things that are too heavy for us. Like maybe I don't have to fix everything."

Now she put down her drawing and held his hand. "Yes. Fixing everything is God's job." They stayed until the last of the light was dwindling and the first stars came out to watch over them.

She was an artist. He was too, in his own way. "You know..." Peter said as she leaned into him, "We're really more alike than we are different."

"Hmm. Like, we both need Jesus. We both need Him to shine His light into the canyons in our lives."

He elbowed her playfully. "Hey, I'm supposed to be the poet in the family."

"Ha."

As they walked to the parking lot, Hope put a hand on Peter's arm and whispered, "Can we come back tomorrow?"

"Definitely," he assured her. "We have a good week to get home. As long as the weather holds, we don't have to rush back."

"Thank you," she said simply. An older couple was heading out to their car too, also holding hands.

The man tipped his hat to Hope and Peter. "Beautiful family," he said to Peter.

Peter touched his forehead back to the man. "A total gift," he agreed. The man didn't even look confused. Just smiled and held his own wife a little closer.

It turned out their cars were parked side-by-side. To Hope, the man said, "And your gift is coming, young lady." She half expected him to look down to her belly like everyone else seemed to be doing these days. But instead, he shifted his gaze towards Peter.

They made two more stops, in New Mexico – first White Sands, which Hope decided was beautiful, but declared that she liked the snow better.

"Speaking of snow," Peter mentioned as they walked to the car, her arm in his, "There's a blizzard predicted this week. We better get home before it hits."

"I wish we could see more. Wouldn't it be cool," Hope asked when they stopped for gas, "to take our kids on a tour of the U.S. someday? Like, all the national parks?"

"All? I think there's, like, 50." Peter made a show of rolling his eyes at her as he climbed back in the car.

"50 kids?!"

"50 parks, you dope." He followed up the rolling of the eyes with a kiss on the cheek this time.

"Okay, most of them, then."

"I'll see what I can do." Peter drove with one hand on the wheel and the other over Hope's hand.

Hope looked at their two hands together; then placed her free hand over her belly. They were far from perfect; but they were a family.

chapter twenty-one

Home. Hope could almost hear the four walls whispering that word to her as she walked through the door of the little blue house three days later.

She dropped her bags and wrapped her arms around Teresa, who hugged her mightily and exclaimed over the growth in her belly. Then Gina, who held her at arm's length and said, "I'm sorry." Hope nodded. There was nothing more to say.

A warm smell came from the kitchen and tickled her nose. Tomato sauce. Hope started down the hallway towards the room she shared with Peter, but something was different about the empty room across the narrow hall from hers. The one that faced the ash trees in front, with the big picture window.

She stepped inside and turned 360 degrees. It was all set up for the baby. A crib with a yellow blanket stood against the wall opposite the window. Lace curtains fluttered lightly as air from the heating vent lifted them. A painting of a giraffe hung in one corner and a brand-new rocking chair graced another corner. There was a changing table, a dresser, a laundry basket... "What the heck!" Hope couldn't help exploding. Her mother-in-law and sister-in-law, who had snuck in behind her, laughed; whether because they were delighted over her surprise, or because Nebraskans never said *heck,* she wasn't sure. Anyway, she didn't need to know why they were laughing; she needed to know how they had done it. And why.

"How did you..." she started, but Teresa held up a hand.

"We had a whole week," she explained, "And lots of help."

"Rob and I put up the crib," Gina started, "And Mama T and

Hazel painted." She gestured to the walls around them. A soft rob-ins'-egg blue warmed the room that had once been gray.

"Wow," Hope breathed, then hugged them both in turn. "I don't know how to thank you." She sat down in the rocking chair to try it out, then laughed out loud. "See?" She pointed to her bel-ly, where a ripple could be seen where the baby was moving. "He likes it!"

The next six weeks passed more quickly than she could've imag-ined. True, there wasn't much to do around a farm in December and January, but the days filled up quickly with doctor's appoint-ments, trips to town, and dreaming and planning the garden with Teresa. Wondering who this baby would be, and what they would name him or her – a mystery, since Peter had wanted to keep the baby's sex a surprise. Finally, along with the blizzard of February 2nd, Hope's baby came.

She held her newborn in her arms, still mesmerized by the miracle of it all. One moment she'd been Hope with a big belly. Now they were two, mother and daughter, one of them a fresh gift from heaven.

She shuddered a little with final contractions as she remem-bered the initial burst of joy that had come when Dr. Neill had handed Hope her baby. "It's a girl!" he'd exclaimed, and Hope had wept with love for this squirming, blue infant. It was a love that overwhelmed her like ocean waves. It was God's love.

But later, when Peter followed the nurses to the sink to photo-graph the baby's first bath, and only Esther sat by Hope's side, the tears came back for another reason. "A girl." Hope sank into the hard bed. Exhaustion took over and with it, her memories. "I think – I had thought it was a boy – expected it to be a boy – because God knew I would mess up a girl. I thought I couldn't handle it," she confided to Esther quietly as she scrubbed at her eyes with the back of her hand.

Esther just looked at her, smiling.

"But now that she's here… I don't know." She winced as she shifted in the bed. "She's just perfect."

"*Yeshua* knew what you needed." Esther put a work-wizened hand over Hope's. "And He will keep on providing, one day at a time, just like He did for the Israelites with the manna in the desert."

The nurses finished washing the baby and handed her to Peter. Peter held her in both arms, smiling and cooing at her; he was a natural. He walked slowly over to Hope and held their daughter up for the two women to see. Hope couldn't stop the wave of love that swept over her when she saw how Peter gazed at their baby; the man at the Grand Canyon had been right. Her gift had come, and with it, the pitter-patter she thought she'd lost.

Esther sat next to her, keeping a hand on the side rail of the hospital bed, watching quietly. Peter handed the baby to Hope, and Hope held her close, tracing one finger down her forehead to the tip of her perfect little nose. When Hope's color started coming back, Esther asked, "You always wanted to know a mother's love, didn't you?"

Hope nodded.

"Well, now you do."

They decided to name the baby Janie. It was more than just a nod to Hope's favorite author, Jane Austen; the name meant *Believer in a gracious God*. "And I pray that you will be," Hope whispered to her little one as she lifted her up to her chest. "We'll get the hang of this, little love." She'd seen women multi-task while nursing; but right now, holding her baby in the right position took all her concentration. She sang a little song she remembered from one of Cora's storybooks. When she was ready to put her little girl in the bedside crib again and get fully dressed, she decided to pull the little Bible out of the bedside table. That Psalm had been bugging her – the one that was in the picture with the windmill. She'd only read the bit that was scrawled across the painting; she hadn't yet looked it up for herself. "No time like the present," she told her little daughter, who cooed like a dove in the hospital basinet.

Hope opened the book up to the 16th Psalm and read aloud. "The boundary lines have fallen for me in pleasant places – surely I have a delightful inheritance." That part she knew. But when she backed up, to the beginning, she read, "You are my Lord – apart from you I have no good thing. Oh," she breathed, "I missed this. Janie, I missed it."

She'd been so focused on where she'd live or what she'd do, that she'd forgotten. The best inheritance wasn't a farm or the keys to a stable or even the skills to be a good wife and mom. The best inheritance was a Person. "You gave Yourself," she whispered in a quiet prayer. A picture started forming in her mind, a picture she'd have to paint later – a Man on a cross, arms stretched wide as if to embrace the whole world.

Hope checked her watch: 7am. Peter had gone home to get some sleep and a shower. The room was warming with slants of light from the window; she walked over and peered through. The line of red was just showing up on the horizon. She closed her eyes and could only hear the faint beeping from monitors far away; but everything else in the hospital seemed to be asleep.

It was her own personal sunrise.

chapter twenty-two

Peter stood with his two-week old baby in his arms. He'd bundled her up and taken her down to the barn so Hope could get some much-needed rest.

He looked around at the tall barn walls; he could see them without seeing the flames now.

He looked down at his daughter's face. It had been hard to feel connected to her while she was in the womb. Only Hope had been able to bond with her during the first nine months of her life. "But now you're here," he whispered. "And in a few months, I'll show you how to plow the fields." He chuckled as they stepped out of the barn and into the open. "One day, this will all be yours." He spread his arms wide. "I'll give it to you freely. Just like God gave you to me."

He headed up the walk to the big house to help Teresa get ready for dinner.

⁓

Work-gnarled hands gripped the steering wheel and guided the old Ford up the hill. She was proud of those hands. They'd done a lot of good in her life. She glanced in the rearview mirror to catch a glimpse of the sunset, and looked instead at two wrinkle-lined eyes; her hands weren't the only thing that had gotten older lately.

She strode up to the front door like she knew the place. What would they think when they saw her? What would they say? But this visit had been delayed long enough. And now, her being here could change their lives... their futures.

Now or never. She raised a bold hand. And knocked.

Peter heard the knock first, and left Mom and Hope in the kitchen, glancing as he went at the red diner-style clock that hung in the hallway. 5pm. Maybe the family had come for dinner earlier than planned.

He opened the door wide, his chest swelling with pride. His wife was home. His baby was growing. The corn seed was ready and waiting in the barn. All was right with the world.

But instead of family... "Miss Hazel. Hi." He stumbled a little awkwardly as he opened the door wide for her. "You come to see the baby?"

She didn't seem to mind his awkwardness at all. Just took over like she usually did. She nodded and gave that same quick smile, pumped his hand in greeting. "Hello, Peter. Actually, no. I've come to see your mother. She here?" Without waiting for an answer, she took off her muddy boots and placed them by the door respectfully. She knew it was a house rule – whenever Teresa was around.

Hazel headed down the tight hallway to say hello to Teresa. Peter heard their greetings – and the exclamations as Hazel met Janie. The Roger and Hazel he knew were too busy to just stop by, especially in early springtime. Why was she here now?

"Yes, I will take a cup of coffee, thank you, Teresa," Hazel was leaning back comfortably in her chair when Peter entered the kitchen and leaned against the fridge. She had a way of filling a room, that woman. Kind of like how Dad had been.

A few more moments of small talk while Hope nursed the baby and Teresa made a fresh pot of coffee. Hazel held her mug close in her hands and took a few sips. "Well, Peter," she said suddenly, turning to him. "Does the brand *JB* mean anything to you? With a horseshoe design over the top?"

He sat at the table next to her and nodded. "Mm-hmm. JB for Jim Bailey. That was Dad's cattle brand."

"Well then. It would seem the two hundred and fifty, give or take, head of cattle that have been tearing up my brother's ranch would belong to you, wouldn't it?"

He looked at her sharply. Hope stopped eating, fork in midair. Teresa's hands stopped washing dishes, tap still on.

"I know it's only about half of what you lost. But it seems those blasted cattle made it all the way to Fort Collins after the fire. Must have scared them senseless. They're skinny as all get out – don't think you'll turn a profit this year – but maybe next year, Peter, if you can fatten 'em up a bit." Her voice softened then and she took a sip of her coffee.

Peter looked first at his neighbor, then at the two most important women in his life. They seemed too shocked to speak. He drew a ragged breath – there were so many questions in his mind. The one he asked first was: "But… it's been over a year. Almost two years. How can it be… Now?"

Hazel shook her head. "That brother of mine." She set her cup down so quickly, a little hot liquid spilled out. She grabbed a napkin to wipe it up. "Wayne is too old to run that ranch. But too stubborn to sell it. Why, he's got over two hundred acres, and he barely putters beyond the boundaries of his front yard. Stubborn Wayne." She looked up at the ceiling as if appealing to the heavens on his behalf. "Anyway, one of his sons came over to visit and decided to take a tour of the property. Your cows have been living off the grass in the south-eastern corner, down by the creek. Not living well, mind you, like I said, they're skin and bones – but living. My nephews will drive them here as soon as the snow melts. It'll be a slow drive, mind you."

Peter's head shot up at this news. That had been his next question – how would they get the cattle back here? "How… I'll pay them back. When they get here. For their time, and work." He didn't know how he would pay them back. Extra overtime, or he could sell the truck, or –

Hazel stood at this. "Don't you dare, Peter." She wrapped an arm around Teresa. "Consider this a gift to my friend here. We farmers' wives gotta stick together." Hazel's eyes suddenly went wet. Teresa went back to scrubbing dishes, but nodded her head ferociously. Knowing his mom, the tears would come later – when she was alone.

Hazel nodded in parting to all of them, then left as unceremoniously as she had come.

The shouts and hollers that erupted when the door clicked sounded like a birthday, and New Year's, and a winning night at a ball game, all rolled into one. At any rate, it was way too much noise for three people and one baby to be making. "The cows are coming home! The cows are coming home!" Teresa shouted as she jumped on her feet. Hope shouted with joy, too, and danced a little, but carefully, with Janie in her baby carrier.

"Wait a minute... the cows are coming home?" Hope sat down and let her giggles escape. Peter looked at her like she was crazy, but he supposed they all were, a little bit, today. He just raised his eyebrows at her. "The cows are coming home... and you finally learned how to pursue me." She gestured to the bouquet of flowers that sat enthroned in a vase on the kitchen table, the one he'd bought her this week, just like he had every week since she'd come home. Then she sat back in her chair and laughed quietly. "Ohhh, just wait till Gina hears about this." She hugged Janie close to her; he thought her face would erupt with the smiles.

She was so beautiful when she smiled like that. He lifted her up from her chair and pulled her over to the window. Led her out with one hand, then pulled her back in with a twirl. He should take her dancing again. "Come on, Mom," he invited Teresa to come and join them. She obliged, and taking Hope's hand, she noticed something.

"Hope," Teresa said, bringing Hope's left hand up to her face and staring closely at her ring, "There is a stone missing from your ring."

"Lemme see." Peter inspected it, too. There was a stone missing. The marquis diamond still rested in the middle... but among the sea of little diamonds that encircled it was an empty spot. "Should we look for it? Or maybe insurance will cover it." As he turned her hand over, the wheels in his mind seemed to be turning over, too. Maybe if he did make a profit with the cattle next year, he could fix it.

"No, I like it better this way." Hope spoke as if from a dream. The peace that radiated from her heart calmed the anxiety in his. "Because, you see?" She held her hand up to the window, where the soft afternoon light bounded in and reflected off the stones. "It's not perfect. Some might even say, *flawed*. But, look." She turned her hand one way, then another, and they all watched prisms of light bounce off the walls in the corner. "It still reflects the light."

Made in the USA
Coppell, TX
20 July 2021

59227666R00152